NAILBITERS

Nailbiters

Tales of Crime & Psychological Terror

Paul B. Kane

BLACK
SHUCK
BOOKS

Black Shuck Books
www.blackshuckbooks.co.uk

First published in Great Britain in 2017 by

Black Shuck Books
Kent, UK

Versions of the following stories have previously appeared in print:
Stalking the Stalker (*Cemetery Poets: Grave Offerings*, Double Dragon Press, 2003)
Grief Stricken (*Noir*, NewCon Press, 2014)
Check-out (*Horrorfind*, 2002)
The Opportunity (*Hidden Corners* Issue 1, 2001)
Cold Call (*HorrorBound Magazine* Issue 12, 2010)
The Torturer (*Touching the Flame*, Rainfall Books, 2002)
Remote (*Redsine* Issue 10, Prime Books, 2002)
The Anniversary (*Tourniquet Hearts*, Prime Books, 2002)
1,2,3...1,2,3 (*Estronomicon* Issue 6, 2006)
The Greatest Mystery (*Gaslight Arcanum*, Edge Publishing, 2011)
Baggage (*Un:Bound*, 2010)
The Protégé (*Hidden Corners* Issue 3, 2001)
Nine Tenths (*Horror Drive-In*, 2010)
At the Heart of the Maze (*The Dream Zone: Special Nightmare Edition*, 2000)
Blackout (*Graveyard Rendezvous* Issue 20, 1999)
The Cyclops (*House of Pain*, 2002)
R.S.V.P. (*The Chronicle* Issue 11, Eternal Night, 2002)
A Nightmare on 34th Street (*Scary Holiday Tales To Make You Scream*, 2003)
Suit of Lies (*The Wildclown Chronicles* Year 2, Issue 1, 2003)
A Suspicious Mind (*FunnyBones*, Creative Guy Publishing, 2003)

978-1-913038-31-1

For my friends Peter James and Michael Marshall Smith,
who walk this fine line better than I ever could.

My thanks to Steve Shaw at Black Shuck Books for taking a chance on this publication, not to mention for the superb cover. A huge thank you to Paul Finch for his wonderful introduction, and a massive thank you to all the editors and publishers who took some of these stories originally. As usual, hugs and thank yous to all my friends in the writing and film/TV world, for their continual help both now and in the past; people like Clive Barker, Stephen Jones, Mark Miller, Christopher Fowler, Alexandra Benedict, Stephen Volk, Tim Lebbon, Sarah Pinborough, Mike Carey, Barbie Wilde, John Connolly, Pete & Nicky Crowther, Simon Clark and so many more. Lastly, a big words are not enough thank you, as always, to my wonderfully supportive family and my lovely wife Marie, who keep me going sometimes. Love you guys tons and tons.

Introduction

I hesitate to say that one of the most recognisable features of Paul Kane's fictional world is its 'kitchen sink' atmosphere because readers might take that as a detrimental comment, maybe even an insult – whereas in fact nothing could be further from the truth.

One of the great strengths of this Chesterfield born-and-bred author, whose father was a coalminer and who grew up entirely immersed in the working class ethos of industrial North England, is that he can find chills – and raw-boned, shudder-inducing chills at that – in what are seemingly the most mundane of situations: a supermarket check-out; a suburban garage; a street-corner boozer; the cramped confines of a telesales office...

Okay, that isn't the whole story. We also visit New York in this collection; we join a manhunt across a hellish wasteland; we investigate crime alongside Sherlock Holmes for Heaven's sake! But for much of the time, quite mischievously, I feel, Kane prefers to tease us on our own everyday turf.

And just take a minute to consider what that actually means.

Fear is not alien to ordinary folk like us. Some unfortunate lives are ruled by fear. But most of our lives are ruled by routine. We sleep, we work, we shop, we walk our dogs, we have a few pints in the pub, and if we're lucky we get to go on holiday once a year. It's not wonderful, but it's not awful either. Hell, things could be a lot worse.

And that is where Paul Kane comes in.

Because Kane's thing is to craftily twist this everyday normality; to infuse the commonplace with the dark and unexpected; with the aid of a few deft key-strokes, to turn the humdrum into the horrific. And that's not easy. It takes a rare talent even among writers of the weird and wonderful.

But it's not just Kane's upbringing in life that has allowed him to nail this recognisable world of the ordinary and then effortlessly transform it into something extraordinary, it's his upbringing as a writer too.

Perhaps I should explain that...

I know Paul Kane personally and, I like to think, very well. We have been friends for a long time, having risen together through the ranks of the British Small Press during that late, lamented 'golden age' of the

1980s/90s, when hundreds of genre magazines and home-grown horror and fantasy anthologies vied for the attention of a relatively small but intensely enthusiastic readership. We were part of an active group (many members of which have now graduated to bigger and better things), who called themselves the 'Terror Scribes', and we would meet on Friday nights and Saturday afternoons in pubs and bars across the North of England. For the most part these were chaotic, smoke-filled drinking dens, crammed with football fans and workers coming off shift, echoing to the blare of the race-meet on the telly in the corner, the clatter of pool balls in the snug, or the shouts of the bar staff as they worked hand-over-fist to supply the noisy throng with a constant river of beer and whiskey.

In such environments as this, shouting to be heard against a friendly but rowdy backdrop, the whole gang of us honed our skills together as fledgling authors, exchanging ideas, performing our latest pieces aloud, offering critiques, proof-reading, editing, workshopping, and of course invariably sinking gallons and gallons of the local brew.

That said, don't be led into thinking that what you're about to get here is *Saturday Night and Sunday Morning* mark II – remember, this is horror. I mean, Paul Kane might hail from the same factory-belt background that produced so many of our angry young men of the '50s and '60s, but I strongly doubt he thinks of himself in those terms. He's certainly never been a 'class warrior'. Everything Kane writes is informed by his past, but his fiction rarely constitutes a polemic, or a treatise on Broken Britain (though there is plenty of Broken Britain in here, trust me). So often it's the case that Kane's everyman protagonists lead mundane and even oppressed lives, but his concerns are strictly with the strange, the weird, the unexplained, the deadly.

Take the householder whose irrational terror of the dark is only made a thousand times worse by an untimely power-cut. Take the shy guy who meets a lovely girl via a dating service, only to discover that when she says she's got baggage, she means it in the most ghastly way possible.

Of course, for all these reasons, *Nailbiters* could be as much a bag of thrillers as horrors. And this is something else we should perhaps take a second or two to admire.

It's fashionable these days to pigeon-hole our fiction. Often this is due to the way modern novels, anthologies and even movies are packaged and sold. Crime and thriller stories can be no less gut-thumping in terms of chills, spills, violence and terror than horror stories. But they look and feel different. At least, that is the way we are supposed to think. Thrillers are connected to the 'real world', we are told. They could be happening right now, right next door to where we live. Horrors, on the other hand, are more of the imagination. There is a harrowing and surreal darkness at the heart of the horror story, which may disturb us temporarily, though afterwards we can always wipe our brow and say: 'Phew, thank goodness that couldn't happen in reality.'

Well, I'm pleased to say that Kane cheerfully blurs these lines. Without ranging into the realms of complete fantasy he can make the most unlikely nightmares seem very real indeed. Check out the woman so damaged by numerical events in her early life that simply counting is now an ordeal for her. And what about the department store Santa who's so fed up with his lot that he no longer just gives presents at Christmas? By the same token, with a few subtle psychological tricks, Kane can transform the everyday into something beyond appalling – take the 'plain Jane' shop-girl so isolated by her peers that she dreams daily of annihilating her customers. Take the run-of-the-mill job application that leads to a life-shattering catastrophe.

And what, ultimately, does all this add up to?

Well, it means you're holding a very special book in your hands. It contains a bunch of stories that will take you to the edge of your seat and beyond. It is laced with the tough, down-to-Earth realism of the classic noir and yet at the same time, often unexpectedly, it hits the full-on horror button hard. You'll be charmed by the quality of the writing but shaken by the subjects under discussion

This won't be an easy read, or a comfortable one, and though you may feel you're in familiar territory, don't be lulled by that either. You're going to need to brace yourself, though if you've already bought this book, I suspect you knew that anyway.

So sit tight. For all its deceptively homely environs, this is going to be quite a ride.

Paul Finch, 2016

Stalking the Stalker

He doesn't know it yet,
But I'm stalking him, stalking her.
As he sits up a tree outside,
Her apartment:
I'm there.

When he raises his binoculars,
I raise mine.
In the street, the crowd,
He follows her.
I follow him.

He loves her – in a way he can't explain.
But I understand because...
I love him.
In fact I'm mad about him.
Do you see?

He's her number one fan,
Her secret admirer.
It's how he signs himself.
But I am his – so secret he has no idea,
That I am even alive.

Once or twice she's turned,
Caught sight of him. Of something...
A figure.
He's turned himself, looking for...the police?
Or for me?

Does he know?
Does he know I'm here, watching him?

Waiting, anticipating?
Can he really see me?
Feel me?

He's clever – that's why I *want* him.
But I'm just as sharp as he is.
I hope it'll make him proud.
I'm every inch the stalker...
Of the stalker.

I walk the walk,
I talk the talk.
I stalk the stalk...
That makes me smile.
So much.

But what's this?
I'm turning myself...
The glint of something,
Of moonlight reflecting,
Off glass: a figure.

Could it be?
No, it's too ridiculous.
I hardly dare hope.
Just a shadow, that's all.
Not...

Not someone who loves me?
Who wants me?
Not a stalker,
Stalking the stalker,
Of the stalker.

Grief Stricken

There he is, Lomax's quarry.

The man chats, flirts with members of staff; hasn't the faintest idea what's waiting for him. Lomax grunts – he'll wipe that look of smug satisfaction off the prick's face. One way or another, that bastard will come to grief.

Images fill Lomax's mind: the cutting of skin; flesh parting; blood spurting and pooling, organs being sliced into, removed.

The man finishes his conversation with his female co-workers, who fawn in front of him, giggling like schoolgirls, pushing back strands of hair over their ears – might as well be sucking his cock right there and then in the corridor, in front of everyone. The man laughs too; Lomax fucking hates that. What right does he have to be happy? What right does anyone?

'Can I help you, sir?' Lomax is startled by the question, didn't hear anyone come up behind him, beside him. *You're meant to be a hunter, what the fuck?* He was too focussed on the object of his pursuit. He turns to face her, and she reminds him so much of... Lomax shakes his head, more to clear his mind than to answer her question. But she can't help him. Nobody can; not even God or the Devil or anything in-between. Not anymore. 'Only you look a little...lost.'

He *is* lost. He has been for some time. But there's nothing this woman can do about it. Only he can do that, work things through – follow this to its logical conclusion. Only then can he find some sort of release.

Lomax knows he has to say something, but isn't sure what. He manages, 'I'm fine, thanks.' It's clear he is far from okay.

'Only you were—'

'I said I'm *fine!*' he snaps, and the woman takes a step back.

Don't give yourself away. Don't let her see what you're really here for, what your purpose is, Lomax tells himself. He smiles awkwardly. 'I'm sorry, it's been a long day. Long week, in fact. I'm here...you know, visiting someone.'

The woman nods her understanding. She's seen all kinds of ways of handling this stuff, of dealing with such heightened emotional states – though not his, he can guarantee that. She won't have seen Lomax's way. It's unique. She leaves him alone, however, so his ploy has worked. He turns back, looks over at the space he'd been scrutinising. The man is gone.

Shit!

Lomax moves forward, his long coat flapping behind him like a superhero. He is anything but. Can't leap tall buildings or dodge bullets, or...or turn back time by flying round the Earth. But he can do one thing, and he does it well. He's a hunter, he finds people. He's been doing it all his life. So find *him*; find the man you're chasing.

The man you're going to kill today.

Christ... Where the fuck has he—

Then Lomax spots him, just a head bobbing down the corridor, but distinctive: that curly brown hair, greying just slightly. That bouncy stride of his, as if he's walking on air. As if he doesn't have a care in the world. He will soon, Lomax will see to that.

I am the bringer of grief.

He pushes past staff and visitors alike. Past the women that man had been flirting with, in their tight, blue and white uniforms. There will be no more of that after today, no more. Lomax will see to it.

He races past nauseating turquoise walls, past wards filled with patients, and spots his prey pressing the button for the lift. *Come on, come on...*

No: Lomax is too late. The metal doors are closing again before he can reach them. But he knows where the man is heading, same place he always does after work. It's just a question of how many stops that lift will make on its way down, how fast Lomax is taking the stairs. Very fast, he has to. He's decided that he's not going to wait any longer, that the deed must be done today.

Flinging open the set of double doors, he hurls himself down those steps, two, three at a time. The rational part of his mind is yelling: *slow down, you could fall and injure yourself* (he's in the right place to get fixed up though, isn't he; problem is, he's also in the right place to get flagged, to get noticed by the authorities, and that's the last thing he needs, not when he is so close).

The irrational part is saying: *fuck it.*

Should have lain in wait down there, but he'd had to be sure. Needed to know for certain his prey was in the hospital itself. *Just because his car is…*

Down, down and down. Below the hospital itself, underneath. The staff car park, so dark and full of shadows, no matter how many panels of strip lighting they scatter about the place. Lomax feels at home here – he knows the layout, after scoping it out on several occasions. Knows where the CCTV cameras are. Knows also that if he pulls up the hood on his sweatshirt and angles his head just right, he can avoid detection, avoid identification.

He fights to control his breathing as he hits the basement level. He's going to need it to be even anyway, for what comes next. There's no room for excitement, for adrenalin. Lomax has to be cool and calm now and—

The blood again, the slices: peeling back skin, sinking the knife further inside. The scars that will be left behind afterward, ugly and ragged. The tears stitched together like Frankenstein's monster. The work of uncaring, unfeeling hands.

No, concentrate. You're in the moment.

First things first, he needs to work out how far ahead his quarry is. The lift's bought the guy some time, but Lomax was quick descending those stairs. He keeps himself fit, you see. Has to, it's the only way to do what needs to be done, fuelled by…

Over there, on his way across the car park. There's no mistaking that confident swagger, coat over one arm. That fucking grin. Lomax moves silently across the concrete, flitting between the vehicles – passing 4x4s and people carriers and sports cars – using them for cover, without ever looking like he is. It's a skill: partly practised, partly organic. And soon he isn't very far away from the man at all, which is good, because already the target has his keys out, is depressing the button on them with a *bee-beep.* The orange sidelights of the sleek, silver Jaguar XF flash on and off momentarily. If Lomax is to make his move, it has to be soon.

Has to be *now.*

He darts between bays, rising and gliding forward at the same time. One hand reaching under his coat.

'Hey... Hey you!' As before, the voice breaks his concentration, and he turns to see a figure heading his way. 'What are you up to there, eh?' Once again, he has failed to spot this person creeping up on him – that's supposed to be *Lomax's* job, the creeping – because he was so intent on what he was going to do. So blinkered that...

His prey is turning as well, closer than the interloper to Lomax. Close enough to see what Lomax's hand is resting on at his belt, and panic. The other man, the figure running over towards him, is closing the gap. Lomax sees that he is also wearing a uniform. Not hospital staff: security. And his baton is pretty much drawn. This really isn't good.

His prey is backing up towards the Jaguar, turning and fumbling with the door handle. He'll escape if Lomax isn't careful. *If you'd been more careful in the first place...* he says to himself, but doesn't finish the sentence.

Lomax sighs, and rushes towards the security guard.

He avoids the baton swing, ducking and coming up again in a single, smooth movement, arm out straight, catching the man – solidly built, but terrible reactions – across the bridge of the nose. It explodes in a fountain of blood. The security man scrunches up his eyes. Lomax knees him in the stomach, crumpling him over; the baton falls from his grasp, clattering on the concrete. They're attracting too much attention, Lomax knows that. This needs to be finished, and quickly. One more blow to the back of the head ensures that the guard isn't getting up again any time soon.

Then it's back to the original focus of his attentions. Covering the distance in a couple of strides, reaching inside his coat, drawing the gun and aiming. The driver's door is now shut, though – the engine of the Jaguar being gunned. Lomax skirts the vehicle, trying the door and hoping against hope the bastard hasn't had time to lock them after him yet.

Click! He hasn't.

Lomax yanks open the door, but the man's ready, fear driving him. He lashes out, knocking the pistol from Lomax's grasp. Then he pushes Lomax back and into the neighbouring car. The glass of the passenger window cracks as Lomax connects with it. He lets out a grunt – not of disgust now, but because of the pain in his back.

His quarry has barged past him, just as Lomax did with the people in the corridor. But Lomax is quick to recover, always has been. He's on the guy in seconds, leaping and toppling him, bringing him to the ground with a rugby tackle. But the man still isn't going down without a fight; not that Lomax would have expected anything less. The guy kicks out a foot, ramming it into Lomax's shoulder. It's enough to set him free again, and he's crawling away.

Enough of this shit! Lomax gets to his feet, walks calmly back to the Jaguar and picks up his pistol. The quarry has also regained his footing and is stumbling, attempting to run. It doesn't matter. Lomax aims and fires, hitting the man squarely in the centre of the back. He goes down, hard.

It's over.

No, not yet. Now they have to get out of there before anyone else shows up. Before more people arrive than Lomax can handle. He is only one man after all, even if he is a predator. Lomax holsters his weapon, goes over to his target and plucks out the dart. *How's it feel to be on the* receiving *end of a needle, fucker?* he thinks to himself. There's no point saying it out loud, the man is unconscious.

Lomax picks him up, carries him to the Jaguar like a best man getting the groom back to his hotel after a stag do. He glances round quickly, then opens the door and deposits his prize on the back seat. He swings into the driver's seat and closes the door.

With the precision of a professional, Lomax reverses the Jag out of the tight spot, manoeuvres it around, and drives up and out of this section. He looks into the rear view only once as he makes his way out of the car park, up and into the world above.

But he fails to see the vehicle pull out of its own space just moments after him.

Fails to see the dark green Ford that follows.

~

As Lomax finishes strapping down the naked man to the cold, metallic surface, he allows himself a half-smile, though it is tinged with pain. *Finally*, he says to himself. *Finally.*

Then he thinks about all the things he has planned, what he's going to do. Start with an incision down the middle, probably. He sees the flesh parting again, the blood. There will be so much blood. So much…grief.

The man's eyelids are flickering. He'll be waking up from the drug soon enough. Lomax has gagged him, not because he doesn't want to hear his pleas for mercy or his screams – those would be so sweet. But because he doesn't want to hear his excuses. He's heard far too many of those.

Lomax taps his knife against his lips. With the man laid out in front of him here, he can't help musing about the events that set him down this path.

Did they turn him *into* what he is? Perhaps. But don't they also say that the capacity to kill is either in you or it isn't? That no matter what the trigger is, some people act, while others don't. How can anyone say *how* they'll react to a certain set of circumstances unless they are in them? It's impossible. It's like…

Like being in love.

You know how you think you'll act, but nothing prepares you for that bolt out of the blue. Or how it will change your life forever. The loss of it changes you too, Lomax knows that. It's as much of an adjustment, though infinitely less pleasant it has to be said.

Once upon a time, another life ago, Lomax had been in love.

It is better to have loved and lost…

Lost, so lost. So long ago.

He'd been married, in fact, his wedding anniversary the 24th March. His wife, Tracey, knew what he did – and though she didn't like it, she tolerated it. She knew this was what he was good at. Being a hunter.

John Lomax. Detective John Lomax.

Deep down, he knew she also respected him for bringing people to justice. Catching murderers and rapists. Lomax never thought he'd be tracking down his wife's killer. Never thought he'd be doing it alone, either, without the support of his former colleagues. But then, if Tracey hadn't gone in for that surgery…

Minor, they'd said; a routine operation. His smile turns into a grimace as he looks down on the man below him: the curly-haired doctor with the laugh, with the grin. 'It's just routine, she'll be up and on her feet again in no time,' he had chirped back then, shaking their hands.

Doctor Brendan Carter, he called himself. In a different hospital, a different city. A different world. A happier place until—

Lomax remembers the time he spent with Tracey before the operation. How scared she'd been then, suddenly – and how right she'd been to be so. 'John,' she'd said, laying in the bed, chewing her bottom lip, 'I have a terrible feeling about this.'

Lomax had patted her hand, told her everything was going to be fine. 'Trust me,' he'd even said. Jesus, how many times did they say that in soaps: everything was going to be all right? It was always the kiss of death. Like saying 'I'll be right back' in some cheesy horror movie, before getting your head lopped off.

But the trust she'd placed in him, the trust Lomax had placed in the doctors – in Carter especially – had been very misplaced indeed.

Lomax fights back the tears, as he recalls waiting in that corridor; thinking that this was taking a long time, longer than they'd said it would. Remembers seeing staff rushing to and fro, as if to answer some emergency but assuming they're for someone else, it's a big place, there are more patients than Tracey having ops. But he'd known, even as they emerged through those double doors, even before Carter could say a word, that she was gone.

'We did everything we could,' intoned the curly-haired man, though was there just a slight trace of a smile playing on those lips? And was he – *yes*, checking out those nurses in the corridor, in their tight blue and white uniforms. For fuck's sake! 'There were...certain complications.'

'What kind of complications?' Lomax had demanded, feeling oddly detached, as if he were having an out of body experience (weren't they supposed to be reserved for people actually under the knife?). It was as if he wasn't even there, like he *was* watching this on some stupid soap.

Carter spouted a load of medical jargon about internal bleeding and trying to locate the problem, though in the end it amounted to one thing and one thing only: they'd screwed up and now he was a widower. Tracey had been his everything, and now he had nothing.

Nothing except trying to get to the truth, trying to get her justice.

Lomax had insisted on an investigation, which the hospital said they'd conduct internally. Lawyers were brought in, but they were useless. In the end Lomax went down to the morgue and broke in, examined the body himself, which was still on ice because of all the fuss he'd kicked up. He'd wept over her cold form as he saw all the cuts, the rough patchwork of stitches that made up her body (they later tried to tell him it was because of the 'further work' they'd done to fully determine cause of death – work that had been conducted *because* of Lomax's questions). But that had just earned him a reprimand, and meant the ongoing investigation would now be shut down. His Super had even suggested taking some time off, that he was too close to all this.

'You've got to believe me,' he said to his partner Temple, a strapping ex-Marine who'd joined the force after injuring his leg on some foreign battlefield. 'There's something more going on here. A cover up... I don't know.'

Temple trusted him, the kind of trust Carter couldn't begin to understand. They'd worked together for a long, long time and on a number of cases – some of them quite high profile, such as catching the train track killer – always had each other's backs. In fact, Lomax had even taken a bullet for Temple on one occasion, something he reminded him of then. So Temple agreed to help him look into all this, on their own time. 'You have a sense about these things,' Temple had said. 'I've always envied that.'

And he had – Lomax had always possessed a flair for thinking outside the box when it came to criminal behaviour. (*Takes a killer to track a killer...*isn't that so?) Something about this whole thing, about Carter in particular, didn't sit right. He and Temple had conducted their own private investigation, fitted in around the cases they had on their desks. And guess what? More suspicious deaths had cropped up, linked to Carter, who had used a variety of different names in the past. 'This is it,' Lomax had said to his friend. 'This is all the evidence we need.' He would finally get justice for Tracey. But they'd been dismissed again, told to drop it – Lomax ordered to take some personal time.

Then, lo and behold, Lomax discovered that Carter had done a runner. Nobody had seen him for a fortnight. So he'd taken that holiday. Taken that and more besides, and gone after his wife's killer. The man had obviously been doing this a long time, courtesy of the perfect cover – everyone trusts a doctor, they do all that they can (well, what if they did a few things they shouldn't? Played God with death as well as life?). And he would continue doing this unless Lomax found him and put a stop to things.

It had taken a while. Taken all of Lomax's detective skills, his tracking abilities, to find the man – posing as one Doctor Gerry Young – and now he would make him pay. Lomax would cause him so much grief, transfer it onto him and maybe then he'd finally be able to find peace. For himself and for Tracey.

Lomax hears the man on the table stirring, his muffled groans through the gag. 'Ah, you're awake,' he says, leaning over him. 'Hello again, Doctor "Carter". Remember me?'

The man thrashes about, but he's held tight by his bonds. He's going nowhere.

Lomax sweeps a hand behind him, drawing attention to their surroundings: an abandoned warehouse he found down by the docks. The perfect place for a little privacy. 'What do you think?'

The man mumbles something and Lomax laughs softly, holds up the knife, which glints in the light from a portable lamp. 'This is my operating theatre, doctor. *My* theatre of pain.' Then he goes on to relate all the things he's intending to do, getting justice for poor Tracey. No – getting *revenge!* Even as he's saying them, Lomax realises how sick it all sounds, but he doesn't care. This is the only way: the one, sure-fire way he's going to assuage these feelings.

'I'm afraid I can't let you do that, Johnny,' comes a voice, echoing through the warehouse. Lomax stands stock-still. For the third time today, he's let someone get the drop on him. Getting old. Old and tired.

Third time's the charm, though, right? And he recognises that voice.

'Temple,' he says, under his breath.

'Long time no see, Johnny. You didn't write, you didn't call...'

Lomax turns, faces the large man striding across the warehouse floor, half in shadow. He cuts an imposing figure, Temple. Shoulders like breezeblocks, arms like iron girders.

'Walk away, Lewis, this doesn't concern you.'

Temple sighs. 'I'm afraid it does. I can't let you kill an innocent man, Johnny.'

'Innocent?' Lomax spits out the word like snake venom he's sucked from a wound. 'How can you say that? This fucker killed my Tracey.' He nods at his captive.

'No... No, he didn't.'

Lomax looks from the strapped down man to Temple. 'What are you talking about? You saw the evidence, same as I did.'

'There *was* no evidence, John. Deaths, yes – but not down to Carter. Different doctors in different hospitals. All accidents, all due to negligence or human error, but not done on purpose. Just part and parcel of the risks you take when you have surgery, that's all. Just stupid, bad luck. Like what happened to Tracey.'

'*No!*' he screams. 'You're lying. Why are you lying? Did they get to you?'

'Who, John?'

'The people who covered it all up?'

Another sigh. 'There are no people, John. There's no Carter anymore, either.'

'No, I know. He's calling himself Young, now. He's there Lewis, right there. He ran away, but I found him.'

Temple continues walking towards Lomax. 'Carter's dead. You killed him, remember?'

No, not yet. But I'm going to, Lomax says to himself.

'It's the grief, John. That's what did this to you. Can't you see that? You have to trust me.'

Trust...

Can't you see? Lomax takes another look at the man in front of him, the curly hair – no, it's straight... Straight hair!

'I can't let you kill another one. Not another innocent man. Not now I've finally found you after all these years.'

Lomax almost laughs out loud at that one. The hunter being hunted himself, and by his ex-partner.

Not like the rest. Not like the rest... All these years, all *these years...* The words echo in his mind, just as they have in the abandoned warehouse. He blinks, and the man's face changes – he sees face after face, in fact. All the people he's murdered. Lomax shakes his head. No, they were all Carter, using pseudonyms.

'Put the knife down, Johnny,' says Temple, coming closer.

'I... No, I'm not going to do that,' Lomax tells him, then sees what Temple has in his hand. It's not a dart gun, this one: it's real. It'll hurt. But can he kill his old partner, kill his friend?

Takes a killer to catch a—

'I said drop it, John.' There's an edge to Temple's voice, suggesting he's not going to ask twice.

Lomax makes his move, rushing him. There's a bang and he angles himself sideways. *Whadya know, I can dodge bullets after all*, he thinks. He can do anything in fact, powered by grief like his. Can take on an eighteen stone ex-Marine, for example, by going for his weak spot – his bum knee – kicking down hard on that and knocking the pistol from his grasp at the same time. Before he knows it, Lomax has plunged the knife he's holding into Temple, forcing it upwards. Temple splutters, warm blood and spittle peppering Lomax's face. He holds his former partner, cradles him as he falls to the floor. He's so heavy Lomax can hardly manage.

'I'm sorry,' he whispers, though he doesn't know if Temple can hear his voice. 'But I have to finish this. For Tracey.'

Once Temple is dead, Lomax returns to the table. To the man he'd once known as Carter. 'Now, this is just routine. A minor procedure. You'll be on your feet in no time,' Lomax informs him. 'Unless there are...complications, of course. But I'll do everything I can.' He lets the words sink in, savouring the terrified look on the man's face, in his eyes, the incomprehensible mumbling.

'Trust me,' Lomax says, then gets to work.

~

There he is, Lomax's quarry.

The man chats, flirts with members of staff; hasn't the faintest idea what's waiting for him. Lomax grunts – he'll wipe that look of smug satisfaction off the prick's face.

One way or another, that bastard will come to grief.

Check-out

Bip

Milk – two pints: 75p

Bip

Sunflower spread: £1.60

Bip

Tea bags: £2.50

The items passed before her eyes, one after the other, like a miniature carnival procession, her hands waving them over the scanner in an automatic, obligatory way.

'Would you hurry up for Christ's sake? My car's on a meter,' snapped the red-faced man on the other side of the till. His words meant nothing to her. She continued on at her leisurely pace until, finally, the last provision had been registered. Only then did she acknowledge his presence and read out the price to him. He paid, hastily pulling out the notes, the coins, and casting them in front of her. The receipt started printing out with the name of the store at the top, followed by the date, and just below that: 'Thank you for your custom. You were served today by Janet.'

'If I get a bloody ticket, I'm reporting you!' It was an idle threat. She wasn't worth reporting. He'd forget all about her as soon as he left the supermarket. Janet had that kind of effect on people.

She watched him stuffing his groceries into the flimsy plastic bags provided, then he scuttled away. At least he hadn't bought any baked beans. If she saw another tin...

No more customers were waiting at the 'ten items or less' aisle. She could relax for a minute or two.

Who would have thought she'd come to this? Check-out girl pricing up goods for ungrateful, unsatisfied, uncaring people. Actually, her parents thought she'd come to this. They told her she'd wind up in a dead-end job working with dead-end people, and they'd been right all along. Much to her regret.

She hadn't always been miserable here, though. At one time she'd relished the prospect of visiting the big, bright store: a glowing treasure trove full of every kind of product imaginable. Janet recalled from her childhood the precious trips with her mother which might end in a treat at the check-out if she'd been good that week. Worked hard enough. The choice was staggering. Rows of chocolate bars, sweets in silver wrappers, bubbly... She could remember thinking that this was truly a paradise beyond compare.

But then, in the eyes of an eight-year-old most aspects of life appear wondrous. Most aspects. Not all. Not by any means.

Ten years of working here had soon changed her mind about the place. Oh, she could still help herself to treats, and free ones at that – just like when she was a kid. The supermarket factored in certain inevitable losses. But it wasn't the same. Janet couldn't bring back those pre-pubescent days no matter how hard she tried.

Janet's parents had produced her quite late in life. Very late in her father's case as he was pushing fifty at the time, with her mother being a much sprightlier forty one. They never told her outright that she was an accident, but they never really had to. It didn't take much working out. After all those years of going without children, Janet was the last thing they'd anticipated...or wanted. Of course, in this life things tend to be thrust upon you when you least expect them.

Janet's mother was forever telling her how difficult the birth had been, how her daughter was so very lucky to be alive at all after the trouble *she'd* gone through. Eleven hours in labour. But, unfortunately, despite her mum's protests, Janet didn't feel particularly lucky.

In fact there were times in her life when she'd felt like the unluckiest person alive.

Janet peered at her reflection in the black, glass-topped scanner. Trapped inside was the face of a small, podgy, dark-haired woman (*too many treats for you, Janet!*) with a sad, dejected expression. The dowdy brown uniform she was made to wear did little to combat her plain image, made, as it was, out of the most hideous starchy material which pulled tight over hips and under arms as she sat at her post.

There was a clear plastic panel on her right, supposedly to separate her till from the aisle next to hers – except she was on the very end one as usual and there was no neighbouring check-out on that side, just a white wall which ran around the corner to the wines and spirits section.

To her left was the conveyor belt, her constant companion for a decade now. She knew the way it moved when she pressed the pedal on the floor (that was exciting when she'd first had a go – a bit like driving, and the closest she'd ever get to the real thing); the way it would stop and start sometimes when it hadn't been used for a while; and the gentle humming noise it made when it was in motion, sending vibrations up the side of her leg that tingled in a funny sort of way.

Below her, under the counter, was a shelf with her bag on it. Inside were some sandwiches, a few bars of chocolate – *free treats!* – a coke and...something else. She wasn't supposed to bring the bag out here with her, but Janet couldn't risk leaving it in the staff room because someone was bound to look inside. They wouldn't care if it belonged to her. Janet broke off a piece of chocolate and slipped it into her mouth. She would almost certainly be in trouble if they knew what she was really up to.

Ah, but it was so nice when there were no customers. No work to do.

Ever since she could remember, her life had been one long trail of tedious tasks to perform. Once she was old enough to stand up straight and walk, her parents had given her chores to do. Nothing wrong with that, it builds character, gives you a taste of what the real world is like. All kids have to pull their weight.

The only problem was that the 'little' jobs increased in proportion to her age, and that of her parents, naturally. By the time she was ten, Janet was cooking, cleaning and washing, while her mum and dad relaxed on the couch watching TV. And it all had to be done just right or there would be hell to pay. Discipline was the key word. After all, her father *had* been a veteran military man.

Janet would never forget his reaction whenever she did something wrong.

'You're for it now!' he'd shout, the bark of a sergeant major. And if she happened to start crying, that just made matters worse. 'Stop your blubbering, lady, and bite the bullet like a good soldier should!'

Yes, but she could not tell anyone about the situation. They had made that painfully clear. Drilled it into her times many, with deeds as well as words. If she did, then the men in blue uniforms would come and take her away to live in a cold, dark place. A cellar with lots of other naughty little children. There she would stay, wishing she hadn't said anything at all, wishing she could go back to her cosy life at home. But by then it would be too late.

She still believed there was such a place even now, though reason told her that the government, or whoever was in charge, would never allow such a business to go on. Would never stand by and watch kids, let alone twenty-six-year-olds, being carted off to a dungeon somewhere to rot for the rest of eternity. Yet she'd accepted what her parents had said without question. If she was bad in any way she would go directly to the dark place. That went for more than just exposing their slave labour schemes.

Janet chewed silently away on the chocolate, staring out into space.

If only...if only...

Believe it or not Janet had been quite a good pupil at school, despite the fact that she sometimes dozed off at the back of the class – blame her busy lifestyle. Needless to say this led to the other kids giving her the cruel nickname of 'Dopey'. It was relatively easy to concentrate on schoolwork when you had no friends, and the fact that she was never released out at night only added to the stigma.

Janet took quite a shine to science and always looked forward to the lessons. Mr Parks had been the teacher and she secretly idolised his chiselled good looks. The kind of man who could sweep a girl off her feet, just like they always did in those pink romance novels her mother read... she sneaked a look at these every chance she got. Some of the passages didn't make any sense to her – 'Ralph cupped her swelling bosom and she was lost in rapture...' – but she understood the sentiment and remembered feeling quite warm after reading certain scenes.

Janet had also enjoyed English, where she could express herself through her writing, although most of her stories were dismissed as being nothing more than flights of fancy. And she'd coped well with cookery lessons; hardly surprising really, the amount of hours she'd already spent in her own kitchen (mess hall?) at home.

If only these talents had been encouraged it might have been quite a different story. But all her parents could do was put her down.

'You'll never amount to anything, lady. You're a nobody so you might as well get used to the idea,' her brutish father was known to remark.

He was right. She never did.

The older her parents became, the more looking after they required. *Pass me this! Fetch me that!* Her father was especially good at dishing out the orders; he'd had a lot of practice. From the moment she set foot through the door at 4:15 to the minute she went to bed, which varied depending on how much work she had to get through, Janet was constantly at their beck and call. It was almost as though *she* was the parent – and a single parent at that – looking after two oversized babies. Just who were the lucky ones in that household, exactly?

But nothing was ever good enough. She could never work hard – or long – enough to please them. Gone were the days when her mother could be bothered to do the shopping. Now it was her turn to go to the supermarket alone. She had to sort out her own treats.

When the time came for Janet to leave school, they'd forced her into work so they wouldn't have to squander their savings on stupid things like food or taxes. So Janet didn't get the chance to do A-Levels or go to university. They couldn't risk her moving away. Couldn't bear to lose their little soldier.

Ironically, she'd spotted the vacancy while she was in the store one week. It seemed like the kind of job she might actually enjoy, here in her fantastical haven away from the world.

And father would so love to see her in uniform.

Janet glanced sideways at the girl on the check-out two rows down. It may have been almost 1 o'clock on a Saturday afternoon, but there were only a handful of staff on – measured out over eight tills. It was done either to cut costs or annoy the customers, she didn't know which. This 'colleague' was maybe six or seven years her junior, though Janet didn't know for sure because they'd never spoken. No one ever really spoke to Janet. The object of her gaze was blonde with green eyes, and she was thin – supermodel thin. The uniform didn't look dowdy on her; *No sir, SIR!* Nobody was ever in a rush when they went through *her* till. Indeed, men would lean on the counter, ogling her cleavage in that obvious way some do, for what seemed like hours. One was there right now. She knew what he was thinking: Stuff the meter, this is more important. The sight made Janet feel sick.

Some people have it so easy, she said to herself. In no time that goddess would be promoted, after she'd batted her eyelids at enough superiors. Within five years she'd probably be running her own store.

Not like Janet.

Janet was on the check-out.

Another customer sauntered up to her till, a laid-back youth with a basket in one hand and his jacket in the other. He slammed down the wire holdall and started unloading his selection.

In her mind she heard the words, *Please don't let it be beans. Not yet.* Over and over like a train on the tracks, heading for an inevitable collision.

Bip

Loaf of white bread: £1.45

Bip

Coffee: £3.00

Bip

Instant mash potatoes: £1.25

He looked at her as she fed the food through. Janet found herself looking back. He had a mischievous grin on his face. The boy reminded her a bit of Mark. Her true love, Mark.

She'd met him here – where else? – when he came to work for a few months after finishing college. Only temporary, mind, but that's what they all think in the beginning. At first he'd been just like the rest and they hadn't progressed past a simple nod as she walked past his shelf displays. But he made her feel funny like the words in that book, or when Mr Parks used to stroll past her in class, usually to answer someone else's question. *Never hers*.

Mark was still working at the store come Christmas time and on the night of the annual party, the first one Janet had ever attended, after telling her folks she was on overtime, something remarkable happened. She'd been inadvertently standing under the mistletoe, on her own...when Mark had kissed her. God, he had actually *kissed her!*

Granted, he'd had a fair amount to drink, but that didn't make any difference. His feelings were clear and Janet had willingly accompanied him home – the dreaded thought of returning to her parents spurring her on.

She and Mark had...done things together. Janet's first time, her first *real* time with a man, was a quick, even mildly painful, experience. She certainly hadn't been lost in rapture. Yet she felt that Mark had been pleased. And afterwards he had fallen asleep while she went round and tidied up his flat. It wasn't a chore when you loved someone, was it?

Without a doubt that had been the best night of her life. Janet felt truly special, *truly lucky*. At last she had found someone and they had found her. She would move out to live with Mark, escaping her mother and father, and they'd spend the rest of their days together in blissful harmony. She had it all planned out.

The next morning she did Mark's washing, then cooked him a big breakfast of bacon and eggs. But before she could say a word to him about her hopes for the future, he'd coldly informed her that the previous night had been a terrible mistake and it would probably be better for all concerned if they just remained friends. By that he meant never speak to each other again.

Had it been something she'd said or done? Janet had tried to please him, make him happy. Obviously it hadn't been enough. It was never enough.

'You'll never amount to anything, Dopey...YOU'RE A NOBODY!'

So that was that. Her parents had been none too pleased about her staying out overnight – in fact they'd been downright furious. But even after all their threats, Janet had told them nothing. They would only have used it against her. Laughed at her for daring to dream.

Mark had started seeing other girls from the supermarket, one of them being the blonde from two doors down, without a moment's thought for her feelings. For how he'd torn her apart. *Used her.* And Janet went back to being invisible again.

Bip

Pork pies: £2.50

Bip

Sugar: £1.05

The youth who reminded her of Mark was still smiling as she passed more items over the scanner. That made five. *I hope he hasn't got more than five left in his basket*, she thought, *because that's against the rules*. Ten items or less, that's what it said above her station.

But had he bought any beans?

Lord, he looked so much like Mark...

He couldn't be Mark. She knew that. He'd moved on, hadn't he?

Bip

Cereal: £1.60.

Bip

Oranges: £1.78

Bip

TV guide: 58p

Was there any wonder she got so despondent sometimes? So fed up with the way the world had treated her that she thought about how she could set things straight?

What she had done had been a bad thing, she understood that. How she'd followed Mark all those times without him knowing it. Breaking into his flat while he was out and...

Or maybe she'd imagined the whole thing.

Janet sometimes thought perhaps Mark had never really existed at all. That she'd made him up because no one would look at her twice, and whenever they did they just looked right through her as if she were...*a ghost*. Was he a character from one of those novels she'd dreamt about so many times?

Mr Parks...Mark? They even sounded the same.

If that was the case, why then was she so afraid of going to the dark place? *The cellar, the cell...* Why did she turn every time the automatic doors went, expecting to see someone in a blue uniform, someone who would take her away because she'd been so very bad? Not just recently, but in the past as well.

'You're for it now...'

No! It was all in her head. All a fantasy...*a flight of fancy*. The strain of this work had taken its toll. Janet observed the supermarket steadily starting to fill up, the lunchtime crowds piling in, faces miserable.

But why the beans? Why were they so significant, she wondered? Was it because she'd eaten them day after day at home, the cheapest food available? *Her 'rations'?* Or was it because she'd seen so many of those mass produced tins going by on her conveyor belt?

For the first time Janet noticed the old couple who'd come to stand next in line at the till. Her mother and father. He opened his mouth to speak:

'You know why, lady. So you might as well get used to the idea!'

Behind him someone laughed; it was Mr Parks.

Then it dawned on her. Beans represented the ordinary, the everyday, the mundane. They reminded her of how dull her existence was and that there was nothing she could do to change it.

Or was there?

The way she saw it, she could kill two birds with one stone. Janet would never have to worry about going to that dark chamber ever again, and she'd show the world she wasn't ordinary at the same time. That she could do something spectacular. One last something.

She'd created the blessed instrument of liberation, a means to an end, because of something her father had said; something he'd seen in combat and spoke of as if he missed the beautiful sight of it. Hadn't been hard. Mr Parks had taught her well and all the ingredients were at her disposal. She'd found them at work and in the kitchen. Once it was finished, the thing spoke softly to her of blue skies and meadows. Of a place where she could be free, where there was no work and plenty of love to go round. Where she could be with Mark forever in her dreams.

And so she'd brought it to work with her every day since, in case. Her baby – the only baby she'd ever know – not a hard labour, not like her mother's...and now, at last, it had told her that today was the day. Everyone was here, ready. Expectant. It was nearly time to:

'Bite the bullet like a good soldier should!' she said under her breath.

'Sorry?' asked the youth.

She played with the lighter, flicking it on and off. Bringing it nearer to the fuse...nearer and nearer to the thing strapped to the hairspray and the bottle of turps. The fuse was sticking out of her bag right now – or was it? She found it so hard to focus... All she had to do was wait for the sign, then the guy who looked like Mark, who might *be* Mark, her parents... (no, the husband was far too thin to be her father, surely?) Mr Parks, the blonde girl, and all the other shoppers – not to mention the entire wines and spirits section – would bear witness to her passage. She'd make the whole store glow again.

'I could see a bright light, and then...'

Just like when she was a little girl.

Janet closed her eyes, imagining the glorious blast with her at the centre. She would finally *be* somebody. No one would ever be able to ignore her, ever be able to order her around, *ever be able to use her* again.

Janet was on the check-out.

Only two items left. She was eager now. Pray it's the beans. *Oh please let it be the beans!*

Bip

Cheddar cheese: £3.50

Bip...

The Opportunity

From my hiding place behind the wall I can see the entrance clearly.

Almost closing time. Last orders will have been called. I only have to wait a few more minutes before they start to emerge.

Figures, bathed orange in the glow from the streetlights. They look unreal. I can hear them laughing. Joking. Pregnant with booze.

I stare across, waiting patiently for the crowds to thin. There I see a woman. *My victim.* It looks like...yes, she's with a group, but they're all going their separate ways. She kisses one or two goodbye, on the cheek, on the lips. She begins to walk down the street on her own. They never learn. Coat wrapped around her tightly against the cool breeze, heels clacking on the pavement. When she gets far enough away from the pub then I'll—

She turns.

Someone is calling out to her. Long hair whips round as one of the friends catches her up, a smaller woman whose goodbyes have gone on much longer than hers did. They link arms; she's going to walk home with her.

Fuck! My mind is already full of things I was going to do. But now I am denied.

Yet I *must* follow them, keeping a good distance behind. To the untrained eye I am just another late night reveller on my way home. A thrill seeker.

They stroll out of the town, down the side streets where the lights are few and far between – some are not even working at all. I'm too far away to hear the conversation but the sound of their giggling carries on the night air.

I am in luck. The smaller woman points to one of the houses on the other side of the road. The pair embrace, then part, waving all the time.

I follow the first woman now she's alone, closing the gap slightly, but still out of sight. I am in the shadows (I *am* the shadows), my pulse racing. And I can... There's that clacking again, louder now, ringing in my ears.

The opportunity has arrived and I must seize it. The waiting is over at last. I speed up. Can she sense me behind her? I'm still some distance away. If she should turn now...

Someone else is coming along the street. I jump into a garden to hide behind the hedge until they've passed by. A man out with his dog. It does its business on the grass verge.

Finally, he goes away. His interference has cost me dear, though. I have to run, fearing that I've lost her.

But no. I have the woman in my sights again, the clacking leading me to her. I'm catching up, quietly, stealthily. Hand in my pocket on the cheese wire. Don't turn around, please...don't. I don't want to see your face.

She's mere feet away. It's now or never—

And she's spotted me. Shit! No...

'Nicky? Oh Nicky, thank God it's you! I thought someone was following me. Scared me a little bit.'

She kisses me then walks on, nearing her house. I stay by her side.

'Just wanted to surprise you,' I say.

'Hmm...can't keep away, eh? You know, I wish you'd come out with me and meet my friends one night. They're beginning to think I've made you up.'

I laugh. Can she see it in my face? Bathed orange in the glow from the solitary streetlight outside her house. Can she see what I had in mind?

'What have you done with the car?'

'Parked it round the corner,' I lie.

She grins. 'Right, well...let's go in then, shall we?'

'Sure,' I say. As I tail her up the steps I wonder if I can hold out much longer. Waiting for the right time. The *perfect* opportunity. I don't know how long I can keep up the pretence. Touching her, 'loving' her. When all I really want to do is...

How long before she discovers who I truly am? Before she sees through my masquerade?

She opens the door with her key, striding into the darkness of her empty home. I follow, as I have done all night. As I have done for weeks now. And I know the opportunity will arise at some point. *It has to.* Maybe tonight. Maybe not.

But it will be soon.

Cold Call

When the call came, Martin's blood ran cold.

He'd been expecting it, laying there in the darkness. Martin had gone to bed a few hours ago, but hadn't been able to sleep. He hadn't slept that well for a good week; since all this began, actually. He'd been thinking about the events of the past few days, and how things had got to this stage. If he could go back right now and tell himself not to take that job, he would. But he'd needed the money, and as a struggling drama post-graduate who was finding it difficult to get *any* auditions, he'd take whatever he could get.

'Here at CompliCalls we cover a wide variety of areas for a wide variety of clients. We also pride ourselves on our selling techniques,' his supervisor had told him on that first day. The man had altogether too many teeth and insisted on showing them every few minutes in a smile that held no warmth, let alone sincerity.

Martin saw selling on the phone as a necessary evil and one he hoped he wouldn't need once that major film, TV or theatre role came up. Then he'd be gone faster than you could say 'Sorry for bothering you, but have you ever considered the benefits of guaranteed protection life insurance cover...?' or 'Madam, I'm calling today to offer you a month's subscription to our book club, absolutely free and, as a welcome, you can select any one of our titles on a trial basis...' The standard blurb he'd been given on a clipboard in front of him to read out.

Martin learnt, as he was putting the headset on, that a certain amount of numbers were called and when one answered he was 'a go!' – the others would be dropped. 'They're people who've ended up on lists from filling out questionnaires and the like, so it isn't as if they haven't asked for this,' his supervisor said, then grinned again. His mouth looked like a piano begging to be played.

That's what happened when people got those annoying calls at home that simply rang off. Cold calling, Martin was informed. Standard procedure. He didn't like the idea, but then he hadn't come up with this system; he was just forced to work within it if he wanted to make the rent and, y'know, eat. He didn't have to worry, though, he was told: his number never showed up, even if people did choose to ring 1471 and find out who the caller was.

Martin's first day was a complete washout. He was beginning to think that nobody out there wanted what he was peddling. Then he struck on the idea of treating this as just another role, another part to play. Martin began to use the acting skills he had to nail the patter necessary to sell this crap. And guess what, it worked like a charm. By the second afternoon, he'd already sold several insurance policies, magazine subscriptions and cheap holidays. He'd just hung up on another 'satisfied' customer – who'd bought something they didn't really need in the first place – when, to his surprise, he heard a distinct ringing sound on his headset. His own phone line was going off. Martin looked around at the other sellers, sitting in their regimented cubicles like extras from 1984. Was this kind of thing supposed to happen? He stood up, looking to see if his supervisor was anywhere in sight. Nope. Nobody had told him what to do if the phone rang at his end, but Martin felt like he should answer it. *Might be something important*, he said to himself.

Oh, it was important all right. Crucial. Life or death... Martin wished he could go back and tell himself not to pick up, just to let it ring off. Things might be so different now if he had.

But he'd clicked the button to receive the incoming call and said, 'Hel...Hello?' in a tentative tone.

'You rang me,' said the voice at the other end. It was normal sounding, if slightly monotonous.

'What?' replied Martin.

'You called me,' the voice informed him. 'Then you hung up without saying anything. Why?'

'Er...' Martin rose once more, looking for his supervisor. 'I...'

'That wasn't a very nice thing to do,' said the voice.

'I'm sorry,' said Martin, hardly believing he was getting into this. 'It wasn't me, the computer—'

'I thought it might have been something important,' the voice said, echoing what he'd just thought.

'No, no...it was just...I sell stuff but—'

'What's your name?'

'Look, I think I'd better hang up now. I'm really sorry for—'

'I asked what your *fucking name was!*' The voice rose, switching instantly from monotonous to angry.

Martin hung up, his hand shaking as he pressed the disconnect button. A few seconds later the ringing began again. Martin let it, assuming the guy would just get fed up and ring off. He didn't; the ringing just kept coming. And Martin couldn't place another call until the line was free.

He got up and walked away from his desk, determined to find the supervisor this time. When he returned with his boss, who told him it shouldn't even be possible to receive calls through his booth, the ringing had stopped. The man, who was definitely not grinning now because he'd been dragged away from important work, said he could find no trace of any number having rung Martin's station. 'But, if it makes you feel any happier...' The supervisor got one of the other centre workers to swap with Martin. He was pleased with how this new young recruit was working out, but told him to make sure this was the last interruption.

Martin thanked both his boss and his colleague, then got on with his job for the rest of the day – gradually becoming less unnerved as he went on.

~

At 10:30am the following morning, Martin's headset began to ring again. It couldn't be the same guy, he knew that, and he was about to report the incoming call when he remembered what his boss had said about bothering him. He let it ring...and ring... Then, frustrated at not being able to get anything done – he was losing commissions here – Martin finally answered it.

The caller hung up.

Technical glitch, Martin told himself. *The computer cocking something up.* He waited as more numbers were dialled and someone answered.

'Good morning, I'm Martin of—'

'So it's Martin,' came the voice from the previous day.

His mouth fell open. 'It can't be.'

'That's twice you've hung up on me, Martin. It's really very rude, you know.' The voice had a calm quality about it, just like the other time, but Martin knew it wouldn't take much to set this man off.

'What do you want?' he asked. 'An apology? I already said it isn't my fault about the first call. But look, I'm sorry and—'

'You can *fucking* stick your apology,' snapped the voice.

'Hey, I've said I'm sorry,' Martin told the voice, starting to lose patience. He wasn't normally a person who stood up for himself, but this guy was pushing him too far. 'Now, could you please get off the line – you're going to lose me my job.'

'Oh, we wouldn't want that now, would we?' said the voice, in a tone that made Martin feel extremely uncomfortable.

He hung up again. Wiping the sweat from his brow, Martin stared at the computer screen. Which one of those numbers the computer had randomly dialled belonged to him, the Voice? He could phone them all in turn, but—

His headset started to ring, and Martin knew it was the man again, just like he knew it was him that had hung up the call before last. He flung down the headset, got up, and backed away from the desk. Martin told his supervisor on his way out that he wasn't feeling very well and needed to get home. It wasn't that much of a lie.

The grin was now conspicuous by its absence as his superior told him, 'That's fair enough. You don't work, though, you don't get any money.' Martin nodded, then left – with his supervisor's words trailing after him. 'And you'd better be here bright and early in the morning, or I'm giving your position to someone else.'

Martin did as he said he was going to do: went home to his small bed-sit. He tried to watch TV, but it all washed over him. Tried to watch his favourite movie, but couldn't concentrate. He barely slept that night, tossing and turning, hearing the Voice just as he was finally drifting off.

Exhausted, Martin went back to work the next day, asking one of the workers near the back if he could swap again. They reluctantly agreed, but only after clearing it with the supervisor. The man simply sighed and nodded. Martin knew he was on very thin ice. But there was no way the Voice would find him after *another* switch.

Yet it did, checking in at about 2:45 in the afternoon. 'You don't get rid of me that easily,' it said.

Martin clicked off the line again, then continued to do so every time the phone rang after that, hoping if he did it fast enough the caller would just get fed up. But he was also on the lines that Martin tried to dial out. *How is he doing this?* Martin thought. *Is he some kind of technical whiz or something? A bored geek with a grudge?* Whatever the case, he was definitely a nutter. Martin reported this new spate of harassment to his supervisor, who fired him on the spot.

'You're obsessed, boy!' he told Martin. 'Imagining things.'

Martin was sad to lose the work, but looked on the bright side – at least he wouldn't have to deal with that loony on the phone again. To cheer himself up, he went for a walk in the park, taking a McDonalds with him to eat by the lake. He was feeding bits of the bun to the birds when his mobile went off; the nice jingly ringtone that always made him feel happy.

Martin pulled it out, opened it, at the same time checking the number and expecting to see either work, one of his acting pals, his folks, or maybe Tina – his semi-serious on-off girlfriend (more off now, as she hadn't called in a while).

It read simply 'unknown'. He answered anyway.

'Time on your hands?' said the Voice.

Martin almost dropped his mobile. 'What? You?'

'Yes, me, Martin. You were expecting someone else?' He was about to bring the phone down from his ear when the Voice said: 'If you fucking well hang up on me this time, you'll regret it.'

Martin swallowed dryly. 'I'm... I—'

'I'm...I...' mimicked the caller. '*Moron!* Nice spot you've picked, though. I like it. Very peaceful. Or it would be if I wasn't so wound up.'

Martin snapped his phone shut, cutting the Voice off. He stood and whirled around. There were a few other people nearby: a jogger, a woman with a small dog, a couple of kids. He saw no-one else. But then he wouldn't, would he.

His mobile rang again.

Martin ran, sprinting up the path and out through the gates of the park.

He took his phone to the nearest police station to report the calls, but the officer on duty didn't seem very convinced. 'Probably just a crank,' he said to Martin.

'No, no...it's more than that. This guy was threatening me. He wants to...to hurt me.'

'He actually said that? That he was going to hurt you?'

Martin thought about it, about the specific words the Voice had used. 'Well, not exactly but... Can't you just trace the calls or something? Find out who's doing this?'

The policeman examined the phone. 'Not really, there doesn't appear to be any record of them even being made.' He showed Martin the screen.

Taking the phone back, Martin frowned, then said, 'I don't understand.'

'Look, son, if it continues to happen come back and we'll see what we can do.' Before Martin could say any more, the policeman held up his hand, and pointed to the door.

Martin left, heading home, but he was constantly looking over his shoulder as he walked down the street. He was already on the bus when the phone rang again. Martin ignored it initially, until he began to draw stern looks from some of the other passengers who were *not* so enamoured with his ringtone. Martin opened the mobile, saw it was 'unknown', and closed it. The phone rang again. He got off at the next stop, the tinny tune following him, so he took out the phone and dropped it to the floor, grinding it into the pavement under his heel.

'What are you looking at?' he shouted at the passers-by who were eyeing him strangely.

After another sleepless night, Martin went out and bought a replacement phone. A cheap 'pay as you go' affair, with a new number he'd let people have in due course. No sooner had he taken it out of its packaging, than it began to ring. Martin didn't even know it was charged up!

Assuming it must be some kind of welcome message asking him to load his credit, he pressed the green phone symbol and put the receiver to his ear.

'How about I stamp on *you?*' came the now-familiar Voice. 'See how you like it, you little shit.' Hands trembling, Martin flung the phone into the nearest public bin. Now *that* was a threat: a definite threat. But Martin didn't see the point of reporting it.

He retreated back home, locking himself away and surviving on what little was in his sparse flat. He didn't dare go out anymore in case the Voice was watching, waiting. In case it tried to contact him somehow, in spite of the fact he had no mobile. A couple of times the doorbell went, but he didn't answer it. Couldn't bring himself to in case it *wasn't* his friends, or Tina.

It was around teatime that the landline in his flat went off for the first time. Martin instinctively reached for the receiver, then stopped; he couldn't believe he'd almost answered it.

The phone rang off, though, after an appropriate time, leading him to conclude that it might not be the Voice at all. Martin picked it up, once he knew it was safe to do so, and dialled 1471. It was a number he didn't recognise, but it was a number nonetheless. Not the Voice. Couldn't be; it wasn't that stupid. Didn't leave traces.

Martin pressed 3 to return the call.

'Miss me?' said the Voice.

'Now I've got you,' said Martin, slamming the receiver down. He had the guy's number. Could take it to the police. Except when he tried 1471 again, the computerised lady informed him that the number had been withheld. 'What? No – it was there a minute ago.' Shit, he should have written it down.

Martin slumped to the floor, breathing quickly in and out. He was going insane, had to be. It was the only explanation. The Voice belonged to him, he was hearing it when it didn't really exist.

The phone rang again, making him jump. Martin considered pulling it out of the wall, but what good would that do? The Voice would find a way in.

The phone rang off again anyway.

Martin hung his head in despair.

~

The phone didn't ring at all the rest of the evening, not even when Martin took to his bed again – trying to get some much needed sleep. *That's probably what's happening to me*, he thought, *probably what's doing this. I'm knackered.*

He lay awake, however, staring at the ceiling; too wired to let sleep claim him. When the phone rang a final time in the middle of the night, it didn't come as any surprise. But it did chill his blood, and the longer it went on the more he shivered. It was not going to stop, Martin realised, so he got up and padded through the bedroom, into the living room – intending to throw it out of the window. But when he reached the phone he actually found himself picking it up.

Enough was enough, and he was about to speak when the Voice got in first.

'Hello again, Martin. Don't hang up.' It sounded more reasonable than it had in a long time, but then it always did do to start with. 'You need to hear this.' The Voice was so much clearer, so much louder than it ever had been before.

Martin gripped the receiver tightly with both hands, almost like he was trying to strangle the thing.

'You need to hear this and you need to turn around.'

Martin could sense someone in the room with him, even before he turned. Could see the shadow now cast on the wall from the streetlamp outside. That was why the Voice was so clear – it was so, so close.

'That's right,' said the Voice, its tone hardening again. 'I'm here, Martin. You can't cut me off this time.'

It was only now that Martin glanced down, spotting the phone lead. Seeing that it had been severed. Martin closed his eyes briefly and swallowed. He knew the Voice was telling the truth. Knew as well what he would see when he did as it asked. The Voice was right, he couldn't hang up this time.

But the Voice *could* cut him off – and that was its intention. To cut him off permanently, leaving behind a dead line.

'Goodbye, Martin,' whispered the Voice.

And, dropping the receiver, Martin slowly turned around.

The Torturer

I'm not sure how long I've been here. A few days, a week maybe? It feels like a lot longer. I've not seen a soul since I arrived, either; shoved inside by rough hands like some kind of animal. I didn't see the men – I assume they were men – who grabbed me, kidnapped me. I know it sounds like a cliché, but it really did all happen so fast. And it was dark, too. As dark as it is here in this...cell. Yes, I suppose that's what you'd call it. One tiny window lets in a little light, just enough so I can make out what the place looks like. Four stone walls surround me, slimy to the touch. It's damp in here and smells of faeces and urine. Mostly mine. There's no bed, so I have to sleep on the cold floor. At night I feel things crawling over me, insects and I think rodents of some kind as well. Needless to say, I've slept very little of late.

My stomach lets out a cavernous growl. I clutch at my noisy abdomen but it does nothing to stop the rumbling. Hardly surprising as I've not eaten so much as a scrap of food since my incarceration. I sometimes wonder if they've forgotten all about me, the people who put me here. Or left me to die for some reason I can't even begin to fathom.

If so, then I'm not the only one.

Even now I can hear distant crying. It might be coming from the cell next to mine, I can't tell, but the very sound of another human being gives me some hope. I've tried banging on the wall and the locked metal door – which must be at least several inches thick – to elicit a response, from either my captors or from the poor unfortunate who shares my fate. But I never receive a reply.

It's like you can feel yourself going insane, in stages. No, not insane. *Not yet!* We were never meant to be alone like this, imprisoned. It's inhuman.

I pace up and down in the limited area allotted to me, trying to think things through clearly; to work out why I'm here. I'm not rich, am I? I don't think I'm famous, so no one will pay a ransom for me. Nobody bears me any kind of grudges that I can recall.

Perhaps it's just an arbitrary thing. My being here could be a random act. Wrong place at the wrong time. Terrorists trying to make a point by snatching the first person they came across.

If only they'd let me go. I wouldn't tell anyone. What the hell do I know to tell anyone anyway? Oh Jesus, why won't they just let me go?

The footsteps are loud. Because of the absence of any other noise (apart from the muted crying), I hear them instantly. The soles of heavy shoes beating out a rhythm down the corridor. Closer, closer. The tapping gets louder...then stops.

I think someone is outside my cell. I've been praying for this moment for days, yet now that it's here I'm backing away from the door. Why am I so scared? I've done nothing wrong. Have I?

A metallic jangling, keys rattling: lots of keys. How many prisoners are there here? One is being inserted in the lock. Thrust in hard and turned ferociously. It makes a sound akin to nails on a blackboard. I quiver involuntarily.

The big door opens, but the corridor is as dimly lit as my cell. I can just about discern two large shapes, possibly the men who threw me in here. Smudged figures, black upon black, come into the chamber. I make myself small in the corner, but they still find me and lift me up. They ignore my protests and my feeble blows bounce ineffectually off their hardened bodies. Even if I wasn't weakened by lack of sustenance, I doubt whether I'd be any more of a match for them.

I'm pulled through the door and my feet scrape along the uneven ground of the corridor. I look up in the vain hope that I might see a face, something to give me a clue. But their countenances are still deep in shadow.

'Why are you doing this?' My question disappears along the length of the hallway to be repeated over and over by a vague imitator. There's no answer forthcoming.

They kick open the door to a side room and deposit me unceremoniously inside. The men have vanished, leaving the door wide open. This is my chance to escape! But as I limp as fast as I can to the exit, the way is blocked by another person. He walks into the room, and brings the stench of evil with him.

Reaching around just outside the door-frame, he finds a light switch.

Instinctively, I look up as the naked bulb comes on. The blaze of sudden light sends me blind. I see whiteness, then purple dots cartwheel across my field of vision. I bring a hand up to shield my eyes and blink rapidly. It takes a good few minutes for me to adjust to my new…illuminated state.

Slowly, I look around the room, and things start to come into focus like props in a low-budget movie. It's slightly larger than my cell – though not much – and there's a table in the centre with two chairs on either side of it. The furniture isn't fancy; it's practical. The kind a carpenter might have in his workshop.

Then my eyes come to rest on the man, a thickset fellow with a wide neck. He appears to have no cheekbones to speak of and two sloping pencil-thin eyebrows meet in the middle of his brow. Below these are a pair of dark brown, almost black, eyes – framed by octagonal glasses with thin metal rims. The glasses seem to magnify not only his pupils, but also the power they have to gaze deep into my very soul.

His hair is greying at the temples. It looks like a military cut that has grown out some. And he is dressed in a black shirt and trousers. In his left hand he holds a clipboard.

When he speaks his voice is flat, almost toneless: 'Please, take a seat.'

I don't know how to react to this, but in the end I obey. With all the grace of a world-weary traveller, I slump down in one of the hard wooden chairs. If nothing else, I may get some answers now.

I wait for him to sit opposite in the other chair. He doesn't. He hovers above me, scrutinising as an owl does with a mouse before the kill.

'Splendid. Now we can begin.' His expression of indifference turns into a sneer. 'Please tell me your name.'

'What?'

'Your name. Quickly.'

'Andrew…Andy Brooks.'

The man stops to write down something on his clipboard. 'You know why you're here, of course.'

I shake my head.

'Oh, come now. You *do* know, Mr Brooks. Think.'

I had done nothing *but* that since I got here. I was no closer to understanding any of this than when I started.

'No? All right, if that's the way you want it. Tell me how you came to be here.'

'Your people grabbed me and—'

'Before that. Tell me what you were doing before that. What you have been doing for the last few months, the last few years.'

He seems impatient, as if he knows this information already. I open my mouth to answer him...and nothing comes out. I'm horrified to discover I can't remember anything before they seized me. Where had I been? On the street? In my house? (My house? I can't even remember where I live.)

The man bends over me, expecting an answer. I want to give him one, desperately; it doesn't seem prudent to do otherwise. But my mind's a complete blank. I know this, truly I do. It's just temporarily out of reach. No matter how hard I try, I simply can't access it.

'Your answer, Mr Brooks.'

'I'm sorry, I—'

He swings the clipboard around, missing my head by centimetres, then slams it down on the table.

'Not good enough. Who do you work for?'

'I...I don't remember. What's all this about?'

'It's very simple. You tell me which side you're on. Make life easy for yourself.' He walks past the back of my chair and I feel his hands on my shoulders.

'I'm not on anyone's side.'

His grip tightens, his fingers inching towards my neck. 'We're all on one side or the other,' he says. 'I'm not a patient man. You should know this. I've been hired to do a job, and that's exactly what I'm going to do, Mr Brooks.'

Despite his proximity, I can feel the anger welling up inside me. Just who the hell does he think he is?

'Listen, where am I? What do you want from me?'

'I've told you that already.' His dispassionate voice is getting to me.

'When am I going to get something to eat?' My humble attempt to sound assertive.

'When you answer my questions. Who do you work for and what have you done?'

'What have I—' The hands close around my neck, forcing a puff of breath out of me. I try to prise the fingers from around my throat, but the grip is like iron. My windpipe is being crushed and I hear myself coughing, wheezing. I can feel the pressure building up behind my eyes. If I don't get air soon I'll—

Then he shoves my head forward so that it collides with the edge of the desk. My forehead throbs wildly and a wetness is running down my cheeks. The liquid is too thick to be tears and I realise it can only be my own blood. My vision becomes blurred again and this time I black out.

In my dream I see people standing around me in a darkened cell. Like the men who came for me, they are just silhouettes at first. One of the number steps up to point at me, except…except his hand is hanging off. It dangles from his arm on a piece of loose flesh, the forefinger raised as it spins round. And now he's stepping closer, into the light. Oh God!

I'm roused by someone slapping my face. It is my interrogator.

'It's not polite to pass out in the middle of a conversation,' he says.

My head is aching fit to burst, and when I swallow for the first time it feels like his hands are still at my throat. Hot bile rises and I turn to the side to spit it out. I can't turn far, mind, because my arms are strapped to the back of the chair. Also, my shirt has been ripped open at the front to reveal a sweaty and pale chest.

'Do you remember what we were talking about before you "dropped off"?' I attempt to nod, but think better of it. The man continues anyway. 'Good. My question still stands. Who do you work for?'

'Told you.' My voice sounds strange, slurred. 'Don't remember.'

'I refuse to believe that.' He stands back and picks something up off the table. It takes me a moment to work out what it is: a length of black plastic wire with a frayed end. The man coils an amount of it around his hand and leaves the rest to droop over his fist.

The Torturer smiles. Then he brings the wire across my exposed skin like a whip. A white-hot fire runs along its tip and burns my chest. I feel pain like I've never experienced before. A cut opens up just below my collarbone. Two more strikes follow in quick succession: one across my stomach, the other just shy of my neck.

I writhe forward on the seat and groan. I convince myself not to scream; it's hard but necessary. I won't give him the satisfaction. Biting on my bottom lip helps a little.

'We'll try again. Tell me what you know.'

Panting, I look into his eyes – those hard nuggets of coal. 'My name is And...Andy Brooks. I don't remember any more.'

Another swipe, across my hands this time. The knuckles weep red tears.

'Tell me.' He doesn't shout, but his speech is louder; frustration begins to emerge.

'N-Nothing to tell.'

The slashing goes on until my torso is raw. I say nothing to him. How can I, when I don't know what he wants? As a last resort he starts on my face. I can't even begin to describe what this is like. My head rocks from side to side with each crack.

Eventually, he is forced to let me go. I'm vaguely aware of being carried back to my cell, but before I leave I think I see someone else in the torture room with the man. But then, I can't be sure of anything in my state.

They leave me be in that dismal cubicle and I can do nothing but lie on my back, trying to will the agony to die down. It doesn't, of course.

I don't know how, but I fall asleep right there and then. Maybe it's the exhaustion, or the body's way of healing itself. I don't know. Don't care.

Anyway, I'm back in the place with the mutilated man. There are more people gathered around him, not just men, but women and children too. Their wounds are abhorrent. I see one girl, she can't be more than twenty-five, with a long piece of metal sticking out of her side, ragged and sharp. It's in much further than any foreign object should be. How can she still be alive? I ask myself.

Another sufferer – I can't tell their sex – is creeping along the floor. At first I think they are looking for something, but then I see they have no legs. Something has torn this being clean in half and organs are slipping out onto the stone as they move.

Yet irrespective of their injuries, they are all coming towards me, pointing. Are they warning me of something behind?

I roll over on my front in the night and the soreness of the cuts snap me sharply awake. Someone is looking at me from inside the cell. I can't see them, but I'm sure of it.

No, it can't be... Just a leftover image from the dream.

I listen for the crying. There it is, much louder now. In spite of this, I still can't work out the source. Is it coming from next door, or a world away?

It isn't long before the men come for me again. I put up very little resistance, even less than last time. As they drag me through the doorway, I turn back to see if anyone is in the cell. Unfortunately, my throat hurts too much and I'm yanked past so quickly that I only catch a glimpse of something intangible.

Back in The Torturer's lair, I am relieved of the last remnants of my clothing: tattered shirt, trousers, socks and underwear. I'm then chained to the wall by clasps I didn't notice there before. My arms are out horizontally straight at my sides and my legs are spread wide. The chains are short; they don't allow me to sag forwards. This uncomfortable position pulls the flesh tight over my chest, intensifying the tenderness of those lacerations.

The men leave me alone with the lights off. I can hear things moving in the room. They make too much noise to be rats. Something touches my leg. A brief sensation, but enough to make me jump. Then it's travelling up my thigh, something with short legs: a spider?

No, it's a hand. I can tell that now.

More fingers join it. They pick at my cuts, squeeze my skin, pinching and kneading. A multitude of eager, grabbing hands all over me, covering my legs, my arms, my face. I want to shout out, tell them to stop. But I know that they won't. The smothering hordes progress; more stroking of digits. What do they want from me?

The light comes on suddenly. I am alone in the room. No hands, no fingers. It was all just a trick. But how could they disappear so quickly? I cast such thoughts from my mind as The Torturer enters.

'Good morning, Mr Brooks.' I can see no emotion in his face today. But the fact that he got nothing from me yesterday has done little to dampen his resolve. 'I trust you slept well. I'm sorry we had to get you up so early, but we've got a lot to do and so little time in which to accomplish it.'

Little time? Does that mean somebody is looking for me? Or is he referring to the short amount of time he has left before I 'expire'?

He walks over to me, hands in his pockets.

'Perhaps you might see reason today. If not, well...' He deliberately tails off, allowing my imagination to do its worst.

'Yesterday was a mere taster of the pleasures to come. But it would be better for all concerned if you just co-operated.'

'Please... *Please*, I've done nothing to you.'

'Nothing to me personally, no. But it's not as simple as that, Mr Brooks. When I'm called in, people expect results. Nothing more, nothing less. And I always get them. You *will* tell me what I want to know. In the end they always do.'

'How can I tell you anything when I don't even remember?'

He ignores me completely and strolls over to the other side of the room. The Torturer stands there for a minute, nodding to himself, then comes back across. As he makes his way to me, he takes a small plastic bag out of his pocket. I can't see what's inside, but it jangles like the ring of keys that open my cell door.

'I ask you once more: who do you work for and what do you do?'

I can only drop my head and sigh. There is more rattling. I look up in time to see him go to my left hand. He takes a number of small objects out of the bag and clasps them tightly. The Torturer drops the bag and produces a hammer from his other pocket.

When he grips my middle finger and pushes one of the small objects under the fingernail, I realise they are long, thin arrows of metal – possibly thick pins or nails. In any event, the point is sharp and scrapes the nerves of my fingertip.

But it isn't until he strikes the nail with his hammer that I really feel it. Holding my finger up, he bangs it right in there, embedding it well below the surface until it almost splits the fingernail.

I find it impossible to look away, even as he does the same thing again and again, planting more shafts of exploding torment beneath my tissue. As a stone causes ripples in a lake, so the pain that starts off in my fingers cascades throughout my entire body. It's like something is trying to burrow its way into my hand and up my arm: a small creature with sharp teeth, feeding on my anguish.

'How's your memory now, Mr Brooks? Anything coming back to you?'

I can hardly comprehend his words. All my concentration is devoted to blocking out my own suffering; it isn't easy. In fact it's impossible. Every twitch of my hand, every spasm, aggravates the pain.

He waits for an answer I cannot give, leaning in to hear my gasps in case I should whisper some important piece of information.

The Torturer bangs his fist on the wall next to my head. 'You disappoint me.'

Over his shoulder I can see people in the far corner of the room. It's only a momentary flash, but I see them: the figures from my dream. Then they are gone.

'I-I don't—'

'Who do you work for? Who? Who? WHO?'

'Don't r-remember.'

'What are you? What do you do? What? What? WHAT?'

He is shouting the last part of each question. As he barks the words out at me, spittle flies from his mouth and lands on my cheek. I can smell his rank breath, like curdled milk left out in the sun. He will get nothing from me.

'Very well.' I watch him go out of the room, slamming the door behind him.

The space around me becomes unreal, melting into a puddle on the floor, and I am lost to the world for some time. Yet I do not dream.

The next thing I know, a coldness strikes me in the face. The icy water, thrown by Him, draws me back to reality. The Torturer is holding a bucket. There are a few more lined up next to the table legs. On the table just behind him is a black bundle of cloth and a glass of brown liquid.

The pins in my fingers have awakened as well, jabbing me with fresh darts of distress. However, the nerves seem to be going numb and it hurts much less than it did before.

'Do try to remain conscious. It makes my job so much harder when you keep dozing off like that.' The calmness has returned to his voice. I can't work the man out. He swings from polite to vicious without warning. Initially, he struck me as a sadistic individual, but now something tells me it's just a means to an end for him, all this...torture.

He turns his back on me and unrolls the cloth across his table. More jangling noises, but heavier. I surmise these are the tools of his trade.

When he turns round again, he proves me right, though I wish to God I hadn't been. He's thumbing a large blade six or seven inches long. It's pristine and glints in the light from the bulb above.

'Do you know how long a person can remain alive during a torture session, Mr Brooks?' I remain silent. 'Neither do I, but I suspect we might find out together.'

He approaches with the blade raised.

~

The next few hours are a blur of blood and barbarity. First The Torturer slices pieces off my legs and arms – thin slices like he's carving a Sunday roast. He uses a variety of brutal tools, including one that reminds me of an apple peeler. Long strips of skin are pulled back, allowing the wine-coloured liquid to flow. Muscles and tendons are exposed to the air as he continues to ask me the questions, 'Who are you? What were you doing before you came here?' over and over, ad infinitum, until the repetition itself becomes a kind of torture for me.

The cuts and defacement of my body don't bother me that much (strange, I know). I believe I'm past my pain threshold already. But I soon discover that is not so.

The Torturer picks up the glass of brown liquid, and I assume he is taking a break for a drink. I'm mystified when he pours a small amount into his cupped hand. But all becomes frighteningly clear as he rubs the vinegar into my open wounds.

Like a man possessed, I buck against my constraints. My screams are loud and piercing in my own ears. All the things I have endured up to this point are overshadowed by his new game.

Again I feel a gloom descending upon me. I can't take much more and my eyelids beg to be closed. Another bucket of freezing water is hurled in my face. He won't let me escape that way, into oblivion. But to some extent I am grateful, for the water does at least wash a little of the condiment out of my sores.

'Tell me what I want to know, Mr Brooks.'

I mumble something incomprehensible. He takes it as 'I don't remember', the same answer I have given all along.

'So you have said repeatedly, and I don't doubt that you believe it...up to a point. But both you and I know that the truth is up there.' He points to my head. 'You've convinced – brainwashed – yourself into believing what you're saying. "I don't remember." You don't *want* to remember, Mr Brooks. Can't you see that?'

I manage a mouthful of words, but only in hushed tones. 'If you know...then tell me.'

'I can't do that. You have to figure it out for yourself. Christ, people like you make me sick. You're scum.'

'But—'

'And still you resist. Why do you think that is? Why do you think I am doing this? It's not for the good of *your* health!' He allows himself a wry grin.

'D-Don't know,' I utter. The figures at the back of the room have returned. Watching them, I feel an uncontrollable fear. Those poor, poor people. Oh God, look at them. Wretches with broken limbs and bloody faces: one small girl clutches at a teddy bear soaked in her own gore; an old woman staggers forwards, her chin a pulped mess; a young man with blonde hair is missing part of his left shoulder, the meat torn away somehow.

'You do know, admit it. Think very carefully, now. Who do you work for?'

I gaze past The Torturer and he looks back at the spot where the people are gathering.

'They know. Don't they, Mr Brooks?'

Why am I nodding? Because he's right. *They* know, I'm positive of it. But how can The Torturer see the crushed souls from my dream? Who now number at least thirty; the room appears to be swelling to accommodate them all.

'I ask again, who do you work for?'

A name pops into my head: Hobson's. I don't know what it means, so I keep my mouth shut.

'Look at them, Brooks,' he says, dropping the niceties of 'Mr'. Even after all he's put me through, I find this one small detail significant. 'Would it surprise you to learn that their blood is on your hands?'

'No! That's not true!'

'You, Brooks, are a murderer.'

What is he talking about? I'm no killer. I haven't got the stomach for it. I just couldn't. The crowd comes up to join The Torturer at his desk. All are pointing like they were in my dream. They blame me, I can see it in their dead eyes.

'And aren't they right to blame you?' The Torturer asks, reading my thoughts.

'No, I...don't think—'

'You don't think, you don't remember. I know that you *do*.'

'How...' I find strength from inside, desperation driving me to ask, 'How do you know all this about me, when I don't?'

He smiles again. 'You know the answer to that, too.'

Riddles, all riddles. The Torturer revolves now and busies himself with his implements for a final time. He chooses one to use: a stainless steel scoop.

Flanked by the ravaged collection of corpses, he sweeps forwards. They urge him on, pointing and pushing. I am more fearful of them than of him. It terrifies me and I don't know why.

'M-Make them go away!' I look from The Torturer to the faces around him, around me.

'You are to blame for their deaths, Brooks. Yes? YES?'

I scream at him: 'No! It wasn't my fault. I swerved to avoid the car... It was on the wrong side...' My breath is quick and shallow. 'I had to...turn the wheel to avoid it, then I couldn't... I lost control.'

'Did you, or did you not, kill them?'

'Yes, you bastard. Yes!'

The people nod quietly to themselves, content with my admission. I remember now who I am, who I work for, and why I tried to forget.

'Please make them go away,' I beg The Torturer.

'There are none so blind as those who will not see. First, tell me what I need to know. I need to hear you say it. Then I'll make the faces disappear.

I tell him.

And as he moves closer, bringing the instrument up to my eyes, I see his face change. It is as if someone is holding up a mirror to me. His visage has become a reflection of my own.

I hear the crying again. It is very loud, very near. I am not at all surprised to discover that I am the one shedding the tears. Before I have time to ponder this, though, I am plunged into darkness. Permanent darkness.

~

I am woken by sounds at my cell door. A banging noise. Someone is breaking in. Someone has found me, albeit too late. They are calling my name.

And they are inside. I cannot see them, cannot see anything anymore, but I hear what they are saying:

'Somebody turn on the light, I can't bloody well see a thing.'

'Watch your step, there's water everywhere.'

'Good Christ! Sir, I think we've found him, here in the garage. He's behind this partition.'

'Oh my... Look at him. I think I'm going to—'

'Has he done this? Fuck! I think he's done this to himself. Smith, don't just stand there, fetch the paramedics. Right now!'

'What's all this stuff? Clothes-line, nails, hammer...and he must have half the cutlery drawer in here with him. Shit! His eyes, he's taken his eyes out!'

'Dr Campbell, your patient's in here.'

'What's that smell? Can you smell that? I think it's vinegar.'

'Oh Lord in Heaven, no. I had a feeling something like this would happen. I tried to warn them at the hospital. Told them he wasn't ready to go home yet. And when he missed his appointment today...'

'Why's he done this, Sergeant?'

'It's that guy who was in the motorway pile-up last August. You remember, the driver for Hobson's Coaches. It was in all the papers. Right, Doc?'

'He blames himself for the accident. A lot of people died. Holidaymakers: men, women, children.'

'That still doesn't explain—'

'It's textbook. He's tortured himself mentally for months, but it seems that wasn't enough. Thank God his neighbours heard the screams. Otherwise...'

'Smith! Where are those bloody paramedics?'

The voices drone on – does someone mention the words 'fantasy' and 'withdrawn'? – but I take no notice. I can see something now. How can that be? I know The Torturer stole my eyes. Nevertheless, I see the host of dead people pointing in my mind. My accusers.

He lied. They haven't gone away at all! They never will.

But what about The Torturer himself? He *has* gone, at least for now. The voices in my cell have chased him off.

Yet I can't help wondering, deep down inside, if he will return one day.

Remote

The office building looks much the same as any other: an amalgam of glass and metal and concrete existing in the same space.

But it hides dark, dark secrets.

Every weekday for the last ten years he has trod its drab corridors, used its lifts and sat in its offices to do his job. Ten years...ever since they found out about him. He is walking to his office right now, following the directions, though he'd know the way blindfolded. First thing Monday morning and his observers will be waiting for him, ready to give him his brief, to run down the company's mission statement. The man takes in very little of his surroundings, as little as possible in fact. They're meant to be drab after all: no pictures on the walls or fancy patterns here. No distractions.

At last he comes to his own office. The title on its varnished wooden door reads: G786. It is not the room number; this is his name. Not the name he was christened with, you understand, but the one they gave to him. The one he is known by at work. The one he has begun to think of as his true moniker. He has no idea what the letter or the numbers mean. It's quite possible that his superiors have no idea either, but it is *his*. It belongs to him.

Grasping the smooth metal knob, he opens the door. Inside is a fair-sized rectangular table, around which his observers are seated. There are three of them, and never the same ones twice: a stocky man with bad teeth and a crown of grey-white hair; a very tall light-ginger man with circular glasses who has the annoying habit of jamming his tongue firmly into his cheek; and a middle-aged woman with a kindly face. As is evidenced by the building itself, though, looks can be very deceptive.

The closest to him, tall ginger, rises first. He doesn't say anything, he just points to a manila file at the head of the table. G786 nods and sits down in front of the file, opening it up to glance inside.

The first thing he sees is a colour photograph of a man dressed in military garb, peak cap and sunglasses. There's a name at the bottom, and a short bio. G786 doesn't take any of this in; there's really no need. He doesn't much care anymore. One guerrilla leader is much the same as another, and he doesn't need to know the ins and outs, the justifications – if indeed there are any. All he needs to know is the country, a vague idea of the whereabouts. He flips through the other papers and finds a map of the area, fairly detailed. Though not as detailed as the satellite pictures that come next, pinpointing buildings, guards, watch-towers...

The place where this target is located is like a fortress. It would take an expert in security and special operations to infiltrate its defences, and even then a successful strike could not be guaranteed – plus a highly trained operative would almost certainly be lost. No, it is much better this way. Much more convenient. Much easier...for them. As for what it is doing to him, well that doesn't really enter into the equation.

Last, but not least, there's a scrap of material pinned to the back of the file. This was very difficult to acquire, cut from one of the target's old uniforms. G786's fingers hover over the square of khaki, but then they withdraw – as if almost touching a flame. Not yet, not yet...

They allow G786 a further ten minutes or so to look through the reports again. He doesn't really read them, just shuffles through for the sake of appearances. It is expected of him, so he obliges. He has no choice.

'So... When you're ready...' prompts the stocky man.

Ready? He is never ready.

G786 nods, and thin ginger walks over to the window to close the blinds. The slats slice into the bright morning sunlight for a moment, striping the grey walls white and yellow momentarily. Then all the brightness goes away.

Tall ginger finally takes his seat again as G786 passes his hands over the papers, his fingers now seeking out the scrap of material at the back. He closes his eyes...and allows the sensations to develop; stops fighting what is supposed to come so 'naturally'. It always starts off with a tunnel, a rolling spiral of colours: of reds, golds, blues, greens, twisting round and around. He accesses this without any problems at all, letting the conduit take him away, lead him in the direction his mind needs to travel. At certain points there are crossroads and intersections, but he instinctively knows which ones to avoid and which to take. The feel of the cloth acts like scent to a hunting dog, linking him to his target, allowing him to cut across great distances in the blink of an eye.

The arrival is always slightly more disorienting. It's instantaneous and he's thrown back into the world without warning. Or at least a piece of him is. He sees the base now, the one from the photograph. He slips past alarms and guards without being seen, because there isn't really that much of him *to* be seen, and he carries on following his senses. He begins to rub the fabric between thumb and forefinger now, centring in on the man from the photograph. Passing through walls, through locked doors, without a second thought.

Then here he is. In a room not much bigger than his office. G786 recognises the target immediately; he is sat talking to another man in a language G786 doesn't understand. It doesn't matter really what they are saying. All that matters is that a sighting has been confirmed. G786 knows what has to come next, even though he dreads it. In his present form it is simplicity itself to enter the target's body. The method has been left entirely up to him, it can be slow and painful – such as an internal bleed – or fast and merciful, like the popping of a brain cell here or there. But whichever course of action is taken, one thing is for certain: he must exit the body before it is over or risk being trapped inside forever.

It must be done, though. No matter how much he wavers, G786 knows this. He wants to get it over with as quickly as possible and so goes for the swifter option. G786 ingratiates himself into the target's head... yet still he hesitates before doing the deed. Even after all this time, there's a part of him that... He mentally shrugs this off. No room for a conscience, for emotions – he continues with the operation. A tweak here, a tweak there. Then he gets out.

The other man in the room is quite surprised by what happens next. His superior suddenly clutches his forehead, eyes clicking backwards in their sockets, and falls out of his chair onto the floor. There is an effort made to save him, naturally, and physicians are even called in to help. But none of it will do any good. G786 hangs around just long enough to make sure his mission has been completed successfully, as if there was ever any doubt, and then departs – searches out the tunnel once more for the return journey.

Back in the office his eyes snap open. 'It's done,' he tells them.

That day he is assigned two more cases, with long breaks between each one, before being allowed to clock out. The first is a senior politician who has risen in the ranks far too quickly and is becoming far too idealistic for their liking; the second is an intelligence operative who has defected to the other side – whatever the other side is supposed to be these days.

Now it is time to leave.

G786 walks to his maroon car in the lot and climbs inside. He pulls out into traffic on the main road, then begins the half-hour drive to the place he calls home, although the significance of the word has long since shrivelled away into nothing. Once, long ago, it had actually meant something. But that was before he had been forced into the programme, ironically by their threats to tear his home life apart. Before his talents had been detected by a routine screening, and before they had enhanced his basic abilities with a daily cocktail of drugs. At first it had been just spying missions, the usual stuff for national security; finding out plans and schemes before they could be used. Locating 'enemy' safe houses and monitoring the movement of certain key individuals. It hadn't been hard work, in fact he'd almost found himself enjoying it. Not many people could do what he did and at least he was putting it to use, for the good of his country. He was also being compensated adequately for his trouble. Looked after.

But then they started to talk about pushing him further. To see what else he was capable of. To train him in other methods and techniques – the kind that weren't so palatable or easy to excuse. To send him on jobs that took a little piece of him away every time he returned, that left him feeling cold and numb afterwards: a shadow of a man.

His car journey mirrors the ones he has taken invisibly that day, except instead of a tunnel there is a road – still, the junctions and turn-offs are the same. One of these brings him to his house, a pretty white abode with net curtains in the windows and hanging baskets over the front door. G786 opens the garage door with the remote control on his key ring, and parks the car inside. He can get to the house proper through a side-door, which opens out into the kitchen.

On the hob is a boiling pan, steam rising in spirals to touch the ceiling. His wife is cooking spaghetti again, as always on a Monday. He hears singing – sweet singing that should touch his heart – coming from the hallway, and suddenly she is at the kitchen door. Even dressed in jeans and an old sweatshirt, she looks so beautiful. Her long, dark hair cascading onto her shoulders like a waterfall. She blinks with those wide eyes and tries to smile. It is not the smile of yesteryear, the smile that first attracted him to her, that he fell in love with so long ago. This is a smile worn away by heartache and pain.

'Hello, Simon.' That's G786's real name. It feels as alien to him now as the house he's in, the woman standing in front of him. She walks across to the hob, turns it down a fraction, then continues across to him.

'Hello, Amy,' he says eventually. Even her name is pretty, but you'd hardly think so the way it comes out of *his* mouth. She rises to kiss him on that mouth now, applying pressure but receiving none in return. He doesn't even put his arms around her, doesn't hold her the way he used to.

She pulls away and returns to the cooker. 'Dinner won't be much longer. Why don't you sit down?'

G786 takes a seat at the kitchen table and listens as Amy makes small talk about her day, about the friends she's seen and the things she's done. None of it really interests him. Then, as she's serving up dinner, Amy asks him how his own day has been – after all this time she still thinks he works for a finance company. He mumbles the usual 'Fine,' but doesn't go into any details. And while they eat she keeps looking at him, trying to find an answer, find some clues. She used to be able to tell what he was thinking by just gazing at him, looking into his eyes; now she sees only a miniature reflection looking back. As usual, she wonders why he has gradually grown so distant, how the man she married could have become the person sitting there now. Had it been something she'd done? Had he gone off her? The fact that she couldn't bear him a child? Or maybe his love had just dwindled away, eroded over time.

That evening they watch the television; he has no preference. Doesn't laugh at the sitcoms anymore, doesn't cheer at the football or get passionate about the news reports. He just lets it all wash over him, and they sit there together on the couch like strangers, Amy trying to snuggle up to him and getting nowhere. It's the same in bed. They undress, climb inside. She makes the first move, hoping against hope, but he presents his cold back to her. *Why doesn't he care anymore?* she wonders. If only he'd care. If only he'd...love her. Instead he sleeps, a mechanical action – a robot recharging. Amy herself lies awake for hours, worrying about what has happened to her marriage, and what might happen in the future.

One thing is for sure, they cannot carry on like this forever.

~

In fact they only have to carry on like this for another two weeks.

G786 reports to the office on a Thursday morning this time. He is assigned one mission – the assassination of a scientist about to uncover a secret that might mean the end of civilisation as we know it...being as it's such a civilised world to begin with – before the alarms go off.

There are only two observers in his office today for a change, a puffy-faced man with triangular shoulders and a slender woman with long, blonde hair, and they both rush out into the corridor. G786 follows, but more slowly. They all believe there has been some sort of attack on the building; that some intelligence somewhere has discovered its true nature and detonated a bomb. As it turns out the wailing throb of the siren is simply an ordinary fire alarm. A soon-to-be *very* ex-employee has thrown a cigarette into a wastepaper bin in one of the downstairs offices without checking whether it was properly out. The offices are meant to be a non-smoking environment anyway, so this was his first mistake. The cigarette set fire to the rubbish inside, which in turn set fire to a desk beside it and the carpet on which it rests.

After the local smoke alarm went off, somebody smashed the glass on a larger one on the wall and it is this that's causing the panic. The sprinklers come on eventually. The standard procedure in any emergency is to get out and ask questions later, so this is what occurs. G786 and his supervisors do not risk the lifts. Instead they join a group of other workers making their way down the stairs. None of G786's fellow numbers are panicking as such – only their observers.

They make it outside safely and stand around in the car park, unsure of what to do next. It takes twenty minutes for the cause of the accident to be discovered and dealt with by internal security. There is no way the proper authorities can be alerted: who knows what they might see inside? The culprit is identified not long afterwards and detained, but the powers that be decide that all other staff might as well take the rest of the day off and return in the morning fresh. This will give security time to make doubly sure the building is safe and fit for the 'workers'.

This is how G786 comes to be driving home at such an early hour on a Thursday afternoon. He takes the same route as always, and makes very good time because there isn't much traffic. He uses the remote and parks his car in the garage, then enters his house through the kitchen door again. The kitchen is empty this time. He walks through into the hall and then checks the living room. Amy is not there. G786 doesn't call out; he simply goes upstairs to use the toilet. While he's up there he checks to see if his wife is around. She isn't in either of the bedrooms or the study. He uses the toilet and flushes.

G786 knows that Amy sometimes goes out in the day. He doesn't know where, because he doesn't really listen when she tells him things. To a friend's house probably or shopping...he doesn't care. Or at least he shouldn't. Except it's strange to return home and not find her here. Every day since they've been married she's been there to greet him when he walks through that kitchen door. Back when they'd first started living together, he used to sweep her up in his arms and kiss every available inch of her face. Why is he thinking about that now? He doesn't usually. He shouldn't. Could it be that...that he *misses* her being here? That emotions he thought he'd suppressed, that he thought had been driven out of him by months and months of doing what he now does, were actually still there? And had been all along...?

He shakes his head. You can't afford to think, to feel. To care. Not when you end people's lives for a living. Not when you are a number rather than a name. A tool rather than a man.

A weapon.

On his way back to the stairs he finds himself pausing outside the bedroom they share. He enters this again. What, is he tired? Does he need to lie down? No. G786 walks around the bed, as if he's never seen it before.

It is a bed they sleep in together, inches apart and yet it might as well be miles. The miles he travels to take out a—

On the bedside table, on Amy's side: a photograph he hasn't looked at in a long time; he's tried not to. Their wedding day. G786 and Amy smiling, laughing, as the crowd throws confetti on them. He knows that he was there that day, but it seems like another man's memory. Actually it *is* another man's memory, isn't it: Simon's. G786 goes over to the picture, touches the frame with his fingers, touches the glass. Hopes that just as he can travel distances, he might somehow also be able to travel through time. Back to that day, to experience it all over again, just to remember what it felt like to—

Why? Why bother? What is the point? What would it achieve? It certainly wouldn't alter his reality.

But it is too late. He needs to see Amy now, if only for his own sake. *She'll be back soon*, he tells himself. Then he can see her all he wants. That's not the same, though; she'll be here with him. It was never the same when she was here. G786 just needs to look upon her face without her knowing. It is a bizarre thing to admit, but true. He can't explain it, either, nor why he is now going to the window to close the curtains, going over to the wardrobe to get something out...a piece of her clothing, a dress, a skirt, a blouse...a jumper. One of her favourite fluffy jumpers. She wears this all the time when the cold weather bites. G786 grabs hold of it and sits back down on the bed.

He concentrates, rubbing the material between his thumb and fingers. G786 closes his eyes and enters the rainbow tunnel, the bright multi-coloured conduit. He zips up 'roads', turns off 'junctions'; but doesn't have to go that far this time. His wife is not in another country or on the other side of the world. She is in the next town. He arrives outside a building, tall and brown; doesn't really recognise the place but knows she is inside. He senses her. It's strange, but G786 thinks little of this. He just enters via the nearest wall, passing through bricks and mortar like a ghost. And enters a wide open space with a counter on one side and a set of stairs on the other.

Ignoring the rest of it, he travels up these stairs without ever having to touch one of them. He flies, up through level after level, up and down corridor after corridor. Until at last he comes to a door. It's one of many, but it's the only one he sees. There is a number on the outside, very much like the one on his office door at work – except this one says 505. This time it's a room rather than a person's number.

G786 passes through it.

Once inside, he sees his wife. But wishes to God – if there is a God – that he couldn't. She is in a room, in a bed. And she is not alone. A man, G786 doesn't recognise him, is on top of her. The sheets that cover the bottom half of his body are rising with him. Slowly, gently, tenderly. Amy's hands are clutching his back, stroking the skin, digging her nails in as he speeds up. Now he is kissing her as he works, his lips brushing neck, and cheeks. Amy's head flops to one side and G786 can see her face.

What's the matter? You wanted *to see her face, didn't you? Only not like this... Not like this...*

Amy is in the throes of ecstasy, and G786 feels almost sick. A whirlwind of buried emotions are churning up inside him. Where before there was nothing – or almost nothing – he now feels love, jealously, anger, betrayal, hatred, and above all envy. Yes, envy. He, G786...Simon, wants to be in that bed with Amy, as he once was, as he could have been all those many, many nights when he'd turned her away, ignored her, forced her to seek comfort in the arms of another. Forced her to find someone whom she *could* love and who would love her; who'd give her what Simon could not. Warmth, humanity even.

It is too much for him to bear. No sooner has he thought about it than he is there: inside the body of this stranger screwing his wife. Simon can feel the beating of the man's heart, faster and faster. How easy it would be to just squeeze that muscle until it burst. But he isn't going to do that. He has other things in mind.

Amy looks up at the slick, rugged face above her. She's never felt so alive in her life – well, not since she and Simon used to... But suddenly something is wrong with the picture. Will – for that is the name of the man she finally gave herself to after months of resisting – is grimacing. Not because he is about to finish, but because of something else. His sweet, handsome face is swelling up. Forehead bloating, eyes bulging. And now his body is following suit. Shoulders inflating and skin stretching taut.

He rolls away and gets up off the bed. She watches as he staggers about there, clutching his head, his chest, his whole torso in fact; not knowing where to put his hands first, or what help they could possibly be when they got there. A trickle of blood is running from the corner of his mouth, then another down his nose. He begins to convulse, crying out in agony as spasms plague his now unrecognisable body.

It is only after Will explodes that Amy starts to scream. Bits of him adorn the walls, the furniture, and her. Free of the stranger, Simon looks down at his wife. The woman he loved, splattered in redness and screaming. *He* has done that, and he will do more besides. For he is not really a person at all, is he? He is a number, a tool, a weapon.

And this is what he does...

~

Monday morning. G786 called in sick for the last day of the previous week, but he is back at work now. He drives to the offices in his car and parks it in the car park. He takes the lift and walks down the corridor to his office.

Inside there are three people waiting. A small man with curly hair, a bearded man with enormous ears, and a woman with a long, pointed nose. They are his observers for the day. The man with large ears rises and points to the file at the front.

G786 sits down and examines the pictures inside. He doesn't really look at them, doesn't need to. Just needs a vague idea of the location – that and the piece of material at the back.

They give him time to look anyway, then the small man closes the blinds.

'When you're ready,' says curly hair.

And he *is* ready now. Oh so ready!

They wait as G786 shuts his eyes and rubs the material. They wait for him to join them back in the real world again, for him to open his eyes, tell them the mission was a success. But all he says when he eventually returns is:

'It is done. It is done.'

Gemini Rising

Property of the Serial Crime Initiative

Evidence Log No. 07–52–1465

Description: *Selected extracts from a journal recovered after the fire beneath Yardley Street police station, Norchester.*

Saturday, March 15 – 1980.

My name is Sebastian Craine Jr, and I'm so alone.

No, that's not true. I feel alone, even though there are people around me. Anton, my little brother, follows me around like a lost puppy. It's quite sad. He's always done that, even though Mother disapproves. 'Hero worship' Father calls it. Intensely annoying, I say… Luckily, he also does what I tell him, so I can send him off on stupid, pointless errands (I'm a patient person, but my brother tests this). Once I sent him off into the garden to count the blades of grass, and he went – he actually went!

Back to the point of this, my diary. Father was the one who suggested it, ages ago, but I was already thinking of doing something similar. Like I needed to get my thoughts down on paper.

I'll start with a little about myself. I'm thirteen years old, I live in a small village called Cambley, just outside Brenton – which is where Father (who I'm named after) works as a doctor at St Augustine's Hospital. Mother doesn't work, she just stays at home all day. She doesn't even do any housework, because we have someone who comes in on a Monday and Friday, a widow called Mrs Thomas. Mother does nothing except play her instruments in her music room: violin, cello, but her favourite is that damned harp. She used to have a career of sorts, playing in an orchestra. I'm not sure what happened, but she doesn't do that anymore.

Oh, and she drinks. A lot.

She thinks she's good at hiding it, but she really isn't. I've lost count of the amount of times Anton and I have returned home from school to find her passed out on the couch. I'm in secondary, but Anton's primary school is on the way home. I have to call there so we can walk home together. I make him trail behind me...several paces.

I quite like school. Well, the learning side, at least. I like finding things out, investigating. I'm good at history and the sciences, but rubbish at maths...and P.E. I *hate* P.E! Mainly because—

[Fire damage]

—enjoy *some* games. Puzzles anyway, jigsaws, that kind of thing, because you can do them on your own. And I'm into comics, which I buy with the pocket money Father gives me. We have a local shop that stocks the popular ones, though they get them ages after America. *Spider-Man*, *Batman*, *The X-Men*, *Hulk*. I love them all. I wish sometimes that... No, it's silly. Just a dream.

I'm a nobody, just like Mr Gregson says.

I'm a nobody and I'm so alone.

I don't feel like writing any more.

~

Wednesday, May 14 – 1980.

Someone new started at school today. Her name is Lucinda. We were in the middle of English – *To Kill A Mockingbird* – when our head of year, Miss Berkley (whose hair is pulled so far back on her head she has a permanently surprised expression) knocked on the door and ushered her in.

Lucinda is almost my height, with auburn hair. She has freckles on her nose and cheeks. Miss Berkley told us who she was, that she'd just moved to the area. She told Lucinda to go and find a seat. The one next to me was free...it always is. Lucinda came and sat down there. I think we're going to be friends. Maybe.

But the strange thing is, as soon as I saw her I *knew*. Even before her sister appeared behind Miss Berkley, so she could introduce her to the class next. Miranda *her* name is, and she's the complete opposite of Lucinda. A negative of her. Where Lucinda's all smiles, Miranda could scowl for England. Miserable cow! She took a seat near the back, glaring at Lucinda as she passed by. Very odd. I've never seen any before. I mean, I've seen them in photos or on TV, just not in person. Not in the flesh.

Twins... Lucinda and Miranda. Fascinating!

But how did I know? How did I know?

~

Tuesday, May 20 – 1980.

I had that weird dream again last night, the one I've been having ever since I can remember.

I'm standing, gazing into a mirror. But the reflection isn't really me, at least not the me I am right now. More like the me I *want* to be. My reflection is...more confident looking, doesn't wear glasses (I've had them since I was seven); I'm standing prouder, taller, instead of slumping.

Usually it's just staring back. But last night, for the first time, it moved. It pointed, as if it was accusing me of something. Maybe of not being him?

When I woke up, my covers were tangled and drenched in sweat. I've felt restless ever since. Like there's something I should be doing. I *need* to do.

God knows what it is, though.

~

Monday, June 16 – 1980.

Fun biology lesson today, we did 'abnormally formed organisms'. You know, mutations, two-headed animals, things like that. Really interesting. Miranda calls them 'freaks of nature', but then she would, being one herself – ha, ha!

I like biology. I didn't like dissection at first, we did a frog the other week. But as Mr Lines pointed out, the natural world is a strange and wonderful thing. Bodies are machines, and it's exciting to find out how everything ticks. Or doesn't, if you've just cut it up... Oh, you know what I mean.

I was quite squeamish at first, but put on a brave face in front of Lucy. Now I'm getting used to it.

I think we have a mouse coming up soon.

~

Wednesday, July 30 – 1980.

Father took me with him into work today, for the first time. Anton was really annoyed he couldn't come, but Mother told him he isn't old enough. I think she was happy just to get a day alone with him. He's her favourite.

It was Father's idea to take me. I think he wants me to follow in his footsteps. Well, he did name me after himself.

I enjoyed riding in the car, listening to the music on the radio – more cheerful than the classical rubbish Mother plays. I couldn't believe how big the hospital was when we arrived, it's massive! Father's a consultant there, he's told me before. But I got to see how well respected he is by the staff. Maybe even feared a little. That feeling must be nice. The respect, I mean.

He took me on a bit of a tour first of all and—

[Fire damage]

—until later when we got separated. A group of people came past wheeling a stretcher, there must have been an emergency or something, but when I looked up again there was no sign of Father. I admit, I panicked. And I know from talking to him later on that he did the same. Anyway, I went off to look for him in completely the wrong direction.

I wandered down corridors, searching for him in that maze. Saw signs for departments I didn't even know existed. Walked past wards full of the sickest people, lying in beds, writhing, groaning. Some looked like they didn't have long left, kept alive by machines.

Finally, I backed up through a set of double doors. It was a little darker in that room than the corridor, and when I turned I could see sets of drawers down the sides of the walls, like filing cabinets.

Something about that place drew me further inside and when I touched the 'cabinets' they were ice cold. Then I turned a corner and saw them. Three 'beds'. Except the patients on these weren't moving at all. Two were just shapes, covered with sheets.

One was uncovered. A young man, stretched out on the shiny surface, completely naked. He looked…blue. I bit my lip, but found myself moving forwards, glancing left, right and behind, because I knew I shouldn't be doing this. Shouldn't even be here. But I'd been left alone…

So alone...and...

His eyes were open, not closed as you'd expect. He was just staring up at the ceiling. The closer I came, the more I could see of his injuries. He had some kind of wound on his side, not that big but it had obviously done a lot of damage. There was one on his chest as well, but this had been inflicted afterwards – then stitched up again. I reached out a shaking finger, touched the skin. It was colder than the cabinets.

'What are you doing here?' The voice startled me and I jumped, pulling my finger back quickly. I couldn't speak, couldn't get the words out. I'd been caught doing something I shouldn't, and that always terrifies me.

I turned, slowly, to see a bulky man wearing a blue coat over jeans and a T-shirt. His eyes twinkled when he saw me, softening. 'Hey...hey it's all right,' he said. 'There's no need to be scared. How did you get here?'

I managed to find my voice and explained. He got the hospital to page Father, who came to collect me, glaring at the man – Colin, he said his name was – like it was his fault I'd ended up there. On the way back home Father made me promise not to say a word to Mother, as if I would anyway (I'm not sure whether it was for her benefit, or mine). Father said he knew it must have been a traumatic experience for me.

'There's no need to be scared,' Colin had said. But, you know what? I wasn't scared at all.

In fact, in a funny sort of way, I kind of liked it.

~

Friday, August 15 – 1980.

I've begun studying medicine and anatomy. Father has lots of books on these in his office at home. He's more than happy to let me read them. I'm not sure whether I'll be going into that line of work, but I do find it all very interesting, the way—

[Fire damage]

—has been troubling me more than seeing that dead man, thinking about those people on those machines. Machines keeping machines – bodies – alive.

I wonder what happens when you die? I used to go to Sunday School when I was little, Mother took us for a while. I remember the teacher telling us that the spirit goes on forever, that it lives on in Heaven. I'm not so sure, looking at those people, at the man who *was* dead. What if the spirit gets...wasted? What if it's just there to keep the machine going, instead of the other way around? Like a battery or something? What if there's nothing afterwards?

Anton was a pain again today, but when isn't he?

~

Saturday, August 30 – 1980.

Been having the dream again...a lot.

I think maybe it's because school starts soon.

Thursday, September 18 – 1980.

My birthday. The worst yet because—

[Fire damage]

—about any of this. I bloody *hate* P.E!!

Wednesday, January 21 – 1981.

That bitch, Miranda!

She just can't accept I'm friends with Lucy, even after all this time. Miranda's the dominant one of the pair, I know that because I've been doing some research into their...condition. Doesn't make things any easier to swallow. It's like she controls every aspect of her life. Always has done as far as I can see.

This morning at break time, I was chatting with Lucy when Miranda came along, pushed me over, and dragged Lucy away.

Everyone laughed.

~

Thursday, January 22 – 1981.

Had the dream again last night.

Every time I see my reflection now, it seems a little bigger, as if it's growing. Growing *stronger*. It's still pointing, accusing, but it was also mouthing something. That's new.

Wasn't until I woke up that I realised what it had been trying to say, and that scared me so much I shivered.

It wanted me to do bad things to Miranda.

It wanted me to hurt her.

~

Saturday, March 14 – 1981.

I'm learning so much from my trips to the hospital. Father thinks I'm studying in the library there, when he drops me off – it *is* a teaching hospital, after all – but really I'm sneaking down to see Colin.

He's worked in quite a few morgues and, strictly speaking, doesn't abide by the rules. Colin told me once that at another hospital, one he'd had to leave, he let students 'experiment' on unclaimed bodies.

He lets me experiment on them, too – I think partly because of who Father is, partly because he just likes me. Colin lets me cut into some of them with a scalpel. It's just like in biology really. He lets me see inside.

They're so pretty.

~

Tuesday, April 7 – 1981.

Bloody Anton! The snooping little bastard!

He found my diary. I walked in on him reading it in my room. 'I...I just wanted to see,' was his whiny explanation. Looking back, I don't even think he understood half of what he was reading. I'm not sure I understand it myself and I wrote it.

I just saw red, I suppose. The next thing I knew I'd grabbed him by the throat with one hand and was squeezing, hard. With the other I'd taken out my pocket knife and flicked it open.

Then I had a better idea.

I've been wanting to test the limits of how far I could push Anton for some time. So I told him to go and play on the main road.

And he went! I don't know if it was because he felt guilty or just wanted desperately to please me, but he *actually* did it. I watched him through the window as he headed up the hill next to our house, towards the road.

It was as he stood there, watching the cars speed by, that I had second thoughts. This was my brother. I was about to run downstairs when I saw one of the cars stop. Someone got out, and snatched up Anton just as he was about to...

That was one of our neighbours, a lawyer called Mr Mowberry, on his way back from work. He brought Anton home, told Mother what had happened, where he'd found him. I watched from the top of the stairs, as Mother slurred her thanks, then clutched Anton to her.

Father was less forgiving. He spanked Anton, drumming into him that he must not play up there, that it was dangerous. 'Why on earth did you do it?' Father kept asking, but Anton just stared across at me when I finally came down, saying nothing. I think Mother caught the glance, though.

I'm going to need a much better hiding place for my journal.

The basement, maybe?

~

Saturday, May 16 – 1981.

It happened again today.

I was visiting Colin when one of the orderlies brought a 'package' in. It's what they call the bodies, I guess so they don't sound as creepy. He was a tall, thin man, with greying hair. Louis, Colin called him.

And I *knew*...as soon as I saw him, from my hiding place (I wasn't supposed to be there). I had that same feeling as—

[Fire damage]

—likes to chat, so I asked about Louis while we were eating our sandwiches. *How* I knew, I can't explain – but I was right. And it must mean something.

Louis has a twin. An identical twin brother called Dennis.

~

Sunday, June 7 – 1981.

I'm not sure how to start this...

I overheard them last night. Mother and Father.

Mother spent the day playing her music, tuning and retuning her strings using her fork – not realising that the reason they never sound right is because she's always drunk.

By bedtime, she was blotto again, falling asleep on the couch. Father sent us to our rooms, but around midnight I heard raised voices. I've always found it hard to sleep and even more so since my dream started to *change*. But I was just beginning to drift off when the argument began. Anton, of course, won't have heard a thing. Once he's asleep it would take a nuclear explosion to wake him... (No, not one of those, poor choice of words.)

Mother had obviously woken, because I heard her slurred bawling quite plainly by the time I reached the top of the stairs, inching down them a step at a time.

Now I could see into the living room, saw Father had a glass in his hand, half filled with scotch (it took quite a bit to drive him to the bottle, I think because he's seen the damage it can do at work). Mother was on her feet, without a drink for a change, finger raised and pointing in his direction.

'...always been something not right about him,' I caught, before Father told her to keep her voice down. Fortunately, I was close enough now that I could hear anyway. I wished afterwards I'd simply gone back to bed. 'You can tell just by looking in his eyes,' Mother continued, voice lower but still full of hatred. 'He's *different*.'

I thought at first they were talking about Anton. He's certainly different, and when you look in *his* eyes you can see there's something wrong. I've known it all my life.

But no. Mother meant me, though Father was quick to jump to my defence. 'That's nonsense, Angela. And you're never sober enough to notice *anything*.' Then he took a sip of his own drink.

'Why do you think I started!' she answered. Now she was jabbing Father's chest. 'You're to blame, it was your idea. What you did, how we... If we'd just waited – but *oh, no!* You had to have a son. Had to have one immediately, like everything else. Well, some son he turned out to be. *Some son!'* Then her face was sad suddenly. 'Secrets have a way of coming out, of coming back to punish you.'

Father drained his glass, storming off to pour himself another. 'You're crazy,' he said over his shoulder. 'Delusional.'

'I'm telling you, it was his fault. *He* got Anton to go up there, I know he did. That...that stranger upstairs masquerading as our boy.' Father spun round, dropping his drink and grabbing her by the shoulders. She began crying, sucking in breaths. He stared at her, letting go. Then he left the room, left the house. I heard the sound of his car starting up outside. Mother collapsed on the sofa, sobbing.

I was in a state of shock, trying to understand what they'd said. No, not understand – part of me understood well enough – more like trying to take it in. Absorb it.

Stranger? That's what she'd called me. If only they'd waited... Father had wanted a son, hadn't wanted to wait.

I inched back up the stairs, wandered across the landing in a daze. I found myself in the bathroom, pulling the door quietly shut, pulling on the light. I looked at myself in the big mirror hanging on the wall.

'You can tell just by looking in his eyes.'

I stared into that mirror for I don't know how long, watching the reflection gazing back.

I was a stranger. To Mother. To myself.

I don't remember leaving the bathroom and going back to bed, but I must have done, because the next thing I knew I was having the dream again. In fact it felt like I'd somehow slipped sideways *into* the dream.

The reflection – the stronger, more confident me – was mouthing something again and pointing, jabbing its finger just as Mother had done downstairs.

When I woke, it was light outside. I wondered for a second or two whether I'd dreamt the whole thing. The argument, the bathroom. Sadly, no. I'd only dreamed about the reflection, about what it was telling me to do.

Not just hurt someone this time.

It wanted me to kill.

~

Thursday, August 13 – 1981.

I've been doing some detective work, trying to find out more about my situation.

I know that I'm not Sebastian Craine Jr. Not really. I'm not their son, not like Anton. *He's* theirs. He came along after they'd...what, adopted me? I have no clue. I can't find any information about it. No papers, nothing. I've tried searching the office, my parents' bedroom. I even looked up in the attic, down in the basement.

So many of the pieces don't fit together. And not only—

[Fire damage]

—figure it out. 'Mother' – can I still call her that? – thinks I'm a monster, that much is clear. She can barely bring herself to look at me. She knows what I did that day, and hates me for it. I *should* hate myself. But I don't. Even less so now that I know the truth about Anton. About me. He's not my brother – never was.

I wish he *had* stepped out into that traffic.

I thought about telling Lucy, if I could get her away from Miranda long enough, but decided against it. So I'm doing what I've always done, jotting down my thoughts, to try and order them.

It's not working, though. Not this time.

~

Monday, September 14 – 1981.

I am *not* a nobody, I'm *not!*

I should listen to my dreams.

~

Thursday, October 1 – 1981.

It's the first chance I've had to write about all this...since it happened. The accident.

It all began with my birthday. Father wanted to take us to the fair camped out near Brenton, to celebrate that weekend. But Mother was in bed not 'feeling well' and I couldn't see any reason to celebrate – apart from everything that'd been happening at school, it wasn't even my birthday really. Father said 'Suit yourself' and just took Anton.

It was while they were out that Mother got up. I heard her clambering about, using the toilet. I never intended to get into an argument with her, but there she was, on the landing, staring through the open door into my room. I got up off the bed, where I'd been doing a word search, and asked her what she was looking at. She just kept on staring, as if trying to work that out. And I lost it again, just like I did when Anton found my diary.

'Who am I?' I snapped, and she flinched.

'How dare you speak to me like—'

'Who. Am. I?' I said, my voice rising with each word.

'What do you mean?' she asked, shaking her head. For once she actually sounded sober.

'I *know!*' I barked. 'Know that I'm not really yours. So who am I?'

She frowned, not understanding how I came by this information.

'*Who am I?*' I repeated, even more loudly. 'Where do I come from?'

She waved her hand, turned away. So I grabbed her by the arm, yanked her back. I held her fast and repeated my question. For the first time ever, the woman who called herself my Mother looked afraid. 'I-I don't know,' she replied.

'Then how did I get here? Am I adopted?'

She bit her lip.

'What? *Tell me!*'

'Y-Your...Father handled it all,' she whimpered. 'The payments and—'

'The *what?*'

Her face creased up, switching from frightened to angry again. 'I wish to God he hadn't bothered. You're...there's something wrong with you, *Sebastian.*' She said my...the name like she was trying to spit a hair from her tongue. 'Your *Father* refuses to see it, because it would make this all his fault, but I've known for a long time. I see it, what's inside you.'

I pulled her towards me with strength I didn't even know I had. 'You have no idea,' I snarled. Then I told her about Anton, about what I'd made him do, that I was glad, that I'd probably do something like it again.

She struggled to free herself from my grip then and—

Suddenly she was at the bottom of the stairs, legs and neck at strange angles. I rushed down, kneeling beside her. She was barely breathing and I knew then she was about to—

'What...what can you see?' I asked, as she stared at me again, this time blankly.

'Noth...nothing,' she managed. Then she was gone.

I should have felt sad, should have felt *something*. But I didn't. All I could think was that I'd get the blame for this, if someone came in right now and found us. I'm not sure where the idea came from to fetch the gin bottle, to pour some over her and place it near her hand – wearing my thick winter gloves, so I wouldn't get any fingerprints on anything.

It was only then that I called an ambulance.

Father and Anton returned just as she was being taken away, after they'd officially declared her dead. Father's mouth fell open, then he'd demanded to know what happened. I just gaped at him, until someone in uniform pulled him to one side. Anton couldn't tear his eyes away from the covered-over stretcher (but it was just a dead body, a broken machine).

An accident. That's all it had been. A tragic accident – the police even said so. I couldn't have pushed her back towards the top of the stairs, shoved her down them, because that would mean—

There's something inside me. And there isn't. If anything, I feel empty.

The funeral's this Friday. Lucy's been really great since it happened, we're becoming quite close. Or would be if it weren't for Miranda.

I haven't asked Father yet about the things that woman said. How can I, without giving away that we fought, that I know?

But I can't help thinking about what she said that night I overheard her.

Secrets have a way of coming out, of coming back to punish you.

~

Sunday, January 3 – 1982

'Happy' New Year! Ha! It's—

[Fire damage]

—imagine what kind of Christmas it's been with Fath…Sebastian how he is. He's taken a sabbatical from the hospital, just sits in his office holding his dead wife's tuning fork, listening to morbid classical music.

He's taken up where she left off with the drinking, and the way he looks at me sometimes… I miss how we used to be, even knowing what I do. And Anton is really driving me insane. He's gotten even worse lately, if anything. Thank fuck Mrs Thomas has stepped up. She now does most things round the house, keeps Anton out of my hair…usually.

I'm looking forward to seeing Lucy at school this week, but not school itself.

I forgot to say the last time I wrote, the reflection in the dream shook its head after 'Mother' died. Not sure what that means. I thought it *wanted* me to—

Accident. Just an accident.

~

Wednesday, March 3 – 1982.
Sebastian Craine Sr might not go to the hospital anymore, but I still do. Colin's promised to show me how they preserve tissue next time I visit.

I'm old enough to go on my own now, pretty much.

~

Friday, April 2 – 1982.
Looks like we're at war. As if the nuclear stuff wasn't enough, we're fighting the Argentineans now. This world—

[Fire damage]

—someone could just do something. Fix things. Make things better. But you'd need to be…

Someone. Just someone.

~

Tuesday, July 27 – 1982.
Oh Christ, oh shit!

I did it. This time, this one... I did it. *I* actually did it. I'm scared and excited and... Not sure I can write any more. I just wanted to—

Later.

~

Thursday, August 5 – 1982.

Things have calmed down a little. Enough for me to try and explain what happened.

If she'd only kept out of things that didn't concern her, she'd still be... She really only has herself to blame. I was supposed to be meeting Lucy, we were going to have a picnic in the meadow. I'd even smuggled a blanket and some food out of the house in a backpack. I could tell, however, even as she walked towards me, that it was Miranda. We've been having...issues for a while now.

But everything came to a head that day.

We had words, she told me to stay away from her sister, that I was a bad influence on her – more like Lucy had been standing up to Miranda recently. Though not enough, obviously, because she'd wheedled our meeting out of her.

The argument grew more heated and Miranda shoved me over again. I fell, hard. When I got up, I had a rock in my fist. It was instinct mainly, a knee-jerk reaction. I swung it and hit her on the side of the head.

Miranda went down, blood pouring from her temple, onto the blanket beneath her. She was mumbling something I couldn't catch, so I leaned in, but it still didn't make any sense. Maybe she was calling me another name? I panicked again a little. Thought about running off and calling 999 from the nearest phone box. But would they even get there in time? And what would happen to me then?

I began to think more clearly, forced myself to. And I thought about what I could do with Miranda out of the way (*To Kill a Mocking...*), about how much easier things would be—

[Fire damage]

—the dream, what it had been wanting me to do to her for a long, long time.

I had my pocket knife with me, and I took this out. She struggled, so I straddled her, held her down while I pushed the blade into her chest. She began to scream so I put my other hand over her mouth.

I've never felt so alive. There was a charge running through me as Miranda's life ebbed away. I could feel a throbbing in the metal, a pulse that travelled up my arm into my body. At first I thought I was just imagining it, but I could sense the actual moment Miranda was about to die.

Strangely I wanted more than anything to save her, then. Not because I felt any kind of regret – I hated her. And it was too late physically, I understood that. But I wanted to put whatever she'd been, whatever she was *becoming*, to use. To direct it, draw it into me, somehow control that power.

Then the moment passed. Miranda lay still and lifeless beneath me.

I'd been so wrapped up in what I was doing I hadn't even heard the footsteps behind. Not until they were right on top of me. I whirled, startled, terrified I'd been discovered.

There, watching me with eyes wide open, was Anton. He'd followed me all the way from home. 'What are you doing here?' I snapped, a stupid, pointless question. He *was* there, and he'd seen everything.

He didn't answer, so I got up. He started to back away, as frightened as I had been moments before. I had two choices, and one of them involved another killing.

The other one was this: 'Hey, it's all right. Don't be scared. Anton, I'm sorry I shouted. But...look, what happened here – it's just pretend. A game. You like games, don't you? We both do.' Anton looked unsure. 'It can be our little secret.' I remembered again what Mother...*Angela* had said about secrets, but I'd already got him. The chance to be involved in something with his older brother that nobody else knew about? He just couldn't resist.

After I'd given him a moment or two, I set him to work. We had to clear all this up, fast. Not just because someone else might happen along – that was doubtful, I'd chosen this area for its isolation – but because we needed to get back home. Needed to be away from here. Anton helped me gather my things, wrap up the body, and lug it through the woods to the lake. Then we looked for more stones and rocks, tied them up inside the blanket with her, and pushed her into the water. She sank almost straight away and I grinned at Anton. He grinned back. Finally, I tossed in the knife.

We headed the long way home, creeping back inside so I could get out of my blood-stained top. The first chance I got, I took those clothes, that backpack and everything inside it, down to the furnace in the hospital Colin had shown me – where they get rid of 'packages' they can't identify.

I also made sure Sebastian heard us inside the house, playing. We woke him in fact. He'd fallen asleep in his office, but came rushing out when we started messing about with Angela's old instruments. I've never seen him as angry as he was then, but it was worth the clout I got – not Anton this time, I noted – because I needed him to remember. It was important.

To remember where we'd been that day.

~

Sunday, November 14 – 1982.

God, the last few months...

I've been lying low, haven't dared write anything in here since... Miranda's parents reported her missing, of course. I knew they would. When the police came knocking at our door a few days after she vanished, I also knew that Lucy had given me up. That she'd told about our 'date'.

Sebastian informed them I'd been around all day on the 27th looking after Anton. He was still in a position of respect, a doctor, even if they could smell booze on him. But my whereabouts were also confirmed by my little 'brother'. It was still part of the game we were playing. I told them I hadn't gone because I knew Miranda didn't want me seeing Lucy, that I didn't want to come between two sisters who were so close. That she must have gone missing after heading off into the meadow on her own. One of the policemen looked wary, but the other seemed to buy it.

There was a search, but nobody searched the lake. It's pretty deep anyway, I remember reading that in a local history book. After a while, and a couple of TV appeals that got nowhere, the police went away again. I don't think Miranda's parents will ever give up, though.

Lucy's...different these days. Even if I did want anything to do with her – and after blabbing, I really don't – she's not nearly as much fun. She *never* smiles. It's like a part of her is missing, the part that used to tell her what to do. Now she just wanders round like she's in a daze. Like Sebastian Sr does most of the time.

I've learned a lot from this experience. Especially from the dreams that followed. My reflection didn't shake its head this time, just mouthed more words – until I was finally able to hear it. Now I understand exactly what a waste Miranda's death was.

Now I know what I must do the next time. How it will bring me closer to the reflection, which is growing bigger each time I see it. I haven't figured it *all* out yet, but—

[Fire damage]

—turned sixteen last month (well, officially, as I still don't know my *real* date of birth). I can leave school soon, whether Sebastian Sr approves or disapproves. Not that I'm being bothered there anymore. People are beginning to look at me differently, as the woman who called herself my Mother once did.

I intend to travel.

A lot.

~

Tuesday, August 30 – 1983.

So much has happened since the last time I wrote in this diary.

Both the dreams and 'Mother' were right. I'm not a nobody, and I am different (though I didn't have anything inside me, not back when she said those words). Pieces of the puzzle are starting to slot together.

I did a test, just like the reflection told me to. I went to a busy place, the market in Brenton. I sat on a bench and cleared my mind. Then I waited and I watched. I saw three that afternoon, a woman and two men. And I could tell, just by looking at them. It's an ability that, as far as I know, only I possess.

I couldn't prove anything that day, but didn't need to. I simply *knew*.

The next step was to attempt what I'd failed to do with Miranda. The key turned out to be that fork, the one Sebastian used to clutch as he increasingly withdrew into himself.

(He's just a shadow, a...reflection of what he used to be; my reflection in reverse. I know I did that to him, but it was necessary. His sabbatical eventually became an early retirement. I don't think he'll ever return to that hospital.)

The knife I'd used hadn't been quite right. I needed something to conduct that energy, that life-force into me. So I 'borrowed' the fork, one night when Sebastian was asleep, prying it out of his hand.

It was a simple matter to sharpen the prongs.

To turn it into a weapon.

Then I—

[Fire damage]

—overcompensated, but I went much further afield to make sure. Mrs Thomas has all but moved in now. She watches over Anton and his father while I disappear for days at a time. Anton doesn't question it, he knows we're still playing the game. Nobody asks where I'm going or where I've been. I think they just assume I've fallen in with a bad crowd. Doesn't matter.

As for money, it's easy enough to forge Sebastian Sr's signature on cheques. He's built up quite a fund in the bank over the years. I know because I saw the accounts while I was still searching for information about who I am.

Anyway, back to the first one I...hunted. Yes, I suppose you could call it that. I tracked him at any rate, got his scent in my nostrils. Followed him, planned it all in advance: what I would wear – all black, including the mask – what I was going to do, where I was going to do it. At his home, where that used car salesman lived out his miserable existence alone. Sad bastard, I was doing him and the world a favour. He was in his forties, so I had youth on my side, but he still put up quite a struggle, even though I came up from behind, grabbing him and choking off his airway with the crook of my arm. We fell forward through the doorway at one point and I remember thinking: *We're making way too much noise.*

Everything changed when I stuck the fork into his back, puncturing his spleen. I felt the jolt, the trembling sensations, same as I did with Miranda, only they were amplified tenfold. And, as I grew stronger, the man I was wrestling with weakened. Not just because he was losing his will to live, but because I was *taking* his will. It was being transferred into me: all his energy, all that he'd ever been...or ever would be. Wasn't long before he was still and I rose, staggering around. It felt a little like that time I'd tried alcohol. I was dizzy, but managed to make it to the front door, closing it.

My whole body felt different and, once things had settled down, I realised that I liked it. A...it's a little hard to describe it, but—

[Fire damage]

—fire this time. It would get rid of everything, just like the furnace in the hospital. He was a smoker, so it wasn't that hard to fake a gas leak accident. From a distance, I watched the explosion, the flames rising. I felt just like them. Powerful. Dangerous.

I was gone by the time I heard the first sirens.

Sadly, the feeling didn't last. I couldn't hang onto it. The dream told me why, afterwards. I needed to *keep* some physical part, only then would it remain.

You see? Still learning.

The time after that was better. The woman, the whore. I pinned that one on her last client, incapacitating him while he was still on top of her, while he was ejaculating. Then I rammed the fork into her throat before she could get a scream out.

Oh, it felt good.

When I was done, I snipped off her little finger; it was all I needed. A body part that she had a pair of. Then I did things to the rest of her, things that would cover my tracks and ensure her customer would go away for a long time after I placed the knife in his hand.

It was only what was left behind: the machinery. I have the important part inside me – working *for* me.

The finger's in a solution I concocted myself, hidden in our locked basement. I've discovered I like it down there, underground. It's like my...sanctuary. My Batcave. At some point I will need to find somewhere better, though. Somewhere I can keep them all. My trophies. My reminders.

Because there will be *so* many more. I'm only just getting started, but already I have two more parts of my collection, pieces of the jigsaw. And I'm getting...*better* (no glasses now), closer to the reflection with each one I take. No, not take. Store, keep safe, borrow. Like the fork.

Old Sebastian simply sighed when he couldn't find it, but I said nothing. He's growing frailer by the day. I am growing stronger.

And I'm far from empty now.

~

Tuesday, March 13 – 1984.

I had to share this one with you. The latest addition to my collection.

Matt Wilson (names to faces now, faces to names), fitness instructor in a gym. I followed him for four days, the posing twat. I did so enjoy our little 'altercation' out in the car park when he was leaving work late. And he was strong; a real challenge—

[Fire damage]

—warned him that he wouldn't like me when I'm angry. Just my little joke. He had balls, though, I'll say that much.

I took one of them from him as a souvenir.

I. Fucking. Hate. P.E!

~

Friday, May 25 – 1984.

Acid is my new best friend, you just have to be careful when you use it.

I spilt some on myself by accident, and it burned me pretty badly. But my arm healed up in under an hour.

Being a freak of nature has its compensations.

~

Monday, September 10 – 1984.

I finally showed Sebastian Sr what I am, what I can do. I figured the timing was right, I'd waited long enough. I'm eighteen very soon, it's a coming of age. Time for a little 'Father' and 'Son' chat. Ha!

So I showed him my new trick.

Showed him what happens when I wear one of the faces...or even two. When I *summon* them. It's handy, I don't even need my mask anymore. I also told him it was all thanks to Angela's fork. Just before he had the heart attack (I was wrong, he did wind up back in the hospital; I *put* him there) he asked me what I was.

'That's what *I* want to know!' I grabbed him by his jumper, lifting him off his feet. Even without my new strength, he'd lost so much weight I could have managed it easily. 'Where did you *buy* me from?' Buy, like I was some kind of *thing!*

I only found out a few things before the attack came on. He got me from a woman up north sometime in late May, 1966. Where *exactly* I didn't discover. But she'd died in labour, giving birth to...

I dropped him then, leaving him to spasm on the floor, gasping for breath.

I have a brother. A real brother.

An identical *twin* brother.

The irony wasn't lost on me either. That I'm like the people I hunt. (No, I'm so much more than that.) I've wondered a lot of things about my twin since I found out: wondered what his childhood must have been like; wondered if he'd felt alone as well.

Wondered if he kept a diary like mine? If we shared any traits beyond a physical resemblance?

Wondered whether he might be a hunter?

And the reflection in my dream... I'm beginning to question if that *is* me looking into the mirror, or him? My subconscious *lack* of him. Now I'm becoming the mirrored image, does that make him the one I'm addressing? Ordering, as I do with Anton? I have a feeling I am the dominant one. Unless he's even stronger than me – than I *will be* once this is all over?

Not possible. But just in case, I'll wait a while before I track him down. I'll know when the time is right, when we're close to the endgame.

Not much to go on, though, those tiny hints at my origins, I thought. Then it struck me. That's exactly what this is.

My origin story.

I watched him die then, this impostor, this man who'd claimed to be my Father, and I felt about as much pity as I did for Angela (now playing a harp of a different kind!). He wasn't worthy, neither of them were. 'Secrets have a way of coming out, of coming back to punish you,' I whispered. 'Some son I turned out to be, eh?' I'm definitely a *stranger*, and proud of it.

I said he ended up back in the hospital, and he did…in the morgue I love so dearly. There's been some mention of Social Services coming in to assess things, but I can handle them. By that time my birthday will have passed (which in itself is a nonsense, my real birthday was months ago!); I'll take over Anton's guardianship, and between us we'll have access to all of Sebastian Craine Sr's wealth. I'll need it to complete my work, complete my collection, honing my skills and abilities as I go. It will take some time, but then I'm quite a patient person – unless I'm tested. Mrs Thompson will continue to look after Anton, until I have use for him, now I know exactly how willing he'll be. How eager he is to play.

But I'll have much more than that. And with great power comes…Well, you know the rest. This world needs to change, needs someone to take command of it. This is a new war, but it's one that's worth fighting.

I'll also have all my 'friends'. They're right here inside me, doing exactly as they're told.

Late May… I just realised what star sign that is, and laughed out loud. A Gemini.

No. *The* Gemini. He has awoken. He is rising.

And I will never be alone again.

The Anniversary

'There now. Isn't that nice?'

'Yes, dear.'

Beryl Sutton finished arranging the flowers in their vase. A dozen red roses as a centre-piece. How sweet! Everything was going to be perfect tonight. *Had* to be perfect. After all, it was a very special anniversary.

'You look a little chilly, love. I'll pop a few more cobbles of coal on the fire, shall I?' she said, not waiting for his reply. Beryl did so love to see a roaring fire; very romantic. What was the point of putting the table up in their living room if they couldn't be nice and warm of a winter's evening?

The coal struggled against her metal tongs as it was snatched from the bucket and tossed into a flaming oblivion. Beryl looked at his card on the mantelpiece (*Words cannot express how much you mean... I'll always be there for you*), then across at Trevor, her husband of thirty years. Her sweetheart. He was so handsome, especially in the glow of the fire, lights down low; no need for candles.

'That better?' she asked him.

'Yes. Much better, thanks.'

Beryl hung the tongs back on the companion set between the brush and shovel, then rubbed her hands together. She'd been looking forward to this evening for ages. Had planned everything right down to the smallest detail. The food: roast beef, Yorkshire pudding and veg. Trevor's favourite. The music: a lovely Richard Clayderman record on the turntable. Her clothes: a lilac two-piece from the catalogue – buy now, pay later. Even a bottle of the finest red wine from her local supermarket; their own brand, naturally.

Who said you had to go out to some swanky restaurant to enjoy yourself? Much better to stay at home, revel in each other's company. It was something they'd always seen eye to eye on, that. Trevor was a homebody, just like her. And she could tell he appreciated all the effort she'd gone to by the smile on his face.

'Can I do anything, love?'

'No, silly. You stay right there while I fetch the dinner.' Beryl wandered through into the kitchen, pausing only briefly to examine her reflection in the hall mirror. She patted those curls which the home perm kit had given her; the copper red tint having also come from the chemists. For sixty she didn't look half bad. Lines around the eyes and neck, but that was only to be expected. God's way of reminding you to enjoy every moment you have left.

'You're only as old as you feel,' she murmured to herself, then continued on. And Beryl Sutton felt like a woman in her twenties; exactly how she'd felt when she met Trevor for the first time. Golden memories they were and no mistake.

He'd been a new recruit at the bank where she worked – secretarial duties mainly, though she told family members otherwise. A striking example of manhood at twenty-five years old, Trevor. Yes, there was three years difference between them. She often joked even now that he was her toy boy.

Women weren't supposed to do all the running in those days, at least not in the little corner of the world where she lived. However Beryl was well aware that if she didn't do some sprinting soon it might be too late; twenty-eight wasn't quite on the shelf, but it wasn't sweet sixteen either. After holding out for Mr Right for so long, he'd finally appeared – just as she'd imagined him. And she wasn't about to let him slip away. She made it plain – in all but words – that she was interested in Trevor: dropping her papers when she saw him coming down the corridor in the hopes that he'd stop to help her; walking by his desk several thousand times an hour; making him extra cups of tea...that sort of thing.

Until at last, the shy young lad of her dreams had asked her out. He later told her that it had been an effort for him to summon up enough courage. But they were both pleased he had. Now, all these years later, they were still together.

Beryl turned off her gas oven and brought out the beef. She'd never been interested in microwaves, no matter how good the adverts said they were. Beryl liked to see exactly how her food was being cooked. She sliced succulent pieces of meat off the side with all the skill of a trained chef. Well, she'd been doing this for some time. Had to, Trevor was simply a hazard in the kitchen. But she didn't mind cooking for him; in fact she loved it. Beryl laid the beef on round Willow pattern plates, one wedge on top of the other, until she'd created a staggered effect. Next she placed the beef back in the oven and rescued the Yorkshire, which had filled out its square tray adequately – a wave-like quiff rising up at each end. A truly mouth-watering sight. Quickly she divided it up, then turned her attention to the carrots, sprouts and beans simmering away on the hobs. Beryl spooned equal portions onto each plate. Last, but not least, she poured on the gravy.

A meal fit for a king...and his queen.

Beryl carried these full plates into the front room and deposited them on the table.

'Hmm...smells terrific,' said Trevor.

Beryl beamed from earring to earring. 'Oh, the wine! Just hold on a tic.' She dashed back to the kitchen and opened the fridge.

She was glad Trevor was happy. That's all she'd ever wanted for him really. To be happy. With her.

Theirs had been a careful but wondrous courtship. For their first date he'd taken her to see a re-release of *The Odd Couple* at the local Odeon. Walter Matthau and Jack Lemmon had been funny enough, but it wasn't really her cup of tea. Given the choice she would've preferred to have seen something with Paul Newman in it. They'd sat near the back, not quite *at* the back, and Trevor had behaved like a perfect gentleman. Afterwards he walked her back to her parents' home and they kissed on the doorstep; only a peck, but it made her night. She knew from that moment on he was hers. They belonged together.

The corkscrew slid easily into the top of the wine bottle. She twisted it a few times then jiggled it out. There was a knack to it. Her brother had shown her one time. Dear Harry, she missed him so much... Out it came. No pop. No bang. Just a disappointing hiss as the air was released. The glasses chinked when she lifted them out of the cupboard. A wedding present from the gang at work; a set of eight, out of which only three now remained. It didn't matter. They only needed two.

The bells of St Mary's rang for them on a Saturday in early October. The best day of her entire life. Trevor had looked like a film star and she was on top of the world, with friends and family all telling her the wait had been worth it. That she'd finally hit the jackpot. Beryl couldn't have agreed with them more. Blissful years followed and it wasn't too long before Beryl found herself blessed with child.

She'd had to leave the bank, obviously, as a baby would mean so much more responsibility at home. But it was what she'd always longed for: a family; a husband; and a gorgeous bundle of joy.

Sadly it wasn't to be, and on 18th February, Thomas Trevor Sutton was delivered stillborn. To this day she couldn't understand it. She'd felt him kicking right up to the last minute. The doctors had told Beryl it would be dangerous for her to conceive again. Next time it might not be just the baby (*just?*). They reeled off some medical nonsense she hadn't understood in the slightest, but she took their word for it; they knew best when all was said and done. He'd be heading towards thirty himself now. She often wondered what he would have become. Whether he would have stayed with her...

Trevor had been mortified, though he maintained the obligatory stiff upper lip, and Beryl had tried not to dwell on what couldn't be changed. There was nothing that could be done. Best to move on, make the most of life. They still had one another. In some strange way she believed it had brought them closer together.

Beryl never had any desire to go back to work. They'd given her job to some teenager anyway, so she devoted herself fully to Trevor. Every day when he came home his dinner was on the table at 6 o'clock precisely. The house was always spick and span in case anyone visited. Not that they ever did – Beryl had lost touch with most of her friends, and Trevor had never been one for mixing socially; kept himself to himself and his workmates at arm's length. Trevor's parents had passed on before he'd turned nineteen, and now that her own mum and dad had gone to meet their maker – with brother Harry not far behind them; if only he'd stopped smoking – they couldn't even have family get-togethers. Not that they'd had many of these before, either.

Beryl clipped the glasses together between thumb and forefinger, and took the wine by the neck to carry it in. Oh, she was so excited she thought she might actually burst. Yes, anniversaries were such romantic occasions. That wasn't to say Trevor couldn't be just as thoughtful at other times of the year, too, especially on Valentine's Day or birthdays, buying her surprise gifts and the like. Just look at the chest freezer he'd splashed out on a few years back. You could get all your weekly, even monthly, shopping in there and still have room for things like the beef she'd cooked today. All right, not the most personal of gifts some might say. But Beryl cherished it. Any such offering was a token of his love. You might not be able to wear it on your finger or around your neck; nevertheless, the principle was the same.

She placed the glasses on the table, one at each end, then proceeded to pour the crimson liquid.

'That enough?' Beryl asked Trevor.

'Plenty, dear.'

Beryl sat down opposite Trevor and took up her knife and fork. The gravy was still hot, so hot in fact that when she popped a piece of beef into her mouth it seared the surface of her tongue.

'I think you've got the right idea,' said Beryl. 'Leave it to cool for a minute.' She smiled at Trevor. He smiled back. Beryl did adore him so.

Naturally, like any other couple on the planet, they'd had their fair share of bad patches. Arguments at times, the occasional raised voice. Usually Trevor's. Nothing abusive, though, and they'd always kissed and made up afterwards.

Take for instance that incident with the clock. The clock that stood on the three-legged table in the hallway. Trevor had won it by solving a crossword puzzle in a magazine (Trevor and his crosswords!): a china carriage clock with a black and white checked pattern on the side. Quite clever really. It was a one-off. Unique. And Trevor was so proud he positioned it where anyone who came to the door – Jehovah's Witnesses, duster salesmen and such – could marvel at his achievement.

But Beryl, stupid, stupid Beryl, had knocked it off when she was cleaning one day. Her hands were quick enough to catch the side of the clock, but not fast enough to prevent the top right-hand corner from striking the floor. The corner broke clean off and left a spider's web crack running down past the clock face.

Panic-stricken, Beryl had tried to glue it back together. But even an idiot could tell.

Trevor had been none too pleased when he came home from work.

'You clumsy… How could you?' And so on, well into the night. Beryl had cried. She didn't do it on purpose and had tried her best to fix it. Couldn't he see that? Eventually he had calmed down, forgiven her careless mistake. But for just a while there she had been worried.

Then, of course, there was all that trouble when he'd been made redundant a decade or so ago. Just as he was doing so well; a promotion assured. All those years of working his way up the ladder only for a merger to take place, throwing half the workforce on the scrap heap.

Trevor had moped around for weeks after that. Had not been himself at all. Who could blame him? Having to go through the humiliation of signing on, being turned down for all those other jobs (*too old, sorry*) and looking back on his past triumphs with nostalgia. Thank God she'd managed to set him up with that nice little position working from home, constructing dolls for a company in the Midlands. It was only a few pounds an hour, depending on how many you did, but it *was* work. It kept the wolf from the door, with enough left over for occasional luxuries – saved him from the dole queue, and ensured that Beryl could have him all to herself every day.

Life was good again.

Beryl hadn't even minded…much…when she'd found Trevor's magazines – hidden behind the wardrobe in the spare room, jammed between the wall and the wood where no one would think to look. Why, if she hadn't knocked one of their old records off the top with her feather duster, sending it plunging down the gap, she might never have found them herself.

Imagine her surprise when she saw the pictures inside. Disgusting, ugly images of women doing unspeakable things to themselves, to men, to each other! Beryl had felt physically sick. Surely they could not belong to Trevor, that was her immediate reaction. Perhaps they'd been left there by the previous owners? But how could she ignore such incriminating evidence? The magazines were far too new, and there was writing, Trevor's handwriting, next to some of the adverts: cheap women who would visit your house to give massages. She couldn't believe it!

But she remained silent, hoping it would all go away.

It didn't. It just got worse.

Tuesday was shopping day. Always had been, always would be. 10 till 11:45. But on the Tuesday after she'd found the journals, Beryl returned home early (at 10:50 to be exact). Whether she'd done so consciously or not she didn't know. All she did know was she'd crept into the house through the back door, and silently padded up the stairs.

Beryl heard the noises before she reached the top step. The creaking of the old wooden bed, the grunting of her husband, and the high-pitched cries of someone else; obviously faked. She didn't want to see. She tried to block out the sounds by putting her fists in her ears. It didn't work. Like Lot's wife she had to look, even if it turned her into a pillar of salt the size of a skyscraper.

Through the rails in the banister Beryl had a good view of the bedroom, *their* bedroom, its door ajar, a woman of maybe thirty with long dirty-blonde hair riding her spouse like a jockey on Grand National day. And Trevor's face: screwed up, the sweat streaming from his balding scalp.

Beryl turned and ran, down the stairs and out of the back door. There she sat on the cold stone step, sobbing her heart out. Trevor had said it was okay if they...didn't anymore. It just wasn't right, not after the baby and everything. He'd never complained. If he had then maybe she...

But now this! How could she ever face him again?

However, face him she did, at 11:45 when she came through the front door, a little less loaded up than usual. Beryl said nothing. She simply kissed Trevor on the cheek. She could forgive him. If that was all he wanted every now and again, well she could turn a blind eye. It was a small price to pay for having him at home with her where he belonged. At least he wasn't having an affair.

Although even that hadn't been the true test of their marriage. This had come a short while later...on the day he announced he was leaving her.

Shocked and stunned, Beryl had stood watching him struggle with his suitcase down the stairs; shirtsleeves and trouser legs sticking out here and there. He never did know how to pack properly.

'I need to get away from here. From this town, this house. From you!

Can't you see how I've wasted the last twenty-nine years? How *you've* wasted them?'

Beryl shook her head. No, quite frankly she couldn't. She'd done everything in her power to please Trevor. He wasn't just going to walk out on her like this. How would she cope without him?

Wasted her life? HE WAS HER LIFE!

'No, Trevor please—'

'This is something I've got to do. It's been on my mind for some time. I'm sorry.'

Beryl recalled the scene, one year ago to the day, while she chewed her carrots. She smiled at Trevor. He smiled back. They'd worked through it together. Come out the other side with a greater respect for one another. A greater *understanding*...although she had to admit he'd scared her quite badly at the time.

Particularly when he'd turned away, heading towards the front door with his case in one hand, his coat gripped in the other. He wouldn't even stop to put it on.

What else was she expected to do? Beryl refused to let him go.

The crossword clock was the first thing that came to hand. It made a wet thudding noise as it connected with the back of Trevor's skull; shattering both the ornament and bone simultaneously.

Trevor had dropped to his knees, the suitcase flung aside as he felt at the wound she'd inflicted on him. His eyes went wide when he turned to face her, as if he couldn't believe what she had done. His mouth a grimace that could almost be mistaken for a smile.

Blood washed down his neck, staining his light blue jumper, turning it the colour of...*red wine*. He fell forward, allowing more of the liquid to seep out, splashing all over her nice clean floor.

Tutting, Beryl had gone through to the kitchen for a cloth.

Trevor, his head pounding, had summoned up enough strength to move. He managed to get his right arm underneath him and push up. His left hand was reaching out for the doorknob. If he could just get out into the street someone would see him and—

But that was when he'd felt something pointed enter his back, rammed in with considerable force. It seemed to take forever for the carving knife to come out the other side, slicing through his flesh and bone, puncturing his heart (*his sweet, sweet heart*) along the way. Even more vital fluid pooled around him. Beryl looked down at Trevor, trying to come to terms with what had happened, to rationalise and justify it. She concluded that he was still here, with her. That was the most important thing.

Then as a 'thank you', she stooped and kissed him on the cheek.

It had taken some cleaning up, that hallway – blood's a swine to get out of your carpet – but somehow Beryl got it all looking shipshape and Bristol fashion again. Alas, there was no salvaging the clock this time. For a while she'd sat Trevor in his favourite armchair. However, some logical sliver of her mind told her that soon he would begin to smell.

That's when she'd struck upon the notion of the freezer. It seemed appropriate. His prophetic gift to her, and now his new quarters. Somewhere he could put his feet up and relax, then come out feeling refreshed and alert. Ready to face the world again.

Although he always stayed at the bottom and the food remained at the top. Couldn't disturb Trevor while he was sleeping.

Because that's all he was doing in there really, sleeping.

Often during the night Beryl would wake up in a cold sweat, believing him to be dead. But how could he be? If he was a corpse, then how come he still talked to her? How was it he'd forgiven her for what she'd done? He'd even told her to take over the doll-making business while he was feeling a bit under the weather; then they'd have enough to live off each week – the money deposited into their joint account at the bank every Friday.

She actually enjoyed the work, too. It kept her mind active. That and the crossword puzzles. As for any official documents that came, well, she had Trevor's permission to sign his name – she could do this blindfolded after thirty years. That's what marriages were about at the end of the day, sharing the load...*for better or worse, in* sickness *and in health*. In a few years Trevor would be on a pension too, just like her. Then they wouldn't have to worry about a thing. They could both...retire.

Yes, life was just fine at the moment. Couldn't be better. The best it had been for a long time now she knew Trevor wouldn't leave her.

Beryl looked at Trevor again. He'd hardly touched his food.

'Not hungry, darling?'

Trevor dropped face-first into the dinner, the hole in the rear of his head clearly visible. Beryl pushed him back on the seat and wiped his face clean with a paper napkin.

'Clumsy,' she said giggling. She didn't have long now; the fire was speeding things up. He would have to go back soon.

Beryl took her wineglass in her hand. 'I propose a toast. To the anniversary of our marriage...and to the first anniversary of our...*fresh* start together. Here's to the next thirty years!'

Beryl clinked the two glasses together. She smiled at Trevor across the table.

Trevor smiled back.

1, 2, 3 . . . 1, 2, 3

The numbers. They were the worst part.

Counting, and the continual repetition. 1, 2, 3...1, 2, 3. But it had to (3, 1, 2) be done. There was no escaping the fact that she *had* to (3, 1, 2) do it. Michelle Blake was a prisoner of the numbers, of the counting. She performed her bizarre acts like a dancer obeying the rhythm of a silent tune. 1, 2, 3...1, 2, 3... or a fitness fanatic following a precise work-out routine. Never any release, never any differentiation.

She mouthed the numbers even now as she placed one (2, 3, 1) foot in front of the other. Forwards and back again, keeping a watchful eye on the pattern of the carpet. Michelle had long since broken the concentric square motif down into (3, 1, 2) a series of arithmetical interpretations. It no longer represented any aesthetic value to (3, 1, 2) her, like everything else it was part of a template she lived by – though many wouldn't even call what she lived a life. When she looked around all she could see were the numbers, those three...1, 2, 3...numbers. Everything fitted into (3, 1, 2) that familiar triad.

1, 2, 3...1, 2, 3. She would make it to (3, 1, 2) the living room door in what, half an hour? That was quite fast for her. During her darkest days it had taken something like two (3, 1, 2) or three (1, 2, 3) hours to (3, 1, 2) cover a few metres. Stopping, starting, beginning again. Never right. Never enough times; she was never able to (3, 1, 2) reconcile it in her mind. If it wasn't done correctly then she knew what would happen. The consequences didn't bear thinking about and the responsibility was hers to (3, 1, 2) shoulder alone.

No, no it wasn't. Not anymore. For one (2, 3, 1) thing she had to (3, 1, 2) stop thinking about it as a responsibility. It wasn't; it was a combination of chemicals and conditioning. Imbalances and habituations. She had to (3, 1, 2) start thinking about it as more of a disorder than a birthright – or a princess being handed a crown and a kingdom.

'Trust me,' she whispered under her breath, in the slight gap between counting, 'this is not a kingdom I'd choose to...3, 1, 2...rule.'

But whether it was a responsibility or not, she no longer had to (3, 1, 2) cope with it on her own. After twenty-five years of being passed from pillar to (3, 1, 2) post, she had finally found the support she needed in Josh. Not Dr Nesbit, not even Dr Josh. Just Josh – plain old Josh, although with the best will in the world nobody could ever describe him as plain. Not with that curtain of blond hair and starry eyes...

Concentrate, Michelle, or you'll never get to...3, 1, 2...the door. Or worse still, she might lose count again and have to 3, 1... *Damn!* Michelle sighed and backtracked carefully, starting again, quite literally, from square 1 (2, 3, 1).

But now that the thought of Josh was in her mind, she found it all but impossible to (3, 1, 2) get rid of it. She'd known him almost two...3, 1, 2...years now. A young therapist who'd heard about her plight and taken a special interest. He was the reason it only took her half an hour to (3, 1, 2) cross a room and not longer. The work they had done to(3, 1, 2)gether had given her new hope. He'd broken down her affliction into (3, 1, 2) its component parts: delved deeper than anyone (2, 3, 1) had ever bothered before, or she'd let anybody delve – because it was Josh, because she trusted him and, if she was honest with herself, was more than a little in love with him.

Josh didn't look at her like she was a freak. Okay, she knew it was part of his job not to (3, 1, 2) look at her that way, but that hadn't stopped most of the medicos she'd known from doing just that. No, Michelle knew it was more than that. He *did* genuinely care about her and that meant the world. Even so, it had taken some time to (3, 1, 2) get her to (3, 1, 2) open up, to (3, 1, 2) get her to (3, 1, 2) remember.

It was a strange thing, she'd thought her memory was lousy. She couldn't recall actions she'd just performed, couldn't bring to (3, 1, 2) mind carrying them out: hence the repetition in case she'd done it wrong or hadn't counted correctly. But Josh taught her that there was nothing wrong with her memory at all. It was her mind purposely rubbing this out so that she would *have* to (3, 1, 2) keep doing the 'Groundhog Day' thing, as he called it. The way Josh explained this was by comparing it to (3, 1, 2) someone (2, 3, 1) who didn't think they deserved to (3, 1, 2) be happy.

'Think about it,' he'd said. 'They unconsciously create difficulties to ensure that they won't ever reach that state. They won't be happy because they're not giving themselves permission to be. Does that make sense?'

Michelle had nodded, flicking the light switch on and off and counting out loud, '1, 2, 3…1, 2, 3.'

'In your case, though, you're not giving yourself permission to be free of this. You're caught in a loop, or a sequence of loops, that you don't want to break out of. At least not yet.' He paused. 'The question is – why?'

Michelle broke off from the switch for a second. 'I don't enjoy doing this,' she told him, then continued flicking the light switch.

'I know you don't, *of course* you don't.' Josh put a hand on her shoulder. 'Jesus, who would? But that's not the point I'm making, Michelle.'

She almost stopped then, but caught herself in time, and started counting faster: '1-2-3, 1-2-3, 1-2-3.'

'You're doing this for a reason. We just have to figure out what it is.' He smiled, and it was the sweetest thing she'd ever seen.

The hard labour had started in earnest after that, trudging through the minutiae of her life. God, *that* had been fun. About how she'd been living in that house for the seven years since her mother left virtually on her own, a recluse from society, surviving only with the aid of social services and various medical staff who would come in and check that she was okay – or as okay as Michelle could be – periodically.

'Thank heavens for takeaway pizza,' she'd said. The joke had been forced and neither of them laughed. 'I don't even have to…3, 1, 2…count the knives and forks for that. Don't even have to…3, 1, 2…make it to…3, 1, 2…the kitchen, just the front door.'

Doctors and the usual 'nutcrackers' – her words – had visited Michelle since she was little. Her mother had made sure she received attention from the best ('She felt she had to…3, 1, 2… Anything to…3, 1, 2…have a "normal" daughter,'). But nobody had been able to (3, 1, 2) do anything for her. In fact half of them didn't have the first clue where to (3, 1, 2) begin. Obsessive Compulsive Disorder specialists came and looked at her, prescribed pills and tried to (3, 1, 2) talk her through the treatments. None of them worked.

'I could hear what they were telling me…1, 2, 3…I knew they were right, honestly I did,' Michelle said to Josh.

'But hearing and believing are two different things.'

'I suppose they are...1, 2, 3...and then you came along.'

Josh tipped his head, slightly embarrassed, before looking up at her again. 'Then I came along,' he said.

She told him about everything she'd been through, about how her mother had been forced to (3, 1, 2) hire private tutors to (3, 1, 2) teach her because she couldn't get Michelle to (3, 1, 2) school – any kind of school. Couldn't get her to (3, 1, 2) go out of the front door. For her the outside world was like a minefield, an overwhelming barrage of things to (3, 1, 2) do three (1, 2, 3) times, times a million. Panic would set in before she even got to (3, 1, 2) the gates of the old house, the numbers coming out as incomprehensible drivel. It wouldn't be long after this that she'd enter a catatonic state, collapse or pass out – probably all three (1, 2, 3). The oblivion that this offered was actually quite nice; it was like when she took her sleeping tablets.

'Mother used to...3, 1, 2...try and get the neighbourhood children to...3, 1, 2...come round and play,' Michelle told him. 'But you can imagine what that was like, can't you? Who wants to...3, 1, 2...play with a kid who keeps getting up and down off the settee or is counting the cushions over and over again? And children can be very cruel.'

As a result she'd never really had any friends, nobody willing to (3, 1, 2) stick around. Nobody willing to (3, 1, 2) try and understand. But then how could she expect them to (3, 1, 2), when she didn't really understand herself?

'What if we were to go back further than that?' Josh had said to (3, 1, 2) her eventually. 'Can you remember anything about your early childhood?'

'Numbers,' Michelle had replied. *Always the numbers.* '1, 2, 3...1, 2, 3.' She knew what he was driving at. When did all this start? But at the time she couldn't honestly tell him. All she'd ever known was the numbers and the counting. Her unique way of viewing what she saw around her.

'Yes, numbers. But what else?' Those expectant eyes, she didn't want to (3, 1, 2) disappoint him. Not Josh.

'Stories. Mother trying to...3, 1, 2...read to...3, 1, 2...me; folktales mostly.'

And Josh had come back with something totally unexpected then. 'I see. Michelle, did you know that a lot of the old folktales had threes in them?'

'1, 2, 3… No.'

'Goldilocks and the Three Bears. The Three Pigs. Red Riding Hood when she confronts the wolf at the end of the story: Gramma, one…' Josh held up a finger. 'What big eyes you've got. Two…' Another finger. 'What big ears you've got – and we all know what happened when she got to the teeth!' A third finger rose and he closed his fist. 'The fact is they mostly followed patterns connected with threes.'

'Oh,' said Michelle. 'My favourite was always the one…2, 3, 1…where the handsome prince would come to…3, 1, 2…the secluded castle to…3, 1, 2…save the damsel in distress. I liked that one…2, 3, 1.' She gazed at him and he grinned.

'You mean like Sleeping Beauty?'

Michelle nodded, still mouthing the numbers.

'One day you'll wake up, Michelle. I promise.' And then they'd moved on to (3, 1, 2) another topic.

It was amazing really, but until Josh had mentioned the 'threes' Michelle had never really thought about how so many sayings in life were related that way. Third time lucky, bad things always happening in threes, letting the phone ring three (1, 2, 3) times before answering.

Father, Son and the Holy Ghost…

'You never talk much about your father.' That was how the conversation began.

Michelle had been stirring her coffee at the time. Round three (1, 2, 3) times, stop, then round again. She'd been doing that for the last fifteen minutes. Josh knew her well enough to (3, 1, 2) realise that any moment now she'd take it out and start tapping it on the side of the cup: three (1, 2, 3) times, over and over. The coffee would be stone cold by now. She said nothing by way of a reply.

'Your records say he died when you were very young, Michelle.'

'My records,' she snapped. 'Is that all I am? Is that what I'm made up of, a set of files in some office?' *A set of files in triplicate.*

It was a reflex action, and a diversionary tactic. 'You know that's not true. Why are you trying to change the subject?'

'1, 2, 3…1, 2, 3…I'm not.'

'Tell me about him.'

'Who?'

'Your father.'

The spoon came out of the cup and Michelle initiated the tapping. 'There's nothing to...3, 1, 2...tell. He died, end of story.'

Except it wasn't, was it? It was only the beginning of the story.

Josh leaned over the dining room table they were sitting at. 'Did you love him?'

'What kind of a question is that?' Michelle tapped the spoon harder against the rim of the cup.

'The kind you're not answering.'

She looked down at the spoon and the cup. The tapping had slowed considerably. 'Yes,' she said finally. 'It was a long time ago, but yes. I loved him very much.'

'What are your fondest memories of him, Michelle?'

Looking up, she searched his face. 'I don't...'

Josh took her free hand, the one (2, 3, 1) not tapping the spoon. 'Think back. You can do this, I know you can.'

And she did. She cast her mind back to (3, 1, 2) a time when she'd been happy. Big, strong hands lifting her up into (3, 1, 2) the air and Michelle giggling with glee. Riding on his shoulders through a park or wood, somewhere green at least. A family day out, a picnic maybe... Michelle wasn't sure. But there was water, she remembered a river, and the sun. A sun she'd rarely seen, a heat she'd rarely felt against her skin in almost twenty two (3, 1, 2) years. She could hear the birds in the trees, see the dappled light filtering through the leaves.

The spoon was hardly connecting with the cup at all. 'He was so proud of me,' Michelle said. 'I was his little Button. He kept talking about all the things I would do, places I'd go...and how clever I was. He was even teaching me—' She froze, began tapping the spoon faster against the rim.

Josh squeezed Michelle's hand tighter. 'Tell me, Michelle. What happened to him?'

There were tears in her eyes, still caught there, trapped. But it wouldn't be long before they broke free and ran down her cheeks. 'People. Pictures of people. Pictures of animals...and shapes...'

Josh frowned. 'I...I don't understand, Michelle.'

'1, 2, 3…1, 2, 3. All the way through. One person, two people, three…one cat, two dogs, three birds. One square, two circles, three triangles.' Michelle reeled off the list like a mantra.

'Is this how you first started to look at the world around you?'

'One person, two people, three…one cat, two dogs…' she repeated.

'What's the connection to your father, Michelle? You have to tell me. It's important.'

Michelle shook her head and carried on chanting.

Josh squeezed her hand even tighter and something seemed to (3, 1, 2) click inside her head. 'Tell me,' he whispered.

When she spoke again, it was staggered, as if it was painful to (3, 1, 2) get the words out. 'In…the…book.'

It took a second or so for realisation to (3, 1, 2) dawn on Josh. 'My God, the people, the animals, the shapes – they were in a book. Michelle, was your father teaching you to count?'

'1, 2, 3…1, 2, 3…1, 2, 3…' Michelle was tapping the spoon so hard it chipped the side of the cup.

'So you were learning to count from a book that you father gave you?' The pictures, the numbers. It certainly explained why she'd started to (3, 1, 2) make those links. Why Michelle had begun to (3, 1, 2) break everything in life down to (3, 1, 2) those three (1, 2, 3) little digits. But not why she'd carried on counting, and the same numbers over and over. Josh pressed her, even though he could see she was upset. 'Michelle, what happened to your father?'

'Daddy…Daddy…Daddy!'

'Something happened to him, didn't it?'

'Phone…three…1, 2, 3…rings,' Michelle spluttered. Then one word: 'Hospital.'

'What were you doing when the phone rang, Michelle? Were you reading from the book? Were you counting?'

'1, Daddy told me 2 practice and never…3.'

'Never stop?' Josh asked. 'Is that why you carried on counting, because he wasn't around to tell you to stop? You felt you had to carry on after he died, to finish what he started?'

She shook her head. 'No…1, 2, 3… *No!*'

'I'm here, Michelle, you can tell me.'

So she did.

Now, as she crossed the carpet and remembered what she'd shared with Josh, what she'd allowed herself to (3, 1, 2) dredge up not so long ago, the tears came again. The splintering of the cup as she knocked it off the table. Josh holding her as she wept. And one (2, 3, 1) final thing: a kiss on the forehead, just like her father used to (3, 1, 2) give her.

She remembered what he'd said as well: 'Sleeping Beauty, it's time to wake up.'

Michelle hadn't done that immediately. It had been a slow waking, but with Josh's help in the two (3, 1, 2) weeks since she'd opened up, she'd begun to (3, 1, 2) see things a little more clearly. Begun to (3, 1, 2) realise that maybe it *was* time and that even though she was still following the patterns right now, perhaps she could turn the tide. Give herself permission to (3, 1, 2) be free of this prison forever. She wanted to (3, 1, 2) be able to (3, 1, 2) cook Josh a meal to (3, 1, 2) say thank you, to (3, 1, 2) go outside and see the sun properly again. Walk through dappled forests again, perhaps hand in hand with the man who'd done so much for her.

Could she simply just stop, though, after all this time? After all these years of counting…1, 2, 3…1, 2, 3…? Michelle was so set in her ways, stuck in this rut.

Sleeping beauty, it's time to wake up.

Time to (3, 1, 2) leave the kingdom behind for someone else to (3, 1, 2) rule.

'It wasn't your fault,' Josh had said. He was the one who'd made her understand. It was just a coincidence; that's all it was. Just a coincidence.

Michelle wasn't far away from the living room door now. It would take her another five minutes at least – 1, 2, 3…1, 2, 3 – or she could cover the distance in a matter of moments. Her choice, her decision.

'1, 2, 3…'

Enough.

'1, 2, 3…'

Enough.

'1, 2…'

Enough!

All was quiet. Michelle stood perfectly still, hardly daring to move. It was as if she'd forced time to do the same, frozen until it saw what her next move would be. Gritting her teeth and closing her eyes, she placed a foot on the carpet. Then another, and another. No counting. No 1, 2, 3. Just walking normally, something other people took for granted. She had a bit of a wobbly moment after the third step – instinctively she wanted to take her foot back, to repeat the motion, do the steps again. But she held fast, carrying on to the door and placing a hand on the jamb for support. She opened her eyes and breathed deeply. It might seem like nothing much to anyone else, but for her it was a small victory. The beginning of a new life perhaps.

Briiiinnnggg-briiiiiing...

Michelle jumped, turning sideways to look at the hall table, her heart suddenly in her mouth. God, it was only...

Only—

Bad things always happening in threes...

In the name of the Father, Son and the Holy Ghost...

Amen...

Briiiinnnggg-briiiiiing...

Michelle bit her lip. She should answer it, should just pick it up and dispel her demons once and for all. Except...except she knew who it would be. What it would be about. What had happened, *again*. She'd abandoned her duties, her responsibilities, and now the kingdom was falling apart without her.

Let it ring one more time, a third time. Just let it ring.

She wondered what she would do now without him.

No, maybe it's not too late?

Briiiinnnggg-briiiiiing...

...3...

1, 2, 3, 1, 2... Not too (3, 1, 2) late, to (3, 1, 2) save him. She'd only stopped for a little while.

Crying, Michelle picked up the receiver. Counting all the time under her breath.

1, 2, 3...1, 2, 3...

1, 2, 3...1...

2...

3.

The Greatest Mystery

My dear and faithful reader. It is only now that I am able to recount the truly shocking events of what I firmly believe to be my dearest friend and colleague Sherlock Holmes' greatest ever mystery. Upon first reading these words, you may feel my claim is somewhat of an exaggeration. What about the case of the Baskerville Hound, you might ask, quite possibly his most famous adventure to date? What about his entanglements with the evil Professor Moriarty (the merest mention of which will later have great significance, I can assure you)? But I have faithfully chronicled the master detective's cases over the years and I can categorically attest to the validity of my statement. I alone was witness to its eventual outcome and, once you have finished this offering, I feel certain that you too will agree about the choice of its title. I can also promise that while I have been taken to task in the past for what Holmes called my embellishment of these accounts – the addition of, to quote the man himself, 'colour and...life' (the latter an irony, as you will soon see) – there isn't a word of this that is not the whole truth. Whether you believe me or not is, in the end, your choice – all I can do is report the facts of this most singular case as I experienced them, no matter how strange they might seem.

The matter in question began with a simple case – although you might recall the air of strangeness and tension against which it was set, in the months approaching the turn of the last century. Indeed, these very events were thought by some to be interlinked, though you will soon realise that this was not in fact so. The real explanation goes beyond that, beyond anything you might have thought possible. But I am getting ahead of myself once more... The case in hand was an apparently straightforward crime, yet as Holmes is often at great pains to teach me, things are seldom what they appear at first glance.

And so, to the details. A lady by the name of Miss Georgia Cartwright called upon us one afternoon in late September, begging that we pay a visit to her cousin Anthony.

'In jail,' Holmes said, motioning for Miss Cartwright to sit down.

When he noticed her look of confusion, he waved a hand and explained: 'The faint marks on your dress and your arms, a distinctive pattern showing you have recently been pressed up against a set of iron bars. Pray tell us of what your cousin is accused, Miss Cartwright?'

'I am sad to say Anthony stands accused of…of…murdering his fiancée, and *my* best friend, Miss Judith Hatten,' she told us, gratefully accepting both the seat and the handkerchief I'd produced to dry her eyes with. 'But he cannot have, he simply *cannot*.'

Holmes sat down opposite her, steepling his fingers. 'If you would furnish me with the facts, Miss Cartwright – and please do not leave anything out. Even the smallest detail might be of significance.'

Sadly, it soon became clear, as she related what she knew, that the culprit could be *none other* than her relation. The night before last Anthony had visited Judith to discuss their forthcoming wedding. Upon hearing a disturbance in the living room, where Anthony had been escorted only minutes beforehand, the girl's only living parent – her father – discovered the young man standing over the body of Judith. His daughter had suffered a tremendous head wound. In Anthony's hand was a poker, the end of which was dripping with blood. Mr Hatten flew into a rage and had to be held back by his staff from attacking Anthony himself, while Miss Cartwright's cousin was held down until the authorities arrived.

Holmes frowned, obviously reaching the same conclusion as I.

'He swears it was not him, says that he cannot remember what happened, Mr Holmes. And I believe him. Anthony is the gentlest man in the world and he did so love Judith. I know he did. He would never have raised a finger to hurt her.'

Holmes raised an eyebrow. 'It is so often the case, however, that we do not *truly* know our friends and loved ones, Miss Cartwright.'

'We grew up together and were as close as brother and sister. I *do* know him, Mr Holmes. Please, I implore you,' she said, clasping her hands together. 'Visit him yourself.'

Holmes glanced sideways, attempting not to let this sway his judgement. But in spite of his somewhat cool exterior, my friend has never been able to turn away anyone in such distress. Yet I have seen him reject far more intriguing investigations, so something about this particular case must have piqued his interest. I wish to God now, looking back, that he'd had the courage to simply inform Miss Cartwright he could not help. If that sounds harsh, believe me it will not by the time I have finished relating this tale.

So it was that we found ourselves in a coach on our way to see her cousin at Scotland Yard's 'charming' prison. The journey at least afforded me some time to glean Holmes' thoughts about the case.

'Surely it would be wrong to get the young woman's hopes up,' I told him. 'The man's destined for the noose. There might not have been witnesses to the actual deed, but being caught with the murder weapon in one's possession implies just as much guilt.'

Holmes steadfastly refused to be drawn on the subject until we'd seen the prisoner for ourselves. Inspector Lestrade similarly conveyed the opinion that my friend was wasting his time, when we arrived and asked to see the man.

'I cannot understand why Miss Cartwright has brought you into such an affair,' said the sly-looking policeman. 'There was nothing untoward in the investigation, I can assure you, Mr Holmes.' His tone was accusatory, as if he thought we were criticising his procedure. Nevertheless, he granted us full access to the man, in part because of all the help Holmes has been to the police in his career – often without due credit – but I think also because he was confident enough that nothing we discovered would make him look inferior in front of his own men. 'The father is baying for the man's blood,' Lestrade called after us, as if he thought that might change our minds.

When we arrived, the young prisoner had a haunted look about him. He was staring at the stone wall opposite, and from time to time just shook his head as if he could not comprehend how he had arrived in that dark, dank place.

'Your cousin Georgia has asked that we speak with you,' Holmes said after making our introductions, but could elicit no response.

'She tells us that you deny any wrongdoing in the murder of Miss Judith Hatten,' said I, at which I did notice a twitch of his eye. Then, suddenly, he was holding his head in his hands, tearing at his hair.

'I did not murder her,' he whispered, almost inaudibly, then screamed: 'I did not murder her!' Anthony looked across at us, eyes as tearful as his cousin's were but an hour earlier. 'P-Please... Please, you have to believe me.'

Holmes stepped closer to the bars. 'Then tell us who did.'

Anthony shook his head again, but it wasn't a refusal; it was simply that he had no idea what to say. What *could* he say, when all the evidence pointed towards him? He would utter nothing more, even when pressed, and we left not long afterwards – Holmes informing the guard on duty that he should be watched.

'I believe he may try to take his own life,' Holmes explained to him.

The guard snorted. 'It'd save us the trouble.'

My friend flashed the guard a threatening look, then turned. 'Watson, let us take our leave of this place,' said he.

As we walked out of the prison, and as I was attempting to match Holmes' stride, I commented, 'You cannot blame the guard. Miss Cartwright's cousin offers no defence.'

'Watson,' Holmes said, suddenly rounding on me, 'did you not see it in the man's eyes? Credit me with having looked enough murderers in the face to recognise one. That man is indeed innocent of this crime.'

'But how *can* he be?' I argued. 'You've heard all the—'

He held up his finger. 'And still he is innocent. I cannot explain it yet, but that is what I believe. He does not remember committing these acts, but I feel certain he *saw* them being committed.'

I rubbed my chin. 'He's definitely a troubled man, but guilt can block out memories. Or are you perhaps suggesting a split personality?'

Holmes pursed his lips. 'You are the one with the medical knowledge, Watson.'

'Well, I'd need to study him more to—' I was interrupted this second time by the blowing of whistles and policemen running past us. There was something afoot, a crime in progress, and even though we were already committed to this first investigation Holmes is never one to let an opportunity to observe a crime – or to lend assistance with the same – pass him by.

We followed the police to a residence but a few streets away. Holmes completely ignored Lestrade's warnings to stay back until they could ascertain what had happened and, dashing after my friend, I too witnessed the tail end of what had occurred.

Later, we would discover that the house belonged to Mr and Mrs William Thorpe, an ordinary couple in every single way – Mr Thorpe being a retired schoolteacher.

Screams had been heard emanating from their home; a woman's screams. As we entered the dining room, Lestrade still attempting to keep us back, we saw that these had indeed originated from Mrs Thorpe, but not because she was being assaulted in any way. No, these were the screams of a woman holding a dinner-knife in her hand, standing staring at the body of her husband, who was lying sprawled out over the dining table. From what I could see, and from later examinations, I can tell you that he was stabbed repeatedly with that instrument. It had been a frenzied attack, redness covering the table and dripping from the tablecloth. However, it would not be the final such scene we would witness during the course of this investigation.

As the police moved in closer, Mrs Thorpe stopped screaming and looked over in our direction. She had that self-same expression on her face that Miss Cartwright's cousin had back in his jail cell.

One of disbelief.

'*Lestrade!*' cried Holmes, but his warnings came too late. Mrs Thorpe looked at the body of her husband a final time, looked down at the bloodied knife in her hand, then drew the blade across her own throat. A thick jet of blood sprayed across the room.

The police let me through then, but there was nothing that could be done for the poor woman; she had made a very thorough job of cutting through both the jugular and carotid arteries. My attempts to stem the bleeding were in vain, and as Holmes joined me we both heard her final gurgling gasps.

'I... ack... I didn't...' she breathed before dying.

~

Though we were fresh to the scene of this incident – able to examine it before Lestrade and his men could contaminate it, as Holmes would say – we found nothing amiss, save for the obvious brutal murder of Mr Thorpe himself.

As you know, I have long been a student of Holmes and his methods, so it was with a heavy heart that I watched him pace the room, sniffing the air, taking out his glass to pay closer scrutiny to a piece of carpet here, the edge of a table there, only for him to concede that – as she must have done – Mrs Thorpe had plunged the knife into her husband during the meal. Holmes pressed a gloved finger to his lips. 'Ah, but it is the way it happened that is the most curious, Watson,' said he. 'Note the way the plates are scattered on the table. The look of shock and surprise on Mr Thorpe's face. This occurred quickly. As if something unimaginable came over the woman. One moment sat eating dinner together, the next...' His sentence trailed off.

I nodded. 'But what *could* have come over her?'

'Once again, you are the physician, Watson. I would suggest that you examine the body of not only Mr Thorpe,' he encouraged, 'but his wife as well. We shall also be needing access to the body of Miss Judith Hatten.' Holmes looked over at Lestrade as he said this.

'I beg your pardon? What has the one thing to do with the other?' the policeman asked.

'Oh, come now, Inspector. Surely you can see the connection here?' The man could not, but I could. Two people murdered by their partners, both surviving halves – though Mrs Thorpe did not survive for long, I grant you – claiming that they did not commit the crime, in spite of all evidence to the contrary. This was turning out to be a case for Holmes, after all, and I could see the recognisable glint in his eye whenever there was a fresh mystery to be solved. Particularly one which would challenge his skills like this.

Lestrade allowed us to examine the body of Miss Hatten anyway, along with the others. But even as Holmes watched my explorations from a distance down in the icy morgue – not far away, yet not too close, either for his comfort or mine – I could offer him no new leads.

'The causes of death are accurate,' said I, 'a head injury in the case of Miss Hatten and repeated stab wounds in the case of Mr Thorpe.'

Holmes looked past me to the grey bodies on the tables, breathing in deeply – something I would not readily advise in such a situation. 'But what of *Mrs* Thorpe?'

I shook my head. 'Nothing that I could see, at any rate. Perhaps an examination of her blood...'

However not even that afforded us an explanation; no abnormalities that would have accounted for sudden changes in personality. Nor did Holmes' trip to the Hatten residence uncover anything, largely because Judith's father would not grant us permission to view the crime scene once he learned who had enlisted our help.

'No matter,' Holmes said as we climbed back into the cab, heading towards Baker Street once more. 'After so long, I doubt whether it would have yielded anything of interest.'

While Holmes attempted to make some kind of sense of the incidents thus far – littering his room with everything from articles on insanity to reports alleging bodily possession by demons ('You cannot seriously be considering that?' I said to him when I discovered his notes, and he just batted me away his with his hand), playing his violin into the small hours of the morning – more incidents took place.

In Kentish Town an antiques dealer named Falconbridge used an ornamental sword to disembowel his housekeeper (a woman he'd employed for many years and – it was rumoured – he also had a strong admiration for) then turned the weapon on himself. At Westminster Hospital a middle-aged builder's merchant called Roberson took it upon himself to secrete a hypodermic needle about his person and inject his elderly mother with an overdose of morphine: a mercy killing, you might assume, but the woman was actually recovering from her malaise and was expected to be discharged within the month. Colleagues of mine who were present informed me that the relative, in a state of confusion and remorse, ran away. His body was later found in the Thames. Finally, passengers on a train bound for Waterloo described hearing piercing screams, only to witness a woman backing out of a carriage covered in blood and holding a fire axe. Her hands were trembling, as she looked left and right, then she dropped the axe and fled, eventually hurling herself from the moving vehicle according to the ticket inspector. Inside the carriage were found the dismembered bodies of her husband and their twelve year-old daughter.

It was the latter, I fear, that had the most telling effect upon Holmes.

As we stepped onto that train, Lestrade now very glad of any assistance we could offer, my friend wavered, almost turning back. But he forced himself to look upon those remains. And I swear to you now, that in all my years serving in Afghanistan I had never seen the likes of it before – nor would I care to again.

'I should have been able to prevent this,' Holmes said, under his breath, his gaze fixed upon the contents of that carriage.

'How?' I asked him, my own mouth dry as sandpaper.

'There *is* a pattern to these events. I simply cannot see it yet.'

When we returned to Baker Street that evening, silence prevailing in the cab on the way, Miss Cartwright was waiting for us. She said nothing as Holmes stepped into his chambers, Mrs Hudson having informed us that the lady was waiting upstairs; Miss Cartwright merely strode towards him and slapped his face. Then she departed.

We discovered not long afterwards that Anthony had committed suicide in his cell by swallowing his own tongue. Lestrade said there was nothing that could have been done, but I knew Holmes disagreed.

I did not see him for some time after that. On the single occasion I did knock and enter his chambers, I found the room empty apart from the usual detritus of the case. However, on the table I also spied the means by which he was administering his seven percent solution; a habit I never did manage to free him from.

Holmes staggered from his bedroom then, still in his robe in the middle of the day – which, I have to say, was not that uncommon. He looked drawn and pale, like a ghost of his former self.

'Holmes, I really must—' But before I could get out another word, he flew at me, enraged. I thought for a moment he might attack, like the people we had been investigating, but instead he simply shouted:

'Get out! Get out! *Get out!*'

I did as instructed, retreating and allowing him to slam the door behind me. I heard a lock being drawn on the other side and considered it was for the best that I should leave him alone, in spite of how terribly worried I was.

An equally concerned Lestrade contacted me several times over the course of those next few weeks, informing me of yet more murders –

drownings, beatings, stranglings – as well as suicides, asking if Holmes would be continuing his investigations. I lied and told him that the great detective was looking into several quite promising leads.

In reality, I feared that he had finally met his match. It is a conviction that I still hold to this day.

When I heard Holmes leave 221b Baker Street, it was the middle of the night. He told neither Mrs Hudson nor myself where he was going, but after his tirade I was not at all surprised. When Lestrade actually called at the house, protesting that he was no longer able to prevent the papers from reporting this insanity that seemed to have gripped London, I had to admit that Holmes was not present.

'Then where is he, Dr Watson? And why aren't *you* with him?'

I said again that he was chasing a line of enquiry, but the Inspector's words struck a nerve with me. It wasn't the first time Holmes had retreated into himself, nor the first occasion he had vanished without warning – and Heaven knows he had justification this time – but Lestrade was right; I should have been with him. I was deeply distressed about his condition, and if there was a connection between all of these bizarre events then I should be working with Holmes to try and resolve the issue.

I set out to look for my friend, searching all the places I could think of that he might go. I even tried some of the opium dens that he has been known to frequent from time to time, especially if he was looking for someone from the underworld of the crime community. During this pursuit, I discovered that he had indeed been spotted in that area of town – and spotted enjoying some of the more questionable vices it had to offer – but had departed some considerable time ago.

It was not until I had exhausted every single possibility that it struck me where I might find him. My years observing Holmes' methods has left me with not an inconsiderable degree of aptitude for deduction myself.

When I arrived at my destination, he was indeed present. Standing, staring out into space just as the 'victims', those left behind after the murders, were wont to do. He looked no better for his absence – worse in fact than he had in his chambers. I approached cautiously, after my last encounter with him, not knowing what kind of reception I would receive.

'Ah, Watson,' said he in a quiet voice. 'My faithful friend and companion. I knew that you would find me here eventually.' Holmes looked down at the grave he was standing next to, the one containing the bodies of the family who'd died on the Waterloo train. 'I am so sorry for my behaviour when last we saw each other. I was...not myself.' He gave a slight laugh, perhaps realising the significance of his words, but there was no humour to it.

Not far away, I knew, were some of the other final resting places of those who had suffered during these past troubling weeks.

I joined him. 'What happened was not your fault, you know.'

He shook his head and turned to me. 'I could not see it until now, but we have been facing my greatest enemy all along.'

'Not...the Professor?' I said, struggling to hide the alarm in my voice.

'I *have* seen Moriarty, Watson, I will not deny it. My own punishment, perhaps. But no...my efforts at the falls were entirely successful. He remains among the deceased. Although through this experience, I have discovered why the murderers – if one can refer to them as such – are so quick to throw away their lives. I know now what they see...afterwards.'

I frowned, conceding that I had no idea what he was talking about. If Moriarty had not returned from the grave – and the dark humour of my own musings was not lost on me, in light of where we were standing – then who exactly were we up against? I ventured my question out loud.

'I've been a fool, Watson. It has been right in front of my nose all along. Literally! The stench is so distinctive. But, you see, I've seen *Him* before as well, if only briefly. You recall the case of the Devil's Foot, which you so expertly set down?'

Good Lord, I thought to myself, *is Holmes making some kind of veiled reference?* Surely we were not facing the Fallen One himself; such a thing would have been even more preposterous than Holmes' theory about demonic possession. As it transpired, our foe was so much more terrifying, and less discriminating, than that. I nodded, remembering the case all too well.

'It happened when I subjected us to the burning powder that was used to induce both madness and...death.'

'Are you saying a similar poison has been employed here to drive people to such acts?'

He shook his head. 'No, no, Watson. The *Radix pedis diaboli* has nothing to do with this affair, save for the fact that the one we must stop was present during that investigation also.'

'I do not follow you.'

'I have never spoken about what I witnessed under the influence of that powder, nor have I asked you what you saw.'

'My dose appeared to be notably smaller than yours,' I told him, remembering how I shook Holmes out of his hallucinogenic trance.

'Indeed.' He looked again at the headstone before him, then cast his eye over the entire graveyard. 'Consequently, I saw our enemy, Watson. A brief...suggestion, you might call it. But nevertheless it was *Him*, of that I am certain.' Was my friend speaking of prophecy now? 'It was a state I have been attempting to recreate during my absence from Baker Street.'

'And were you successful in your endeavours?' asked I, when all I really wanted to do was voice my concern. The state Holmes was talking about almost cost him his sanity, if not his *own* life.

'I was indeed. I saw that which I was seeking, and more besides. I finally know what I must do. Actually what *you* must do, Watson.' I still wasn't following his line of reasoning and I told him so. He placed a hand on my shoulder. 'Right now, I have more need of your skills as a physician than a detective. Do you trust me, old friend?'

'Of course, Holmes.'

'Then I would ask you to visit your surgery, with the express intention of collecting the items we shall require for our task, and meet me back here tomorrow at sundown.'

'Task, Holmes?' said I, still puzzled.

'Yes.' He fixed me with a stare that I have never forgotten from that day to this. Then he said, more serious than I have ever heard him sound, 'Watson, tomorrow evening I would ask that you kill me.'

~

The logistics of Holmes' plan will soon become apparent, but you can appreciate my asking him to elaborate on his exclamation. However, he would not, merely stating that the following night he would require me to end his life by stopping his heart.

'I simply refuse,' I told him.

'Then more innocent people will die before this is all over,' Holmes said to me. 'The killer has a taste for this now. He is using more and more "hands on" methods, from what I can ascertain. He is taking pleasure in the tactile aspect of ending lives. If you will not do this for me, Watson, then do it for the victims yet to be claimed.'

Reluctantly, I agreed, returning to my surgery to gather what I would require. The safest way I could think of to stop Holmes' heart temporarily was by way of administering an injection; a lethal concoction of my own devising, for which I also had the antidote. For Holmes had explained that he only required me to impede the beating of his heart muscle for a short amount of time. 'Long enough to lure our prey out into the open,' Holmes informed me.

Quite how 'killing' my friend would achieve this, I did not know, apart from the obvious parallel it had with friends and loved ones suddenly doing the same thing across our city. Did he wish to recreate the madness of extinguishing life in such a way? If so, he could scarcely have chosen a more apt person to perform this action; Holmes has always been, and will forever remain, my best friend.

The wait of a day passed slowly, as I contemplated what I was about to do. In a few hours I would achieve what every single one of Holmes' adversaries had failed to do. Even Moriarty. I would murder the great detective, and he was going to let me – had *asked* me to do the very deed! The merest thought of it boggles the mind, does it not?

Nevertheless, I found myself once more travelling back to that cemetery as another thick fog descended upon London. The sky was darkening and the overall effect succeeded in chilling me to the bone. As I walked through that graveyard, knowing full well the people contained therein could not harm me, I still found myself shivering. When Holmes stepped out from the depths of a bank of fog and tapped me on the shoulder, it was very nearly I who found his heart stopping that night.

'You gave me an awful fright,' I told him.

'My dear Watson, please forgive me.' In spite of the circumstances, and by the light of the lamp he was holding, I detected the hint of a smile playing on his lips. 'Did you bring the required items?'

I nodded, showing him my medical bag.

'Splendid, then we shall begin.' Holmes took me over to where a flat slab of stone was located, somewhere for him to lay as I carried out his request. He placed the lamp beside him so that I could see.

'Holmes, are you quite sure about this? I still do not understand why—'

He silenced me with a finger. 'Please proceed. I know that I am in the most capable of hands.'

Sighing, I took out the hypodermic and a vial, siphoning off a massive dose of my poison. Holmes, for his part, rolled up his sleeve and I saw exactly what the cost of his experimentations were; red welts on his arm, digging into the lines along his vein. I frowned, but said nothing, instead taking up his arm to give him the injection: quite possibly the last I might ever administer to him.

As the needle went in, Holmes reached over and patted my hand gently. Neither of us said a thing as he shut his eyes and waited for the drug to take effect. I sat there and noted the look of complete peace on Holmes' face. It was the first and only time I had seen him so content.

I took his wrist and felt for a pulse. It was still there, but faint.

'I never got the chance to tell you this before, Holmes,' I whispered, still keeping hold of his wrist as the beats slowed. 'But thank you. Thank you for everything.'

Then, suddenly, the beating ended.

I bowed my head, choking back the wave of emotion I felt at seeing my companion as dead as those corpses I had examined after the murders. Then I experienced it, a sudden jolt – so fierce I almost let go of Holmes' arm. I wonder now if I would have seen what followed had I done so, for I firmly believe it was the physical connection to Holmes at the time his spirit departed his body that allowed me to bear witness to what transpired. Yes, that is correct – you did not read wrongly. I can finally unburden myself of the knowledge of what happened in those ensuing moments. It is a memory I have carried with me now for so long.

A shape began to coalesce beside the slab, indistinct at first and shimmering – but as I blinked, refocusing on it, a familiarity began to reveal itself. A head, shoulders, arms, legs...it was a body, glowing white in appearance, and transparent. But eventually it took its true form. It turned to stare at me, and it was then that I saw the unmistakable visage of none other than Holmes himself. He mouthed something upon seeing me, but I could not hear him at that point and was too much in shock to reply anyway. I wondered whether Holmes had somehow infected me with his madness, for this must surely be what it felt like to experience insanity.

There had hardly been enough time to adjust to this new development when something else happened. The fog parted, close by, and at the same time began swirling round, taking on a form itself. It was difficult to separate the darkness beyond our lamp and the glow of Holmes' spirit from that which was bending the mist to its will. I soon realised my mistake, however, because again this was not a thing of our world. It was nebulous in appearance itself, mist-like though not *of* the mist enveloping us. The only reason I could see it at all was because of my physical connection to Holmes.

Like the latter, it too settled on a form eventually: tall and black, wearing what looked like robes but were not made from any kind of material known to man; rather fashioned from the same miasma as the rest of it. Its hands, when it reached out, were in contrast white and thin, almost bone-like but lacking substance. A finger whipped out, pointing at my companion's shade.

And its voice, when it spoke, sounded like thousands of voices speaking at once in my mind. '*Sherlock Holmes*,' it stated simply. '*I have come for you.*'

All the times he had cheated Death, in particular that celebrated occasion at the Reichenbach Falls, and now I feared that it had sought Holmes out – all because I had ended his life. But Holmes was right, there was a distinctive smell; it was one I recognised all too readily from my time serving abroad, and my career as a doctor on these shores.

'No,' I heard my friend say then, in a voice that was his but not his. 'I have come for *you*.'

There was silence then, as if the creature in front of Holmes did not quite know how to reply. That silence was filled eventually by an explanation of sorts.

'It wasn't quite enough for you, was it?' Holmes continued abruptly.

'Taking lives like this. It wasn't...satisfying.' He uttered the last word with all the contempt it deserved. 'You have watched for so long as we have found new ways to kill each other. Watched and come for us when needed. All the while wondering what it might be like to actually kill, to tighten a cord until the last gasp of air emerged from a mouth, to plunge a knife through someone's heart until it beats no longer, to hack a child to...' Holmes paused. 'I saw your pattern, you see. This isn't the first time you have slipped inside; you've worked your way through battlefields, have you not, choosing those who would not readily be missed. The poor, the destitute. I have seen them all. They told me what you have done. Yet that was not enough for you. The sweetest sensation, the longest and strongest high of all, comes from the murder of a loved one. To feel the connection severed at your hands. *Your very hands!*'

Listening to Holmes' explanation, something I have done on many occasions at the conclusion of a case, everything fell into place. The reason why Miss Cartwright's cousin, Anthony, had done what he did – the reason those others did the same. It was a disturbing revelation to say the least.

'*You dare to pass judgment on me?*' came the voice that was a thousand voices, almost screeching the reply. It was filled with indignation that Holmes was even talking to it.

'When your actions result in...' Holmes' spirit looked over again at where the family from the train had their plot. 'Yes. Yes, I do.'

There was a snarl from the black, mist-like shape, and it flung itself forward, just as Holmes had done back in Baker Street after wallowing in depression and indulging too much in his seven percent solution (or more?). The intent was different here, however, and we could both see it.

The shape raised both hands, in an effort to grab Holmes, to take him back with it, to drag him away and undo his very existence. I wished there was something I could do... But there was! I could bring Holmes back as he had instructed. We knew the identity of the killer, we just could not do anything about it – and never would be able to, I feared.

It was time to administer the antidote and restart Holmes' heart.

He looked sideways and could see what I was about to do. 'Not yet, Watson!' he cried, then those hands grabbed him and Holmes was grappling with Death itself. Not in any figurative sense this time, but as he would have done any other criminal he was tangling with. Though how would he be able to defeat such a creation?

'You...have been...with me...every step of the way,' Holmes grunted as he struggled with his enemy. 'But even...you should know...there are consequences...to one's actions.'

Something was happening behind me. I took my eyes off the spectral pair, to glance around. More shapes in the mist, breaking through in fact: one after the other. It did not take them as long as Holmes or Death to form. They had been waiting for this moment and were eager to strike. Not only were there the victims of Death's atrocious crimes, such as Judith Hatten, Mr Thorpe, the husband and child murdered on the Waterloo Train, but also those who had been so tormented by their spectral appearances that they had taken their own lives – and, I had to wonder, given a helpful push by Death itself? So there followed Anthony, Mrs Thorpe, the mother who'd turned that fire axe on her beloved husband and child, and more besides. I watched as those Holmes had spoken about, the earlier victims, both the murderers and the suicides that had gone unnoticed, unreported – the ones who had told Holmes their tales – all came marching through the mist. But they were also joined by those who'd been lost during the last few weeks, while Holmes had been attempting to get to the bottom of this very mystery: the ones Lestrade had not been able to keep from the morning editions. They surged through that graveyard as one, a phantom army heading towards Death, all craving revenge.

The black figure – whose face was still unclear to me, and I would imagine to Holmes – turned towards them, letting go of my friend. The horde encircled Death, crowding in and raining down blows that I did not think would have any effect, but evidently did. They were backed up by the power of those trapped between life and...whatever was on the other side. It suddenly dawned on me then exactly why Holmes had wanted to wait a day. It was October 31st, All Hallows' Eve – the time of year when these spirits would be at their most powerful.

'Now, Watson!' shouted Holmes, limping away from the scene. 'Bring me back now!'

I snapped out of my daze, not wanting to let go of Holmes' hand because I wished to witness the last of this, wanted to see Death's end. But, of course, I should have known that Death is never, ever truly gone. How could it be? It is the other side of the coin to life. I saw the dark figure being smothered by ghosts, then let go and watched as the vision faded. While I worked – injecting Holmes with the antidote then pounding on his chest to get his heart beating again – I heard a faint voice. A voice made up of so many more. *'We* will *meet again,'* Death promised Holmes, *'and not even your friend will be able to save you then.'*

The words filled me with dread.

I couldn't see the 'spirit Holmes' anymore, couldn't see any evidence of the battle that had taken place, but it did not matter to me at that point. I beat on Holmes' chest one final time, and he sat bolt upright, taking in a lungful of night air. He began to cough, though whether it was the result of coming back or the fog still surrounding us, I had no clue. But I held on to him anyway, until he was strong enough to sit up on his own. 'Rest a little, Holmes,' I warned him.

'I'm...I'm fine,' he told me. 'Thank you, Watson.' Then he clasped my arm.

I nevertheless had to half-carry my friend through the graveyard and through the fog, into a more public place where we could hail the cab that would take us back to the relative safety of Baker Street.

Holmes spent the next few days recuperating, enjoying the ministrations of both myself and Mrs Hudson. When Lestrade called on us once more, I was able to inform him of the conclusion to the case. 'You should not see any more deaths like those,' I assured him. I could not promise him the madness of the population would not continue, as indeed it did in the final stages of the 19th century until everyone was certain the world would not end. But of the murders committed by loved ones and subsequent suicides, there was no more sign. Due note had obviously been taken of the repercussions. As I already mentioned, the matter was put down to the singular time of the year and our calendar. I would not be pressed further on what had been amiss with those people, in spite of Lestrade demanding answers from both myself and later Holmes – for one thing, I did not know where to start; for another I was positive he would have us both committed if we spoke of what we'd uncovered. Nor did Holmes and I talk about what had happened and what we had seen that day. To do so seemed somehow to invite the premature return of the culprit.

So you see, it is only now, with my friend passed on and myself nearing the end of my years, that I am committing this to paper. Even then, I doubt very much whether it shall see the light of day. Instead it will probably be dismissed, I fancy, as a work of fiction less credible even than some of those by Mr Stoker or Mr Verne. The final ramblings of an aged adventurer.

But I know the truth.

Holmes once spoke about his greatest foe without realising it, before he ever encountered the thing, during a case a long time ago. 'The Adventure of the Six Napoleons' I believe it was, though my memory is waning, I must confess. He was in the mortuary then, not the graveyard, but he mused: 'I am just contemplating the one mystery I cannot solve. Death itself.' How prophetic those words should turn out to be.

Because although he may have prevented more innocents from going the way of Judith Hatten and the others, spared future 'murderers' from the blame and guilt of something they had not done, Holmes had far from solved the mystery of exactly what Death was – nor what happens when we take our final breath.

The voice had been right, of course. It *had* seen Holmes again, and I had not been able to save him. But that is a story for another time.

For now, I have entrusted my recollections to the page and all that remains is for me, myself, to await the hand of Death on my own shoulder.

Perhaps then, at least, I will discover the mystery of what Holmes already knows himself.

Baggage

He was just carrying around too much baggage, that was the problem.

It was worrying Nicholas, even right now. If this one worked out the way he thought, he'd give up completely on finding any kind of happiness. Resolve himself to a life of being alone.

That was what had motivated him to start looking in the first place; the fear he'd probably end his days sad and lonely; no wife, no kids. Nothing. If he could only make some kind of a relationship work, then—

It wasn't so easy, though, was it? Nicholas couldn't help feeling bitter about his previous failures – especially those in his youth. It wasn't as if he was hideous or anything, in fact he'd been told he was quite attractive. He was just incredibly shy, and liked to treat girls with respect. Inevitably, that had led to them either taking him for what little money he had, or taking him for granted.

Even those he'd thought were nice had stabbed him in the back. Take Julie, for instance, back when he was twenty-one – and still a virgin, though he did his best to hide it. They'd worked together at the coffee shop, and he'd been sweet on her for so long. She'd kept him dangling, saying they should just be friends. On the rebound, however, she'd dragged him out to buy her drinks one night, then dragged him back to her place. He hadn't been able to hide his inexperience then; couldn't conceal the fact he was terrified. And when he asked her if she was *really* sure, that she'd always said they should just be mates, she'd taken it as an insult and told him to get out. The next day, he was the butt of all the jokes at work, while Julie had already moved on to her next conquest.

He'd learned from this mistake, but it hadn't been any better once he'd finally popped his cherry. Nicholas treated all the women he'd dated well, and what had he got in return? 'You're just too...nice,' they told him. 'Too clingy. I need my space.' At the same time they accepted all the nights out he paid for, all the gifts. It drove him to spend years not bothering with the opposite sex for fear of getting hurt.

But man wasn't meant to live by himself, so every now and again he'd get drawn back into the fray. It was easier than ever now the internet was around. He'd found himself surfing the dating sites in his spare time, signing up for free and checking out who might be a suitable match. The first time he'd found what he thought was a nice woman – liked to spend cosy nights in, watching movies – he'd bucked up the courage to mail her, then hadn't even received a response. Despondent, he'd kept away from the site for a fortnight, before finally receiving an email to say he'd had a reply.

Valerie had been away on holiday when he mailed, and yes of course she'd like to talk more. She'd seemed ideal, but when they actually came to meet it had been a disaster. Not on his part – it never was – but because she wasn't what she'd said at all. Turned out she liked nightclubs and picking up blokes by the dozen. She hadn't been on holiday either, she'd been in contact with at least a dozen men on that same site (and Lord knows how many others on different ones).

Reluctantly, and in desperation, he'd tried a few more profiles, each one more disastrous then the last. GSOH? You'd need one to cope with all the catastrophes: most didn't know what they wanted from a man (or from life in general), others were just plain crazy. Some had lasted a few days, others a few weeks, but inevitably he got the same response he had out there in the real world. Towards the end, and now seeing forty approaching like the edge of a cliff, he'd also been getting a new brush off: 'You're just carrying too much baggage.' He'd ask them what they meant, and they'd tell him they could see it on him – like he was dragging around the weight of all those romantic fiascos. You get to a certain age, it's only natural for a person to have some history. Right?

Not as much as him, apparently.

In a strop, he'd given up. Closed all his accounts and walked away from the whole scene. Then another one of those damned emails had arrived in his inbox. From *Date-a-Match*, the one site he must have overlooked – perhaps one of the first he ever signed up to, way back when. 'Gina' had read his profile and wanted to chat. She was new to the area and it seemed like they might have things in common. Nicholas' finger had hovered over the delete button, but something made him click 'open' instead. To his amazement, he then found himself clicking on the link to her profile.

No picture, but his eyes scanned over the words: 'Honest and loyal' (yeah, he'd heard that before), 'looking for that special someone' (doesn't exist) and 'have been hurt in the past' (hasn't everyone?). In spite of the fact that last line rang warning bells, said she might be on the rebound just like Julie, Nicholas mailed her back and they struck up a conversation. Like him, she was giving it one last try. Fresh city, fresh start and all that. Nicholas found himself warming to her. They actually did seem quite compatible, and eventually she gave him her mobile number. He rang it and they ended up chatting for three hours, about everything and anything. Forgetting himself, Nicholas found a huge grin appearing on his face as they revealed more and more of themselves, the guards slowly dropping. What he was hearing in Gina was a kindred spirit. Someone who appeared to have suffered just as badly as him on the dating scene.

'I can't explain it,' she told him. 'None of this makes any sense to me.' It could have been him talking.

Now they'd arranged to meet, at a local wine bar one Saturday afternoon. Gina was late and Nicholas feared the worst. That was what set him thinking about the 'baggage' problem. Whether Gina would see it, just like the others – realise he was a bad bet and just walk back out through the door. He hadn't even thought about how she might look yet. She'd seen his picture on his profile, but he hadn't seen one of her.

Thankfully, when she arrived, apologising for being late – she'd been doing some more unpacking and lost track of time – she was exactly how he'd pictured her.

Her beam when she sat down at the table lit up the whole room, and when she kissed Nicholas on the cheek he felt tingly all over. Again, they sat and talked, and the afternoon fell away. Nicholas found himself opening up to her about his previous attempts at dating, even laughing at some of the most painful memories.

'Sometimes I worry,' Gina said, playing with her long, chestnut hair and taking a sip of the Chardonnay he'd bought her, 'that nothing will ever work out all right. Don't you?'

Nicholas nodded, having a drink of his lager. Then he looked at her, concerned he was putting out those vibes again: that she'd see he was carrying too much baggage; that he was damaged goods. But she said it first: 'I'm always being told I hold on to too much from my past. You know, from the guys who hurt me.'

And that was it. That was the moment he knew Gina was the woman for him. A female *version* of him, in fact.

That was when he began to fall for her.

Before they knew it, the barman was calling last orders and Gina looked at him, a little the worse for wear after her wines. 'I don't usually... I'm quite a cautious person, but, well, my place isn't too far away if you want to come back for a coffee...maybe?' She smiled again, but it was a nervous one.

Don't do it, he thought to himself. *Don't ruin things by asking if she's sure.* He remembered Julie, and although it had probably been a good thing in the long run he still thought to himself 'what if?' But he was a different person now, why shouldn't he go back with Gina?

'Look, it doesn't matter,' she said, smile fading.

'Yes,' he replied, a bit too quickly. 'That would be lovely.'

The smiled returned.

So they got a cab back to her home, a rented two bedroom that was slightly further away than she'd implied. 'Ignore the mess, won't you? I'm still getting straight,' she said, leading the way inside. He would have said 'What mess?' but it *was* pretty cluttered. Gina had been right when she said she was still in the middle of unpacking stuff. There were boxes and bags everywhere.

She told him to wait in the living room, while she fixed that coffee. He hadn't expected an actual drink, but was glad when she went off to the kitchen. It gave him time to calm down a little. He knew things were going way too fast, but for once in his life he was willing to take that chance.

For Gina, only for her.

When she sat next to him on the sofa, the tentative kiss that followed felt natural. Like something that was meant to happen. 'Hmm, that was nice,' he said. Then Nicholas suddenly realised he really needed to pee; the coffee mixed with lager had gone right through him. 'Hold that thought,' he said, excusing himself with another kiss. Gina nodded, relaxing back on the sofa.

Looking for the bathroom, he made a wrong turn, stumbling into another small room instead. He'd flicked the light on before he realised, noting more bags and crates. The spare room obviously, where Gina had dumped the worst of the detritus from the move. He was about to flick the light off again when Nicholas caught sight of something. One of the holdalls closest to him was open a fraction. Maybe it was his imagination, or the drink, but he thought he saw a finger sticking out.

Nicholas frowned, moving forwards. Wanting to reassure himself that it couldn't be, then needing to see more when he realised he was right. His own fingers shook as he reached out for the zip, but before he could pull it down he looked past the bag to another one beyond. There was the tip of a foot emerging from that one, toes clearly visible. Next to that was a closed suitcase, but there were tufts of hair trapped where it had been closed.

He didn't need to open that first zip now, because he knew what was inside. The sickly-sweet smell of air freshener alone, which Nicholas was suddenly aware of, gave it away. Masking another smell entirely. It made him cough. Now he knew why Gina was usually such a cautious person.

'I told you to *ignore* the mess,' he heard from behind. 'What a terrible shame.'

Whirling around, he saw Gina with a kitchen knife in her hand. Then suddenly she was plunging it into his chest. He looked down, mouth open. All he could think was, at least it wasn't in his back.

'I knew it was too good to be true, that sooner or later you'd discover just *how much* baggage I was carrying from my past. It's probably just as well, Nicholas; they all end in disasters, my relationships. Better to strike first, before *I* get stabbed in the heart. Too bad. I was beginning to like living here, as well.'

Nicholas shook his head as he stumbled backwards and fell. It could have been different for them. Might have worked out.

Christ, what was he saying?

'I'm sorry,' she said, blood dripping from her knife. There were genuine tears in her eyes, but no trace of that smile. 'I really, really am. I honestly thought...no, it doesn't matter.'

Nicholas' eyes, conversely, were bone dry. From the floor where he lay, staring up at her, one thought was nagging at him: still he was wondering what might have been.

If he could find anything positive about the fact that he was dying, it was this: Gina, it seemed, was fated to live with all of her previous encounters. Couldn't part with them, no matter what. And he would soon add to her burden, his body crammed into a bag, suitcase or crate. Ironically, it would probably be the longest relationship he'd ever had or would have with a woman...especially now.

Gina had so much baggage, but she'd actually done him a favour.

Because now, as the darkness took him, Nicholas realised he had finally, at last, been freed from his own.

Forever.

Graffitiland

When it happened, it was quick.

Dean had always prided himself on being pretty aware of what was going on around him. Even when he was pissed, even when he'd taken blow in the past, he was always one step ahead, could tell when things were about to turn in a club or bar, when trouble was brewing. It was one of the things that had kept him alive all these years; kept him one step ahead of the law as well. And he'd known when to move on, when he'd outstayed his welcome – just as he had down South, when he'd cut and run. When his bosses were looking for someone to take the heat for that armed robbery which had gone oh so wrong. That's when he'd done a runner and made his way here, to Granfield. Here there was even a chance to be a bigger fish in a smaller pond, as opposed to a tiddler that was going to be first on the hook when the time came.

Here there was an opportunity to start afresh, to re-invent himself. And that's exactly what he'd done – got his feet well and truly under the table. In fact life couldn't have been going better really; he had money to burn, had a girl who loved him; had trust and respect. Then this...

Quick and professional – no calm before the storm. No moment of clarity when you knew the wind was going to change, or the tide would turn. As he stepped out of the casino in the wee small hours, about to lock up as he often did, they'd come out of nowhere. He'd not had a chance to fight back before the men in ski-masks had hold of him in a vice-like grip. Dean figured they were here for the money, the takings that were in the office; might have been better waiting until the end of the month if so, rather than a slow Tuesday at the beginning of it. 'Y-You're making a big mistake,' he managed. 'D-Don't you know whose place this is?'

They said nothing, made no demands that he take them to the safe, that he give them the cash. They'd simply placed a bag over his head, before securing his hands behind his back with a plastic tie. Had taken his phone and wallet, then wrestled him towards the sounds of a vehicle pulling up, its tyres screeching. Next he'd heard a door being yanked back on rollers – and he was shoved inside what he assumed was the back of a van. At least a couple of the men who'd done the deed piled in there with him, before the van took off again.

'Hey...look... I don't know what this is about, but I'm sure we can figure something—' the blow to the face shut him up immediately and Dean tasted the familiar coppery flavour of his own blood. They didn't want him to talk; fair enough. It had been a lie anyway when he'd said he didn't know what this was all about; he had an idea, definitely. He had enemies – in this line of work, who didn't? – and so did his employer. One especially, they'd heard about: a guy called Malcolm Rains who was up and coming in their field, fancied himself as pretender to the throne...like there was ever any chance he'd snatch that.

They drove for what seemed like hours, but was probably no more than about fifteen, twenty minutes. Dean's heart was racing – he had no idea what was going to happen to him at the other end of this ride. Maybe they'd just want a 'nice little chat' as they said in this business. Maybe they wanted to send his employer a message. Maybe they just wanted to recruit him, although they were going about it a funny way if so. Grabbing someone off the street and smacking them in the mouth was not a good way to get on somebody's good side.

When the van finally pulled up, it did so with a jerk and Dean was pitched forwards. Then hands were there, strong hands picking him up again. Not just to right him, but when the side door slid back again, to drag him outside and deposit him on the ground. Dean fell over sideways, but was soon lifted up once more, so that he was on his knees – hands still firmly tied behind his back. It was a stance he'd seen often on the news, usually followed by the person being executed by terrorists in some foreign land.

He knew he was risking another punch, but felt the urgent need to speak again. 'Hey...hey fellas, listen. You can still let me go, I can walk away from this and there'll be no retaliation. I haven't seen your faces, I don't know who you—'

'Shut the fuck up, pretty boy,' said a gruff voice, 'before you get another slap.' Beneath the hood, Dean frowned; even though the person speaking was trying his hardest to disguise this voice, there was something very distinctive about that rough Geordie brogue.

If he hadn't been earlier, now he was really crapping himself. Before he could say anything else that might land him in hot water, he heard another vehicle in the distance. It sounded smaller, the engine more efficient. Having grown up around cars and been able to hotwire them before he was even out of nappies, Dean recognised the noise an expensive model made. It was a noise he'd heard before. A noise that caused him to swallow dryly.

It brought back memories, that sound. Of an afternoon when he'd been chauffeured around Granfield, taken on a tour of the 'sights' – the old parts and the new, with very little in-between. A guided tour of an empire, of places owned – of people owned, as well. This had been back even before he'd been put in charge of operations like the casino, trusted with a certain level of responsibility within the organisation. 'You see all that?' the man he'd been with, sat next to in the back while they were driven around, had said. 'It's mine. It belongs to *me*.' Then he'd grinned a chilling grin.

Wasn't an exaggeration, and wasn't just ego (although he had a healthy one of those); the man doing the talking did have this town pretty much sown up. There wasn't a pie that was baked here the guy didn't have his fingers in before, during or after the fact. It was why Dean had gone to see him straight away when he hit Granfield – or at the very least requested a meeting. It had taken a while and some persistence, but he'd finally got past the barriers and been invited to one of the clubs for a drink. Thankfully, the man had taken a shine to him, seen something in him – regardless of the fact he couldn't go into details about where he'd worked before.

'There was some...unpleasantness,' Dean had explained. 'Not my fault, but I was going to end up taking the fall.'

'So you got out? Very sensible... Not very loyal.'

Dean had nodded. 'I'm extremely loyal, sir. Just not a patsy. Nobody likes being a patsy.'

'Agreed,' had come the reply. 'Neither am I... But I am a damn good judge of character, and I like you Dean. I might be able to find something small for you.'

Dean had been delighted, had nearly shaken the man's hand off –

almost kissed it in fact for giving him this break. 'I won't let you down, I promise.'

Except he had, hadn't he. After so long, almost seven years, Dean had let the man down spectacularly. Which was why, when the car pulled up nearby and the hood was taken off Dean's head, causing him to blink rapidly to focus, he hadn't been shocked at all to see the man getting out of the back of that Jag. To see the driver, Roberts, and another large man Dean didn't recognise wearing glasses, climbing out of the front seats, too – flanking him:

Danny Fellows. Self-appointed mob boss of Granfield. *His* boss… Some called him The Kingpin, after the comic book character, though never to his face – mainly because he was sensitive about his receding hairline and he would probably severely damage you for the comment. He wasn't as stockily-built as his two-dimensional counterpart either, but you certainly wouldn't have called him weedy. Danny worked out quite a bit, mainly in that private gym located in the basement of his house – sorry, mansion – just outside the city. Dean also knew for a fact that although he was more often than not surrounded by bodyguards, the man could also take care of himself; there was even a rumour that he was highly trained in several martial arts.

More because he didn't want to make eye contact than anything, Dean looked about him now at his surroundings. It had indeed been a van that delivered them all here, a dark transit with a door on the side which was still open. The men who'd snatched him – three of those, too – had all taken off their masks. Dean recognised a guy with a beard called Crouch, who he'd seen around but never really spoken to that much, and was now sitting half inside the van smoking. Another man nearby, with a square jaw, was called Haggard – one of Danny's bodyguards. And the Geordie voice he'd recognised belonged to Milburn, a real nasty piece of work by all accounts – muscle Danny used to demand protection money from people.

Dean tore his eyes away from the group and looked in the other direction, trying to gauge where he was. The light wasn't great, which was making identification that much harder, but he saw the remains of a few buildings – their windows put through – grass that hadn't been cut in an age, and an iron bridge that looked like it would barely hold one person's weight without buckling. But it was the lettering and art covering absolutely everything that really gave it away; spray-painted legends like 'Sweet Dreamz' and 'Growlers Rule' (which was Granfield's Hockey team) competed for space with pictures of dragons, a young lad in a baseball cap and a devil with a pitchfork.

Not a foreign land at all. This was the deserted patch of town – well, deserted as far as the ordinary population was concerned; there were people living here, they just didn't show themselves...mostly – that had come to be known as Graffitiland, for obvious reasons. This was where the wannabe artists came to ply their trade, and where the disaffected youth of today blew off steam. Countless people had lost their virginity in Graffitiland; many more had almost certainly lost their lives. But what was *he* doing here?

Dean had a horrible feeling he was about to find out.

Danny, Roberts and the man he didn't know had covered the distance between them in the time it had taken Dean to figure out his location. Danny was wearing a burgundy suit that would have cost most people's wages for the year, and jewellery that would have kept the average family afloat for many more. He pulled his matching long coat tighter around himself against the cold. In contrast, Roberts and the other guy were dressed head to foot in black, which was also coincidentally the uniform of the men from the van.

'Danny,' began Dean. 'What's... what's going on? I don't understand what—' The man standing only a few metres away now held up a hand to silence him. It was more effective than a punch in the face, because he knew if he uttered another word, he'd be on the receiving end of much worse. Danny then moved that hand, gesturing to the man on the other side of him that wasn't Roberts.

'I don't believe you've met Mr Waterhouse, have you.' He wasn't looking for a reply, just stating a fact – the edge to Danny's voice even sharper than his suit. 'Mr Waterhouse, this is another associate of mine, Mr Ashby. He's been in charge of the running of my casino here for some time.'

Mr Waterhouse – hair cropped short, like a military cut that had grown out some – nodded a hello, as if they were meeting at a dinner party.

'Leastways he *said* his name was Ashby when we first met. I suspect, given his circumstances, that he might not have used his real name. Something you'll probably be able to relate to, Mr Waterhouse... Now, we recently had a very interesting conversation, Mr Ashby with—'

'Dean,' he breathed, couldn't help himself. 'My name is Dean, you know that.' Danny and Dean; best of buddies, like a sitcom or something. 'That's what you've always called me...' There was a whine to his voice, a pleading quality he couldn't control.

His boss shot him a sideways look, and he regretted having broken his silence. But all the man said in reply was: 'I only call my friends by their first names, Mr Ashby. *You* know *that*.'

Dean hung his head, then shook it.

'Now, as I was saying, we recently had a very interesting conversation with someone you know, Mr Ashby. A young lady of your acquaintance by the name of Victoria.'

Shit! thought Dean. But at least they were getting to the core of it, of why they were all here. It just depended how much they knew.

'She was most forthcoming, wasn't she Mr Waterhouse?' The man with the glasses nodded.

Shit! thought Dean again. *Shit, shit, shit and shit!* Then he asked himself: *Why?* And not even he was sure what he meant by that. Why had she'd blabbed, perhaps? Why did she have to come along, exploding into his life? Why did he have to have a weakness for them, for the ladies? More specifically: why did he have to have a weakness for that particular one?

Victoria...Vicky. In spite of himself and what was happening to him, Dean's mind flashed back to his first sighting of her, when Danny returned from a business trip and was showing her off at the casino – giving her the same tour he'd taken Dean on after they first met. She had flaming red hair, and had been poured into a green satin number with a deep V accentuating her cleavage: a very expensive necklace with a ruby hanging from it was nestling in the valley. Every now and again, Danny would lean in and whisper something, and she'd laugh. Dean hadn't been introduced to Vicky that night, but he'd felt like he knew her just from the things Danny had said: about how she might be the one, about how she was the only girl who'd ever been able to keep up with him, in and out of the bedroom. The temper on her!

'Fuck me, she's amazing,' he told Dean once. 'Fiery, you know? Hot stuff!' But then, inevitably, he'd witnessed the obsession with the woman peter out, as it had done with so many in the past. Watched Danny head off on business trips where there would be other women on tap, while Vicky was left behind to occupy herself as her lover cheated. It was during one of these trips that Dean had been given the task of helping Vicky occupy herself, taking her out shopping and maybe for a bite to eat. Dean had protested at first, he had too much to do at the casino, but apparently there was nobody else available and Danny had specifically requested it. Trusted him to do it.

The connection, the...spark had been there right from the moment their eyes met. They'd both felt it, but neither had commented – how could they? But then that day, going around town, followed by an Italian, it became apparent they had so much in common: not just the same taste in movies, music, but backgrounds (Vicky had been basically dragged up as well, by a single parent who hadn't really given a shit). Soulmates, if you believed in that sort of thing. The kind of person you pictured yourself getting old with; pictured yourself dying with.

Oh, Vicky was 'the one' all right, just not Danny's one. She was Dean's.

They hadn't done anything about it at first, however; too dangerous. But when Dean couldn't get her out of his head, when the aching, the burning for her was too much to bear, he'd called again at a time he knew Danny was away once more for the weekend. He'd driven her out to a hotel in Redmarket, booked in under a pseudonym and paid cash for the room; for what had been probably the most intense sexual experience in his life. As they'd both laid back on the bed, panting and sweating, they'd already been arranging the next time they could see each other... But they had to be careful, very careful – use burner phones to keep in touch, for example. Not one thing that could be traced back. They were playing with fire, after all.

They'd seen each other, what, maybe half a dozen times before the subject arose of the future. 'He doesn't love me, you know,' Vicky had said to Dean. 'Not like you do. He never could.' There was truth in those words, but what they could do about it was anyone's guess. You didn't piss on Danny Fellows and get away with it. Maybe when he was done with her, when they finally split – and they would, Dean assured her; he'd seen this all before – then they might be able to pick up…after a reasonable gap. 'He'd *never* let us be together, you know that as well as I do!' Vicky had snapped, that famous temper of hers rearing its head.

There was a way, but it wasn't until a couple more rendezvous had taken place that they began to contemplate actually doing it. They could take off together, sure, but the only way they'd be left alone would be if Danny Fellows *thought* they were dead.

'Fake it, you mean?' he'd asked, and Vicky had nodded.

'Why not?'

Because the risks were enormous, that's why. And he'd better be bloody well convinced they were both stone cold or he'd come after them. Vicky had suggested a car crash perhaps… But that was really as far as they'd got. Talk, just talk. Dean had even started to think about whether it was worth it at all, choosing to spend the rest of his life with fiery Vicky, potentially on the run, versus a cushy number here with Danny. Of course, that option wasn't without its pitfalls either, but at least he knew where he stood with Danny. Or had done.

Vicky…bloody Vicky. He'd bet any money that at least some of this had come out in an argument, maybe even the one Dean had been hoping for where his boss had chucked her. His thoughts returned to the present, mainly because he was being addressed directly.

'…think I wasn't going to find out about it all? Christ, I've know about you and that bitch for a while.'

One, maybe even two or three steps ahead of Dean; he'd finally met his match. Had his boss even engineered this, to test his loyalty? No way – how could he have known the power of attraction between them? Unless…Vicky was on his payroll? Nobody was that good an actress, though, surely? He'd looked into her eyes as they'd made love – not had sex, nothing so trivial – and he'd seen it…hadn't he?

He thought about saying: 'She means nothing to me.' But that would have been the biggest lie of all.

'Oh, what a tale she had to tell – everything by the end of it. Mr Waterhouse here is very good at...getting people to open up, aren't you?' A tip of the head from Mr Waterhouse. 'Was that what the trouble was in your previous place of employment, Mr Ashby? Was that connected with a woman?'

He shook his head. There'd been a woman all right – many women, but only one at the end. Only one he'd run out on, left without even saying goodbye. She'd been nothing like Vicky, mind. But what did Danny mean about Waterhouse? Just what had they done?

The answer to that question came when Danny took something out of his pocket, using his handkerchief to hold it. Then he'd cast it onto the ground before Dean, so he could see it properly. The necklace with the ruby in it, Vicky's favourite – the piece of jewellery she loved the most. It wasn't just the ruby that was red, though, or dark maroon in this light; the chain was now too, splattered with...

Bloody Vicky.

Dean began to rise, though it wasn't easy. 'You son of a... What did you do to her?' The words were out before he could keep them in check, an emotional reaction – and suddenly one of the men who'd grabbed him was by his side. He couldn't tell which one, but he felt the blade of the huge knife under his chin, coaxing him to behave.

'Easy there, Mr Ashby. Save your strength, you're going to need it,' said Danny, as cool as you like.

What for? Torture? Mr Waterhouse's speciality? thought Dean.

'You see,' his boss continued, turning and talking to the man in question, 'our Mr Ashby here is a bit of gambler. That's how he came to be involved in the casino; in fact he won the position in a late night game of cards. Do you remember that, Mr Ashby?'

Dean couldn't even nod, it would have slit his throat. He'd always been good with cards, the thinking ahead thing again in practice – that and taking risks. So he'd won, *in spite* of Danny's cheating... Danny didn't play fair. 'You did all right, kid,' he'd told Dean that night. 'I'm impressed.'

'I took a gamble on him. A simple game of chance... And that's what I'm going to offer you tonight, Mr Ashby.' He gestured for the blade to be lowered; Dean looked to the side and saw that it had been Milburn holding the Bowie; a further gesture and the knife was cutting through the tie that held Dean's wrists together. 'Relax. Victoria is still alive, I assure you...for now.'

Dean reached out and picked up the necklace, held it in his hands for a moment. Then he looked to the side and saw that beyond Milburn, Crouch was rooting around inside the van – bringing out pistols, machine guns, one of which he handed to a waiting Haggard.

'Did you ever see that movie... now what was it called, *Target* something?' Danny shook his head. 'Doesn't matter. It had Van Damme in it anyway, he was being chased. It's always stuck with me. Anyway, the game is this: You will run, and my men will hunt you,' Danny Fellows explained; it didn't sound like much of a game to Dean. 'If you get to the other side of Graffitiland, or make it to the morning, you get to be with Victoria forever. That's right, I'll let you be together – and I promise I won't come looking for you. I'll even throw in the money you were planning on stealing, casino takings for the month wasn't it?' Vicky had floated something along those lines, but again nothing had been firmed up yet; they'd run out of time. 'Or the equivalent anyway. That sound fair?'

'Only if I get one of those, too,' said Dean, nodding towards the weaponry being handed out. Crouch was even strapping on a belt that had grenades attached to it, for Heaven's sake!

Danny clapped, laughing for the first time tonight. 'Oh, Mr Ashby, you do amuse me. Is the fox armed when the dogs come for it, when they rip it to shreds? Is the fucking bird armed when you blow it out of the sky with a shotgun? The relationship now is, them: predators...' He pointed at his men tooling up, then at Dean. 'You: prey. Get it?'

'And if I refuse to run?'

Danny looked at him as if he couldn't believe the question had been asked.

Dean shook his head. 'I really wish there was some way I could... I'm sorry,' he said as sincerely as he could.

'I'm not. You've taught me a valuable lesson, Mr Ashby – that I'm not as good a judge of character as I thought. That I need to be on my guard more than I have been. Otherwise...' It was Danny who shook his head now. 'You've got a twenty minute head start, I suggest you get going.'

Dean took one last look at his old boss, at the men who would be coming after him. Then he tucked the necklace in his pocket, turned, and began to run into the wilds of Graffitiland.

~

The first thing Dean did once he'd waded through that long grass, checking his watch all the time as he did so – glancing back over his shoulder to see if the men who'd be following him had set off – was try and find a weapon himself. He'd need one, whatever he decided to do. And he hadn't worked out what was for the best yet, just running to reach the other side of this Godforsaken place – to civilisation, if you could call it that – or hole up somewhere and hope that Fellows' men didn't find him.

No one to blame but yourself, he told himself as he ran. He'd made those choices, knowing what the consequences were – and still he didn't think it would come to this. Thought the risk, the gamble of being with Vicky would be worthwhile. But there was still a chance of coming through this; Danny Fellows was a man of his word, and if he said that getting to the other side or evading those guys (don't even think about the guns, the grenades) until dawn was all – *all?* – he needed to do, then that was that.

'Shit!' Dean said out loud this time, looking about him in the dimness of the few streetlights still working in this part of the city. He stooped to pick up a piece of discarded wood, tapping it against the palm of his hand; it promptly broke in two, only as strong as balsa really – rotted through. 'Shit,' he repeated, under his breath.

He looked back, up and over the sea of grass, saw that the area next to the van was empty. That the men had probably set off, though he couldn't see them. Wait…there they were, going up the path towards that bridge – obviously braver than him. They'd head him off if he didn't get a move on. Dean abandoned the idea of a club for now, making for the first of the disused buildings ahead – thinking that there might be scope either to cut through or find somewhere to hide. Trying to think ahead, though his mind was racing faster than his feet, his heart pounding away in his chest.

Dean couldn't find a door, so he resorted to climbing up and smashing through one of the windows – the job had already been half done for him – taking off his jacket and using that to clear the glass. He shushed it as it shattered, not because he was worried about attracting undue attention (those maniacs behind him obviously didn't give a shit, with their guns), but because he was frightened of giving his position away. His trousers caught on the ragged edges as he fell through, ripping up the side, and he swore again.

There was even less light in here, but he could just make out a set of stairs ahead of him and a corridor leading through what he guessed must once have been some sort of office. This whole area was a testament to a decline in Granfield's fortunes a while back, before even the recession had hit home – certainly before the more modern parts of the city began springing up. When he got to the stairs, they looked about as strong as that wood had been outside, otherwise he might have thought about hiding up there – but did he really want to cut himself off from the ground level?

Best to push on through the building, he decided, though that proved harder than it sounded. One corridor fed into another, and soon it was blacker than ever. He wished now that he hadn't given up smoking a couple of years ago, because then he'd still have his lighter – they'd taken away his mobile or he could have used his torch app. It was as he made his way through to what he thought must be the centre of the building – he didn't really have a clue and was becoming more and more disorientated by the minute – that he saw a faint glow ahead of him.

Cautiously, Dean crept towards it, turning a corner and taking a peek. There, against a background of more pictures and words on the walls (one declared 'It's Always Darkest Before the Dawn'), huddled up in what looked like a sleeping bag besides the remnants of a fire, was a figure. Empty cans of lager and vodka bottles were strewn over the floor where this person (man, woman...it was difficult to tell) had made their bed, perhaps as some kind of early warning system, but more likely because they'd drunk themselves into oblivion. Dean couldn't say he blamed them. Still, he'd swap places in a second right now, because nobody was after this bum, nobody was coming with machine guns to riddle them with—

He suddenly had an idea – what if he was to trade place with this person? Offer them what he had, his clothes, money... Then he realised that his clothes were probably in a worse state than the tramp's at that moment, and what money he'd had on him was in the wallet they'd taken back at the casino. An IOU then? Get serious. They'd probably figure him for this person anyway, and at least want to look at his face – then they'd pump him full of bullets without a moment's hesitation.

Could still use the tramp, though. What this person had was of value to Dean, if it wasn't to them. Wood that was alight, a bottle he could smash and use as a weapon at close range. Might not be that bloody huge knife, but he'd seen as much damage done with one of those in his time in pubs and clubs. Would have been on the receiving end himself on a couple of occasions, if it hadn't been for thinking ahead. Dean moved forwards as quietly as he could, bending and reaching out for one of those bottles...

The tramp wasn't as out of it was he thought, however, and stirred, rose up – squinting to see Dean. 'Wasssatt?' slurred the individual, still of indeterminate sex. As Dean grabbed the bottle, the derelict was crawling towards him, lunging for him – perhaps thinking he was trying to steal the precious alcohol, not that there was any left inside.

'Get back... Get off me, I don't want to hurt you.'

'Wasssdoing?' came the reply, and the tramp made another attempt to grab Dean. He hefted the bundle of rags backwards, probably a little harder than was necessary – and it fell back, hitting its head against the wall where a butterfly had been spray painted. The figure slumped down and didn't move. Dean swore again, sighed, but went over and felt at the neck for a pulse. There it was, strong and steady; he hadn't killed the tramp at least. Then he stepped back and gathered up a piece of wood which was still lit at the tip.

'Sorry mate, but my need is greater than yours.'

Dean entered the next corridor, finding the way much easier now that he had a light source. There, at the end, was another window – this time there was no glass, but there was wire mesh that had obviously been placed there at some point for security purposes. Only someone had busted through it in the middle, and it was relatively easy for Dean to open up the leftover spokes to climb through.

No sooner had he started to do so than something pinged off the side of the building to his right. Another ricochet followed, definitely a bullet, but closer – aimed at the fire in his hand. Dean tossed that away outside, but also dropped the bottle, which smashed completely; so much for the weapon. Then he saw another spark from the end of a rifle, fired by one of the men that had set off after him. Dean scrambled backwards, leaving the lit wood behind. Really stupid; the flame had provided light, but also made him an easy target.

The man was there in seconds (alone, so perhaps they'd split up?) but by this time Dean had retreated and was on the inner side of the window again. He pressed himself up against the wall, observing as the bloke – he could now see it was Crouch – approached the fire on the ground and looked around, looking for Dean. Then the barrel of the gun was poking inside, a torch beam following, flashing around the room; Dean tried to control his breathing, not give himself away. There was a noise from outside and Crouch pulled the gun back to check it out. Dean let go of the breath he was holding, risked a glance through the window again.

Crouch was gazing in the opposite direction, waving the torch around out there – figuring that Dean must have run off. Dean's eyes caught sight of those grenades again, then flitted to the wire on the window, and he grinned. He had an idea...

Have to do this quickly, he told himself – working hard. Working one of the loose wires free and bending the end of it into a hook. It would be just like those duck games; the ones at travelling fairs when he was a kid. When he wasn't pinching people's wallets, or on the slot machines, he really enjoyed this particular game. Could always snag those ducks... Snag this one now, he thought to himself, and you'll win something even better than a cuddly toy.

The wire was out and stretching towards Crouch – at one point when the man moved forwards, Dean didn't think it would reach. But then Crouch stepped back and it was on again: just a little further, a little closer. Dean stuck his tongue out of the side of his mouth and—

There, done: the hook was in, curled around one of the grenade pins. In the end Dean didn't even have to pull, because Crouch whirled around, maybe sensing someone was behind him – too late, of course. Dean only just had time to duck down under the window as a volley of bullets struck the wall.

Moments later there was a bang and, even as shielded as he was, Dean was jolted into the centre of the room by the blast. He waved his hand to clear the smoke, coughing – grateful for the fact he'd been thrown clear when he saw the mess the explosion had made of the wall: the rubble and the hole. But that was nothing compared to the mess it had made of Crouch.

Dean rose, stepping over the remains of limbs – the ground covered in blood. Bile started to rise in his throat, but he didn't have time for that. Even if they'd split up – and he didn't know that for a fact – they would have seen or heard the explosion. Time he wasn't here... There was nothing useful in the detritus that he could see, so Dean staggered across the open space in front of him, letting out a silent thank you when he reached the relative safety of another building.

~

The place was like a labyrinth.

He'd never realised that this part of the city was so fucked up; it was like another dimension, another world. Like something out of a twisted horror movie. As he slipped between buildings and through them, he felt further and further away from his goal, from getting to the outskirts of Graffitiland. Plus he felt as if eyes were on him: the forgotten inhabitants of this world, or maybe the pictures themselves monitoring his progress? Still, he was doing pretty well to avoid his other two pursuers. And he was one down...

As time ticked on, he began to think again about maybe bedding down somewhere – hiding until the threat had past. Hoping that they wouldn't find him first. There was an old battered husk of a car nearby, its tyres slashed – and even that had been covered in graffiti (across the side was the lovely phrase 'Skream For Me!'). It occurred to him that if you stood here long enough, then you were fair game for the artists; either that or it just happened organically. But it would probably make a decent hiding place, for now at any rate – because Dean was also getting tired. No sleep and a trek through this place, on top of coming down from an adrenalin rush...

So he'd clambered inside, slumped across the backseat. Eyes heavy, he'd almost dropped off – when there came a rustling from outside. Dean levered himself up, looking out through the dirty windscreen which was doing a decent job of concealing his presence. There, not far away and cradling his machine gun in front of him like a baby, was Haggard. They'd definitely split up, Dean thought to himself.

He would have let him just go past, wander off and continue searching – if the man hadn't paused, looked around, and spotted the car. Decided to head towards it to search the thing. Dean scrambled over into the front seat, thinking fast – if not exactly thinking on his feet, thinking on his belly. He risked another look up through the windscreen; Haggard was approaching, gun raised just in case.

Dean reached under the steering wheel, thankful that this was an old model – and hoping that there was still a little spark left in the battery. He waited, waited... If this didn't work, then he was well and truly screwed. Wait...wait...

Touching two wires together, he created a different kind of spark – the engine rumbling into life. Haggard was reacting, training his rifle on the car and readying to fire. Dean flicked on the headlamps, knowing that – again – if they were dead, he wouldn't be far behind them.

Light filled the area in front of the old banger; full beam, right in the eyes. Haggard brought one hand up to his face, to shield them – his other raised the gun upwards and sprayed the air above with bullets. By the time he brought it back down again, Dean had exited the vehicle. Bullets peppered it, taking out one of the headlamps but leaving enough light for Dean to see Haggard and run at him, pitching the man sideways. Recovering enough to defend himself, the still blinded Haggard hefted his rifle like a staff now – bringing it up and into Dean's face, causing him to step back; to spit more blood out of the corner of his mouth. Then Haggard swung out with the weapon, turning it into a club, but missed his target completely.

'*Fucker!*' shouted the large man, blinking and swiping the air in front of him with the rifle once more. Dean looked about him frantically for something to use against Haggard, finally settling on half a brick not far away from his foot. Dodging a final swing of the rifle butt, Dean slammed the masonry hard into Haggard's temple. His blind eyes rolled up into his head and he dropped his weapon. A couple more blows finished him off and Dean stood back from the felled man, breathing in and out quickly.

'There! What d'you think about that, eh? *Eh?*' The only response was the man's right foot twitching spasmodically in the throes of death. Dean stared at the corpse, blinked a couple of times. Wasn't like Crouch this time – that man had practically killed *himself*. And it wasn't the first time Dean'd had to kill in his line of work, but that didn't mean it happened often – or that he enjoyed it, as some on Danny Fellows' payroll clearly did. Hadn't had to do it for a long time, either, but Haggard had left him very little choice.

Haggard had also left him a gun. Dean reached down and picked up the firearm, pointing it and pulling the trigger to test it.

Click!

Nothing happened. Maybe it was out of ammo, so he checked Haggard's body for magazines, but couldn't find any. Perhaps it wasn't out; perhaps it was just broken. Dean really didn't know the first thing about machine guns anyway. Now, if it had been a good old-fashioned sawn-off...point and fire. Simple.

It was as he was examining the weapon that he felt something prod the back of his head; the barrel of another gun. So much for knowing what was around you, for thinking a step ahead. Somebody had crept up on him and was about to blow his brains out. Probably all that shouting, Haggard's shooting. Didn't matter now. Didn't matter.

'So, there you are, pretty boy,' said the man in a Geordie accent. 'Finally. Led us a bit of a merry dance, haven't you?'

'Just...just get on with it, Milburn,' said Dean. 'Do it if you're going to.'

There was silence for a moment, before the man said: 'Now where's the fun in that?'

Why was Milburn toying with him? He had no idea how close this guy had been with Crouch or Haggard, so maybe that was the reason? Make him suffer before ending it?

'Drop the rifle and turn around,' ordered Milburn. Dean was reluctant at first, until the man shouted: 'I said *turn around!*'

Dean did as he was told, faced him; faced the pistol pointing at his head.

'Now then, we can talk sensibly,' said Milburn, his voice changing – softening. 'If I lower this, I need to know you're not just going to attack me. Kill me.'

'Wha...' Dean's brow was furrowing.

'After all, I could have just offed you here and now. So, we good?' A nod, though the frown remained. Milburn's gun started to drop. 'Okay... You want out – you're almost there. Just through that alleyway, and beyond that the plaza, then you're on the edge of Pleasant Moor estate.' From what Dean knew of that place, he might well be jumping from the frying pan into the fire, but he should at least be able to find a phone box.

'You're...you're just letting me go?'

Milburn nodded now.

'Why?'

'Does it matter?'

It wasn't a guilty conscience, people who worked for Danny Fellows didn't suffer from those. Revenge for something? No. Then it had to be...

'Can I smell bacon?' said Dean, but Milburn didn't answer. If he was right then it meant that Dean wasn't the only one up to things behind Danny's back. That he really wasn't that good a judge of character; that this man was sticking his neck out, even though it meant potentially giving himself away. Milburn turned the gun around, handed it to Dean.

'You just point and fire. Easier than one of those things anyway,' he told him, gesturing towards the machine gun on the floor. 'Less to go wrong.'

'If...if you are what I think you are, you'll be in just as much shit as me soon.'

'So... point that thing and fire,' said Milburn, tapping his own shoulder. 'Make it look good, but not *too* fucking good.' When Dean frowned again, he added: 'Don't worry, I'll be found. And the chicks dig scars.'

Dean, once again, did as he was told – pointed and shot Milburn in the shoulder with a BLAM! He went down, grimacing. 'Are you...?'

'*Go!*' snapped Milburn through gritted teeth. 'Get the fuck out of here – hurry!'

He didn't need telling twice. Dean headed off for the alleyway – almost there, the end in sight, and all three of Danny Fellows' men down. Home free, then he and Vicky could get the hell out of Dodge.

Dean paused at the head of the alley then looked left and right. All seemed quiet, the plaza surrounded by more buildings decorated in the customary way here. One mural in particular caught his eye, this one on the plaza floor itself: angels with wings battling demons amongst the clouds. The eternal struggle of good vs evil; to be honest he wasn't sure anymore which side he was on.

'Right,' he said to himself. Not far now, but a risk, a gamble – it was awfully exposed. He ran, sprinting as best he could across the concrete square. Before he knew it, he was nearly halfway. Dean began to laugh. He'd beaten bloody Danny Fellows, shown what—

The shot came out of nowhere, Dean didn't even hear it this time. But suddenly his left leg was out from under him. His thigh was pouring blood, leaking all over the plaza; all over the demons. Dean heard footsteps from off to the side, looked up and saw Roberts holding a pistol with a silencer on the end.

He'd assumed, wrongly, that he was just dealing with the three men – probably because Danny had called them the hunters. Should have known the bastard wouldn't play it fair. Roberts said nothing as he approached, gun still raised and pointed at him. Dean kept his hand underneath him, his own gun hidden until the last moment – then he raised himself up and fired. Bullet after bullet. Roberts' body danced, like a puppet being worked by a lunatic master, before dropping…

And Dean clicked on empty.

Breathing hard again, he started to inch forwards – leaving a trail of redness behind him. He had to reach the other end of the plaza, before Mr Waterhouse showed up or something else stopped him. He was aware again of eyes on him, looking out from the derelict buildings of Graffitiland. As he crawled he came across an angel's face, and – though he had never been the religious sort – he prayed then. Prayed he might make it out of here, have a chance to redeem himself. If he went now he'd just end up with the demons, burning in Hell for all eternity.

Crawling, crawling. Almost there, almost at the edge of the plaza – in fact he could see the outskirts of Pleasant Moor now, just waiting for him like a mirage in the distance. He made it past the concrete bollards, to the curb of a road just beyond it that marked the very edge of the 'land' he'd made it across. Dean was laughing again, hysterically this time.

Then he stopped when he saw the car parked up not far away. When he saw Danny Fellows leaning against it. Danny pushed himself off and walked round to the boot, popping it and taking something out which he held behind his back. Then he walked over to Dean. Of Mr Waterhouse there was no sign.

'Shame about Roberts. I suppose I'll have to drive myself fucking back now,' he moaned. 'I have to say, you're no Van Damme... But you did all right, kid. I'm impressed.' He could see Dean was looking beyond him, looking for the other man he'd brought – the final man. 'Oh, you're wondering where Mr Waterhouse is? He's already begun the clean-up operation with his own team. You see, he has many skills, Mr Waterhouse. Torturer, fixer... I'm not sure what I'd do without him, if I'm honest. By the time he's finished it will be like we were never here at all – he'll even sort that bullet wound of yours, good as new.' Danny suddenly looked up at the sky, which was still quite dark – but showing the first gradual signs of lightening. 'Shame you didn't make it to morning.'

'I...I made it across... across Graff...Graffiti...'

'Graffitiland. Yes, *yes* you did. Which means, I suppose, that I should make good on my promise. And I will, Mr Ashby; I won't let you down.' He brought the object he had hidden behind his back around to the front.

It was a can of petrol.

'What...what are you...' Dean spluttered, as the can was upturned and he was doused in the stuff. The stink of it on his clothes, his skin, up his nose.

Danny said nothing, just took something out of his coat pocket to show him. It was small and black and he flicked the side; Dean squeezed his eyes shut, then opened them when he heard a beep. The black box had a small screen on it, with a red flashing light. 'I suppose you're wondering how we found you, how we always knew where you were? Tracker...on the necklace.' He smirked. 'The one you couldn't leave behind. *Hers*.' Dean reached into his pocket, took out the piece of jewellery and gaped at it.

Danny's cheating... Danny didn't play fair; always several steps ahead.

'Not that I'm into all that techno stuff myself. Prefer to keep things simple.' He put away the monitor and took out a box of matches.

'No... wait...you... you said... said you'd let me go... Said—'

'I never said I'd let you go. I said you could be with Victoria, that you could be together, and you could have your money. That still stands.' He bent, practically shoving his face into Dean's. 'It's like you said yourself, nobody likes being a patsy. Game's over.'

Then he stood, took out one of the tiny pieces of wood and struck the head with his thumbnail (yet another spark). Before Dean could say anymore, he'd tossed it at him. The thing flew in slow motion, over and over, and his eyes trailed it. Until he'd...

Finally met his match.

It hit his leg and caught almost immediately, spreading up him, washing over Dean and foiling his attempts to pat it out with his free hand – *playing with fire...*

The heat reached upwards, tearing into his torso, getting to the core of him. Darkest before the dawn? Not here, not now – and the burning hot liquid stuck his clothes to his flesh, which was bubbling away on his bones; finally he was smoking again. The fires of Hell couldn't even approach this, he thought in his last moments.

Aching... burning for her... (even as he clutched the necklace tight).

Screaming...'*Skream For Me!*'

Then his mind, for some reason, recalled yet another part of Graffitiland, something he'd seen even before he'd begun running:

'Sweet Dreamz' it said...

'Sweet Dreamz'.

~

'I've eaten better looking kebabs on the way home from a bender.'

DS Chris Burton, tactful as ever, stood looking at the mess the accident had made of those two bodies. DI Erica Wright sighed. There was no one she cared about, nobody she trusted more, but sometimes Chris could be a proper knob. He'd be cracking jokes about 'the burning issue' any minute now... They were at the stretch of road leading out of the city that was notorious for crashes, a black spot the locals called 'The Death Trap' – and it looked like this couple had taken the bend at speed. The car hadn't been spotted for a good few hours – not many people braved this route for obvious reasons – and by then the fire had all but burned itself out. Now it was just a blackened husk, the people who'd been inside it crispy to say the least.

They'd know more about what happened when Ted Giddens and the SOCOs got back to them, but it looked pretty cut and dried really. Whoever had been driving had lost control, skidded into a tree, and that was all she wrote. Cut and dried...or was meant to look like it. Erica was always very suspicious of things that appeared to explain themselves like this. That coupled with the fact there'd been vague reports of a 'disturbance' the previous evening near the misnomer that was Pleasant Moor; something about fireworks being let off. Uniforms had been sent in to try and ascertain exactly what this was, as there were no CCTV cameras within miles of that place, but they'd come out after speaking to some of the residents none the wiser. And that was before they'd ventured into the so-called Graffitiland itself, where the meth-heads and alkies who inhabited the place spoke about angels, demons...the Devil himself walking amongst them. One had even tried to make a complaint about somebody stealing an empty bottle of booze and some fire. God almighty...

But there were other rumours floating around about that day which were probably more relevant. Like that of a certain casino manager – Ashby, they'd known him as – making off with Danny Fellows' main squeeze, taking with him a bundle of cash. Not something that would have gone down well with someone they referred to back at the nick as the Tony Soprano of Granfield; but even if they did discover that was this pair (and the singed notes scattered around the car were a bit of a giveaway), it was doubtful they'd be able to pin it on Fellows. The guy was just too slick, always two or three steps ahead of everyone, especially the law.

'Shit way to go,' said Chris, breaking into Erica's thoughts.

'Hmm?' she said.

'Like this...' the man who looked like he'd just stepped out of the fashion pages of a magazine said, pointing at the wreck. 'Such a waste, an accident.'

'I suppose you want to go out in a blaze of glory?' Erica said.

'As opposed to just a blaze,' he replied with that practised grin, the one that made him such a hit with the ladies. 'Yeah, definitely. Go out fighting, y'know?'

'How d'you know they didn't?' said Erica under breath.

'What's that?'

She shook her head. They had no evidence, Fellows was just too good at covering his tracks. Erica looked at the skid marks on the road. Too good at creating new ones; false ones. No, she knew the drill by now: this would be put down as an accident like Chris had said, the same as a good many more they suspected weren't at all. Just an accident, nothing more.

'Still, I suppose it must have been quick,' said her DS, folding his arms, watching their team flit about the car, the bodies – one of which, in the passenger seat, was wearing what looked like an expensive ruby necklace. 'That's something, I guess.'

'Yeah,' Erica replied, not really listening to him. Her mind still wandering, still thinking about Fellows, about Ashby and the girl – about the love they must have shared to have risked this (something she could only dream about). Wondering what the truth of this puzzle was; its core... Something that made her one of the best detectives Granfield had ever boasted.

Wondering if they would ever really get to the bottom of it, no matter how hard they hunted. Whether Fellows would ever get his. They were questions, though, for another day. And, as the sun dipped beyond the horizon, Erica wondered whether they'd be answered as quickly as these people had died.

Whether that day would be tomorrow.

Or if it would ever come at all.

The Protégé

Did I ever tell you how very proud I am of my boy?

No? Well I am.

He's not my real son, of course, leastways not in the flesh and blood sense of the word. But there's a bond between us that's stronger than such things. We're closer even than me and my old man used to be…and that's close, let me tell you.

I found him exactly fourteen years ago to this day, while I was out on a job. He'd have been no more than two at the time. The lad was in an upstairs bedroom, crying. I just couldn't let him suffer the same fate as his parents. I always knew one day I'd be blessed with a child, someone to keep alive the family name, but I never imagined it would be this way. Just goes to show you. Anyhow, as soon as he caught sight of me he quit his bellyachin'. There was this look in his eyes, like he knew me somehow. I just *had* to take him with me.

It's not been easy bringing him up on my own, 'specially as I've not been able to tell anyone about him. And all the travellin's meant that he's never really had any friends – any *real* friends. Only me. But that's just the way things are; that's how it should be. Never did me any harm as a little 'un. Plenty of kids much worse off.

As for schoolin', I've taught him all I know. Everythin' important. All the things Pop taught me – about how to survive. Everythin' except the reason why. Never did find that out myself. I have a feelin' maybe *he* will, though…eventually.

I took him out to work with me when he was still only a nipper. Had to, no babysitter see? He never made a sound or kicked up a stink. Just sat there and took it all in, like he was storin' it up for later. I'd sometimes steal a look at him as he watched me, those big round eyes darting left and right. You've no idea how much it delighted me when he'd laugh and clap at my antics. He enjoyed the show, all right – it's good to enjoy what you do for a living.

But I never let him forget the seriousness of it all. The danger… Mind, nothing drove this point home like that one time when I clumsily allowed my attention to wander, showin' off. When I was taken by surprise and the boy was very nearly left to fend for himself – you shoulda seen the way he fussed over me, took care of me till I recovered.

As he grew, I allowed him to take a more hands on approach to the business. Helping me out. He took to it like a duck to water, welcoming each new job, handling himself with professionalism and pride. Getting each detail right, never slipping up. It's almost as if he was born to the work.

Now my boy has come of age. He's almost a man.

Almost.

The time has arrived to let him branch out on his own. I just know he's going to do so much better than me. Oh, he'll have so many adventures.

But before that he has to pass the test. His first solo job, no help from me. Not even an encouraging word.

Ahhhh! Shit, he's so damned quick I never even felt it slide in. Not until he began to twist. Ramming me up against the wall, one hand over my mouth to stop the screams. My God, I never even heard him creep up on me until it was too late. Barely had time to turn before...

As I drop to the floor I glance down at the glinting point of metal sticking out my stomach, and the thick blood escaping. Exactly the same technique I used all those years ago when Pop's time came.

My boy grins down at me, looking for my approval. I nod. He took me fair and square.

He rummages around for another implement in his bag. I wish I could remain conscious to see how he handles the vivisection on his own. But I know deep down in my gut – *heh* – that he will do just fine. Better than fine, in fact.

I laugh, bubbles of red air bursting out of my mouth, mixing with the gore in my throat. He knows what has to be done.

I'm so very proud of him, my boy. My – dare I say it? – my protégé.

For today he becomes a man.

Today he has made his first kill.

Nine Tenths

He'd been watching the place for a few weeks.

In his line of work, patience and persistence paid off. You couldn't afford mistakes, because they got you caught. So he'd camped out, watching. Always watching.

As far as Ren could discern, the new owner – a middle-aged man who was going both grey and bald at the same time – lived all alone in that big place. He was usually out in the evening (some kind of shift worker, perhaps?) but when he was gone, he'd be gone for hours. Ren would watch him leave in that sporty Mazda number, during which time he'd phone the house at random intervals to see if anyone picked up. No-one ever did, and there was no sign of any wife or family at all.

No sign of anyone.

Ren also made recces, gaining access to the wall at the back through the wooded area beyond. What would have been a selling point when buying the place – a nice, quiet, isolated spot – was a major bonus in his specialist field. The wall was fairly standard size, offering no obstacle to him: he'd been climbing like a monkey since he was small. He'd been doing this almost as long, graduating in the ranks from petty thief to professional burglar. One gig these days could last him a good few months, because he chose them so carefully and always scoped his targets out.

The house itself was alarmed, which he could spot from the outside. It would be easy enough to cut the lines to that though. What he was also able to do on those research missions was take a look through the windows and see whether it was actually worth breaking in. It was amazing how many properties looked like they'd be Aladdin's caves but turned out to contain nothing of value at all.

This one was different. No sooner had he pressed his face up against the glass than he spotted the works of art on the wall; the LCD TV and home cinema system, not to mention blu-rays; the music system, racks of CDs; the various statues and ornaments scattered about the place that would make a mint when he sold them on (so much stuff that he considered bringing someone else in...but decided ultimately that he could handle it). This was a person who enjoyed the finer things in life.

It was also while he was looking through his third or fourth window that he spotted the locked door, just off the hallway which led into the spacious kitchen. In Ren's experience locks always meant that there was something of worth on the other side – and he hadn't come across a lock yet that wouldn't yield to him. It would probably be where this guy kept his serious money. There might even be a safe on the other side. Again, Ren had the tools and the skill to handle any kind of job.

So he'd waited for the man to leave once more that night, tested the phone for the final time, and when there had been no answer, he'd made his move. Did he feel any kind of sympathy for the people he stole from, any kind of guilt at what he did? After this long? Hardly. Besides, Ren had always subscribed to the philosophy that possession was nine tenths of the law. Once he had all he wanted loaded up into his van – parked down the side of the house, out of view – it would *belong* to him. And if he chose to sell it on...well, that was his affair. He'd lose no sleep over it.

In his black clothes and mask, he blended into the shadows – not that there was anyone around to see him. Ren brought along the tools necessary to disable the alarm, which took only a few minutes. Next he pulled out his glass cutters and armature, to gain entrance through the back door. Long gone were the days of him trying to use a screwdriver to jimmy doors on his estate. Now he had much more finesse.

He'd popped the locks and bolts on the door in a matter of seconds, gaining access quickly and stealthily. *Start with the larger stuff*, he told himself – he'd brought along a trolley to pile it on. But there was just something nagging at him about that locked door. Beyond it, there might be cash – or better – that would render all that hefting redundant. *Have a look inside there, first. Go on.*

Ren couldn't resist. It was like a magnet was drawing him to the door. The lock was again a fairly standard one, but probably hadn't come with the house. He checked the seals for another alarm, just in case, but there was nothing. The lock sprang open and he pushed on the door, flicking his small torch into the blackness. There was a set of steps leading downwards, into some kind of cellar. A wave of cold air greeted him.

Ren frowned. Was it worth going down there, when he could just load up on the ground level? Hell, he hadn't even checked the upstairs yet – who knew what kind of finds there were? To his surprise, Ren found his foot on the first step. He'd come this far, he had to know what was so priceless it needed to be kept down here.

His beam flashed over a room, with metallic cupboards on the walls. *Could be storage*, he thought to himself, *the kind they use in banks*. In all his time, he'd never pulled off a bank job, so maybe he was in over his head. *Don't be silly, you still know how to crack those kinds of locks*, he reminded himself.

But there were metallic shapes in the middle of the room as well, plus what looked like floor-to-ceiling storage cabinets. Ren moved further down into the basement, one ear still cocked for any noises upstairs. These days if you were caught by the owner of the place, and they attacked you, *they'd* be the ones going to jail. But he'd rather avoid that kind of messiness if he could.

He couldn't see properly using just the torch, but found a light switch on the wall not far away. Ren hesitated before throwing it, but decided that the light wouldn't extend upstairs. Now he could see the room as a whole, the cupboards and the table not far away – the edges of which he'd only just brushed with the torch.

Ren wasted no time in trying to open the cupboard doors. They were steel, and remarkably cold, but he managed to fling open the one nearest. It was full of glass vials, each one containing liquid. He picked up the closest and read the label on the side. Ren had no idea what it was for, but he did know one thing: drugs were drugs, no matter which way you cut it. He'd been right, there was a fortune waiting just in this cupboard alone.

Moving to another, he opened it and found containers. White, plastic, that opened up at the top. They ranged in size from the very large to the really small; each with a temperature gauge. Ren frowned again. He should just fill his backpack from the first cupboard and leave. But he wanted to see if there were any more of the vials in the cupboards.

He made for another one on his right, tugging it open. The metal finally came loose and Ren stared at the contents of the cupboard. He staggered backwards, hitting the edge of the table. He felt nauseous, but tried not to throw up inside his mask. Breathing long and slow, he opened another cupboard. This one was even worse.

Ren swallowed, a sour taste in his mouth. He turned and looked at the larger cabinets. Against his better judgement, he reached out his hand. Before he could stop himself, Ren had opened that door too. He caught only a glimpse of what was inside, before he felt the blow on the back of his neck.

But that glimpse was more than enough.

~

When he woke, Ren still felt sick, but it was a different kind of nausea.

He tried to move, then realised that not only was he doped up, he was also strapped down. *Are you happy now?* he said to himself. *You got your drugs, all right.*

A face appeared above him, the grey-bald man whose home this was. Just behind him was another figure, much larger, the one who must have struck him from behind. They were both dressed in aprons, wearing rubber gloves.

'Ah,' said the owner, 'back with us?'

Ren attempted to say something, but found that his tongue and lips were completely numb.

'You've kept us waiting, almost as long as you did deciding to rob us in the first place.' He smiled; it was a terrifying sight. 'That's correct, we've been watching you for some time.' Ren tore his eyes away, then wished he hadn't. The cupboards were still open, the contents clearly visible.

'What? Oh yes. You're probably wondering what I do, what pays so well? I sell them on, you see. In just the same way *you* sell things on, I'd imagine. It's a specialist field.'

Could he be comparing what they did? It made Ren's stomach churn to think about it. He never...he'd never do anything like that!

'About ninety percent of each "unit". The rest...' His eyes flicked over to the larger cabinet. Ren looked too, seeing the poor thing inside again. 'It's just a hobby of mine really, isn't it Maynard?' he said to the larger man, who nodded.

Ren was able to take in the full length of it now, the oddness of the body with its parts stitched upon parts – the bits that were left over from this man's organ stealing operation. There were both male and female bits, spliced together: it had three eyes, each covered in cataracts and not viable for selling on; two mouths, one almost where it should be, the other on its cheek; but just two holes where its nose should be. Ren gasped as it moved, the warmer air obviously wakening it. Those three eyes opened and looked at him, blind but pleading, as it moaned and strained against its own bonds.

What kind of madman was this?

'We're not so different, you and I. Finders keepers, isn't that what you people say?' *Not quite*, thought Ren. 'You were on my property, and now...' He held up his scalpel. 'You *are* my property.'

Ninety percent (nine tenths) sold on. The rest—

Ren tried to struggle again, but realised it was useless. As the scalpel came down, he had to concede that the man had a point. It was his rule as well, wasn't it? His law?

The law of possession.

But that thought didn't comfort him much as the blade sank into his flesh, cutting deep – some of which he felt, some he didn't.

Nor did it help in the slightest when, at last, the man reached for his power tools. Nonetheless, they were his final thoughts.

Nine tenths, Ren turned over and over in his mind as he lost consciousness.

Nine tenths...

At the Heart of the Maze

'The melting voice through mazes running;
Untwisting all the chains that tie
The hidden soul of harmony.'

John Milton – *L'Allegro*.

The walls of The Maze were smooth and warm. He touched one and felt a bolt of electricity pass right through him. Jumping back, he continued on his journey. Trying to work out where he was.

Trying to get to the centre of The Maze.

That was all he knew of any significance. He had to get there no matter what. His sanity depended on it. He looked up at the sky. It was dark, night-time, yet somehow The Maze itself was brilliantly lit. The weight he was carrying on his back was becoming heavier and heavier with each step he took. The straps of the bag dug into his shoulders, almost cutting into him. He tried to ignore it, hitching the lump up higher so that it hurt his spine less. At this rate it wouldn't be long before he'd be stooping like an old crone.

But he steadfastly refused to give up.

Ahead of him was another bend. So many twists, so many turns. He'd lost track of the way he'd come, of the entrance – if, indeed, there was such a thing. He couldn't find his way back now even if he wanted to. And that was clearly out of the question. No, the only thing he could do was forge on. Stagger blindly around this place until he came to his destination.

He followed the path, his feet supported by the pliant surface. At least that was working in his favour. The spongy nap seemed to cushion his steps, massaging the skin on his bare soles. Now if only he could quench this terrible thirst...

Almost immediately he came to a fountain. About waist height and made from stone that was blue-grey in colour, it was a dainty shape, resembling a flower, with a long flute-like stem and an opening at the top where mouth-wateringly clear water spurted out. Sublime!

But as he approached, ready to drink deeply of its spray, he saw the water thicken and turn a ghastly shade of red. It bubbled out of the fountain, jets of blood rocketing upwards from its gash. This nauseating stuff rained down on the walls and floor of The Maze, covering everything in sight. He held up his arms as the liquid struck him, protecting his face.

Retreating, he glanced at the ground where droplets the size of hubcaps were falling. Floating in the puddles he saw white spherical things, pockets of air given form and tone. Each one glistened as it rolled around and around, joined now by shreds of skin. And suddenly the eyes, some green, some brown, some blue, were looking directly at him. Not the first strange spectacle he'd seen in here, by any means.

From somewhere came the sound of a beating heart.

He turned and ran, bumping into a wall in his haste. It pushed him sideways and he toppled into the next junction. When he picked himself up, he discovered he was looking at a lane with several offshoots. How was he supposed to know which one to choose?

All would be revealed soon enough, he reckoned. Slumping forwards again, he set off down the passage.

'Hey!' The voice ran past him, then doubled back and smacked him in the head. It sounded like it had come from behind, but you could be sure of nothing this deep into The Maze.

He looked around for the source. Again: 'Hey! Hey, Sonny.' A familiar voice. Though it was warped by the strange acoustics in here, there could be no mistaking that inflection, or the use of his nickname. Only one person had ever called him 'Sonny'.

The face of his Aunty Meg pushed through a side-wall, twice...no, three times its normal size. The pinkish-blue material stretched tight over her disgusting features like cling film, bursting at the mouth in strings of drool; those huge purple lips and rotten teeth threatening him. 'Come and give old Meg a kiss,' she said, her fetid breath knocking him backwards like a hurricane.

Sonny tried his damnedest, but he couldn't look away. She opened and closed eyelids crusted thick with mascara, tangled like a spider's web...with the spider still in it. She pursed her lips, the craggy face looming further and further out of the wall, chasing him. Meg wanted her kiss. Oh, she wanted it so badly.

Christ, he could not allow that. Turning his back on the woman's obtrusive head, Sonny raced as fast as he could in the opposite direction. Cackling laughter followed him and he knew that if he should suddenly fall, or stop for some reason, Meg would catch him up. Then that mouth would smother him completely, suck him dry as it had done so many times in the past.

Sonny turned corner after corner, losing himself in The Maze again, hoping that one of these turns would offer respite.

In time he came upon another unusual scene. The path he'd settled on now led him to a dead end. But instead of just a wall blocking him off, he saw a kitchen rooted to a patterned floor, all fused with The Maze like some bizarre work of art. In it was a woman with mahogany hair.

She worked earnestly at her table, slicing pieces of fruit. Sonny watched her take an apple, remove the pips, then divide it in two, and eventually into four. When she was happy she dropped the pieces in a crystal bowl. A punch bowl. Laughing, she took a sip of the wine set beside her in a glass. She switched on the radio. The woman was in a party mood.

Sonny hobbled up to her. 'I'm sorry, but do you know the way...'

There was no point carrying on. It was obvious she couldn't see or hear him. He waved a hand in front of her face. Not even so much as a twitch. She began to dance to the Latin-American rhythm, hips swaying as she picked up the next piece of fruit: an orange.

This time when she brought the knife down, a trickle of red squirted out from the skin. She appeared not to notice this and pressed harder. More of the gummy juice escaped, dribbling down the sides. The two halves fell apart.

He couldn't believe what he was seeing. Standing in for the usual triangular segments were miniature human organs: lungs, liver, kidneys. And on the left-hand side was a perfectly formed heart. It puffed out with every beat; the arteries around it swelling fit to burst. But before that could happen, the heart simply stopped pumping. The music ended at the same time.

The woman stepped back, showing the first signs of fear. And for just a moment he thought he saw her features change so that they corresponded with those of his long-lost mother, his long-*dead* mother. But in the moments after that she resembled no one. Her face was wiped like writing on a blackboard, leaving behind only a faint trace of the dancing lady she had been.

Repulsed, Sonny made to leave, though not before the woman reached out with her hands open, begging him for help. There was nothing he could do except escape from the nightmare, save himself. She started to scream, ripping and sucking noises coming from behind. It was already too late for her, he'd realised that as soon as he saw her face. The forces at work in this place would be dissecting her even now, doing the same to her as she had done to the fruit in that bowl. To the orange.

Sonny twisted his left hand round to support the bag on his back, in an effort to run faster, to be away from here. To find the...heart.

The woman's cries died down after he negotiated the next bend. He looked back to find that the way behind had been sealed off. What chance did he stand when The Maze kept shifting, altering its shape? Was it a conscious thing? Perhaps he was being diverted for a reason. Something was either hindering or helping him; he just couldn't decide which.

Again there was but one thing to do: tramp on and hope for the best.

This road offered him the option of two routes, a left and a right. For a good few minutes Sonny lingered at the intersection, head pivoting, weighing up the alternatives. In the end he went left. No particular reason, it was fifty-fifty.

Another room, or part of one, was his reward. This time it was a bedroom. But it was too sterile, too ordered. Standardised, like there was another one exactly the same on the other side of The Maze wall. Then another, and another. A hotel suite? The pale pink bed-sheets, hideous wallpaper – blended seamlessly with the blue-grey Maze – the lack of any kind of personal items at all seemed to justify this hypothesis.

But what was it doing here?

Ask no questions and I'll tell you no lies.

Sonny heard footsteps behind him, hands turning a doorknob on a door that wasn't there five seconds ago. The door opened, but no one entered. No one he could see at any rate. He felt something, two 'ghosts' drifting past him to the bed. He watched as the sheets rose in the middle, bulging until human outlines could be seen beneath. The moaning sounds of lovers bombarded his ears. The shapes moved in a natural way, a couple combining, enjoying the carnality.

There was much more to see, but the sheets were preventing him. He walked slowly towards the origin of the noise, intent on lifting the covers. Knowing that underneath lay a woman and her partner intertwined. It excited him, stoked his imagination.

Their cries were louder now, the motions faster. His hand was out, ready to uncover their shimmering bodies, the pleasant tangle of limbs. But he froze when he saw the colour of the sheets. The pink was darker around the midsection; sweat perhaps? No, darker still. Like paint or dye...or blood.

Sonny couldn't bring himself to go any further. Some small part of him knew what he would find if he did. The bad things that lived in The Maze had already 'changed' them, before his eyes, under the sheets.

But they weren't going to let him escape that easily.

'NO!' he shouted as invisible hands drew the fabric back. He could barely assimilate the baseness of what he was seeing. An assortment of body parts, skin rent, carved pieces scattered all over the mattress. Wallowing in a lagoon of gore. The bits were moving, caressing each other as best they could. And on the pillow lay two mouths, one lipstick-coated, the other with stubble dotted around the top, which were still making the sensuous sounds of love.

Again there was a thumping like that of a beating heart.

He had to get away. This abomination was refusing to gel with that which had aroused him so. But in his hurry, Sonny overbalanced and fell. The bag ensured his descent, dropping backwards onto the floor. He rolled around there for a moment, an upturned turtle. Then he felt himself sinking. Helpless and hopeless, the hotel room disappeared as the ground slithered up all around him. Sonny frantically tried to pull himself out, but the bag on his back was caught. His legs were the next to go, followed by his torso. Electricity buffeted him and he shook with the intensity. Sonny's face was the only part of him sticking out now. Was The Maze going to do the same to him? Pick him apart as a schoolboy might tear the wings off an insect – just for the hell of it.

Sonny sucked in a few last breaths, and then disappeared.

Everything was black, but a cerise blackness; the same as when you shut your eyes on a warm sunny day. *Inside* The Maze he was content. After the initial struggle had proved fruitless, he'd let it take him. It seemed like the right thing to do. Sonny felt like a babe in the womb, except this womb was enormous and constantly fluctuating. His senses were stretched to capacity, unreality filling him up. Surely he wasn't here, and yet where else could he be?

Where was The Maze taking him now?

The answer to that question came sooner than he thought as he was pushed upwards and outwards, shooting through the layers of The Maze to stand upright in another corridor. The floor healed itself up around his feet. It had helped him as much as it could, brought him this far. The rest was up to him.

But man, the weight on his back was unbearable now that he was mobile again. Ten times heavier than before. He struggled to build up a pace to start with. And he understood that if he should fall over this time, he would never get back up. No way could he reach the centre on his hands and knees. Too much; it was asking too much.

The mezzanine opened out ahead.

It knew he wouldn't be able to resist. He had to find out what was beyond, even if it killed him...which was looking more and more likely with each passing moment. Groaning, Sonny staggered on. The ground that had embraced him before was now green and waving. Grass, a meadow of fluttering blades and flowers – daises mainly, but a handful of dandelions added their yellowness to the scene as well. Giggling, the sounds of birds in the trees (trees? what trees?) and a far-off dog's barking were audible.

By a river, which ran concurrently along The Maze rampart, he saw a woman in jeans and a T-shirt standing with her young daughter. This was a special time for them; a weekend, bank holiday, spent enjoying the tranquillity of nature. But there was also danger here. Sonny sensed it. The woman was playfully chasing the girl, both laughing. Unaware that there would be another chase soon.

Clickety-clack, clickety-clack; faint in the distance. Urban life infringing upon their fun out here. Both Sonny and the woman listened to the train. He couldn't see any tracks around, no bridges. So where—

The mother held her child to her breast, arms around her. An urgent need to protect.

But from what?

And the train was nearing. It was so loud now. With a blast of wind it whipped past Sonny. He fought to stay vertical. Yet as it went by it seemed to do so in slow motion. The black metal was only half-right, only half-real. It had no undercarriage and there were no tracks for it to move along. The Maze itself was providing the necessary momentum.

A hand appeared at the window of the closest car, spreading fingers that slid down and left ruby patterns on the glass. A moment later and the victim's head appeared, his eyes wide, muscles of his boyish face stretched tight as he tried to scream; an imperceptible something pulling his hair back. Sonny saw the neck rise above the frame of the window. And...

Nothing more.

That head continued to climb up the pane, but there was no body attached to it. Nevertheless, the severed ball was still opening its mouth and eyes wider (they do say that you can survive for so long afterwards, that it is possible to look down and see your own headless torso below), until ultimately the face melted like hot vinyl. Then the window exploded in a shower of glass and carnage.

The train sped up, travelling past a newly-formed station.

No, not a station – the beginnings of a public lavatory diorama. But hanging on hooks in the cubicles were bodies – just bodies – opened up, insides unveiled; cuts on display at the butchers. Each one wriggled and squirmed, but they could not reverse what had been done. Could not piece themselves back together again.

Sonny simply stared, his attention drawn to the train again as it headed for the figures by the river. They ran, the woman pulling her daughter behind, a last-ditch attempt to break free. Their faces were blank now. Didn't they know that no one could escape The Maze? The train's front was distorted, bending and flattening. Becoming pointed and lethal. The rear carriages took on the shape of a hilt and handle. Grass and daisies and dandelions were carved up in the blade's wake.

The ground wept.

No matter how fast the two of them ran, the train-knife matched and doubled their speed. The outcome was inevitable; in a sense it had already happened. The tip of the dagger speared them both and they slid back like meat on a barbecue skewer. It was over in the blink of an eye, leaving nothing but the sound of a thumping heart.

Sonny's initial horror had deteriorated into fascination. He'd seen so much in here it had desensitised him. The thing that had been following him, committing these atrocities – The 'Other' – was everywhere. All seeing, all knowing. But he wasn't afraid. It would never harm him.

He knew then that the centre of The Maze was close. There was just one more corner to turn. A corner which appeared before him, leading to...

The tool shed.

Like everything else in here, it was semi-solid but still part of The Maze. Its door was creaking slowly open, slats of knotted wood a guiding hand to welcome him; more an entranceway than anything. To get to the centre. He heard the deep-seated chuckling of his father. Sonny knew he had arrived.

It was a funny thing, but the weight on his back was no longer a hindrance. In fact he could hardly feel it anymore. There was no point now; the game was lost. It couldn't prevent him from doing what must be done. Sonny stamped confidently through, his assignment clearer and clearer. Roaches and woodlice the size of small rodents crawled over dusty shelves. There were a variety of tools hanging up in the shed: clippers, axes, drills, hammers. He grabbed a couple of items he would need to perform his duties, and the back of the shed fell away. He moved into the hub, the nucleus.

The Heart.

It was ring-shaped, encircled by those same soft Maze walls. In the middle was a hill-like protrusion, and spiralling around that in concentric circles were much smaller mounds of dirt. Next to each one was a name, carved sloppily across the Maze floor. Some made no sense – strangers to him – others he read and recognised: these were the people he'd known. There weren't many. His parents, Meg, a handful of close 'friends'.

He took the shovel and began to dig. It wasn't long before there was a hole next to the last mound. Wiping the sweat from his brow he ditched his load on the ground; the weight from his back. It was a brown bag with something inside, something curled up – the merest inkling of definition, but that was all.

He opened the drawstring at its neck and pulled down the sacking.

Then he reached for the other object he'd brought. A saw. Sonny worked diligently on the curved thing until it relinquished its whole. Now only parts remained: a finger, toes, a torn piece of thigh, an ear...eyes. (The eyes followed him all the time.) And the things he'd found when he'd opened her – *it* – up: organs, entrails...heart. Everything went into the pit and was covered over.

But even as he patted down this fresh hump he heard a muffled voice say, 'You can't bury the truth!' Sonny ignored it and stood back to admire his handiwork – a reflection of something he'd done before he entered The Maze.

The bigger mound in the centre started shaking, thumping. He remembered what was buried there and cowered away from it. A heart, *his* heart – symbol of his own enshrouded compassion.

And the presence he'd felt all this time, that which had done those awful, awful things – not so awful now, though, eh? – finally caught up and joined with him.

He wondered if it would always be like this. Would he always have to travel the canals of his own brain each time? Relive every incident, every slaughter, in a surreal and warped way before disposing of a fresh sacrifice and moving on?

Or would it get easier the more times he did it?

One thing was for sure – and The 'Other' told Sonny this so he had to believe it – only after his new victim was buried could it start again. Only then could the process begin anew.

But soon he would wake up to find that The Heart and The Maze had gone – for the time being. Replaced by another world.

A world full of wonders.

Where anything, absolutely anything, was possible.

Blackout

When Kelly awoke everything was black.

To start with she thought perhaps she was in bed and it was the middle of the night. But everything was so, so dark. Not even the streetlights outside were shining.

And she was alone.

It wasn't until she raised herself up and something heavy dropped from her lap that she realised where she was. Where she *had been* before she'd fallen asleep. Reading on the sofa, curled up enjoying her book.

Damn, I must be getting old, she thought, *nodding off without warning just like Mum used to do.* Or maybe it had something to do with the fact that she'd been up since six, dutifully seeing Jeff off at the station.

In any event it was a shock to wake up and find such a stifling gloom bearing down on her. She couldn't see her hand in front of her face, let alone any of the familiar, comforting objects in her living room.

Kelly never had liked the dark. As a child she'd pleaded with her parents to leave the table lamp on for her at night, and they had done so for a time. But as she got older they said it was a waste of electricity. Kelly was a big girl, and big girls weren't afraid of the dark. It couldn't hurt her. It wasn't alive or anything. And the daytime Kelly agreed with them, there was nothing to be frightened of.

It was the night-time Kelly who was the problem – whispering lies in her ear, forcing her to see things that weren't there.

Oh, but it is alive! And so are the things that lurk within.

Was there any wonder she'd wet the bed until she was almost in her teens? The fears didn't go away just because you were older. The blackness didn't go away – ever.

Of course Kelly hadn't thought about any of this for ages. Her nights were no longer sleepless ones. No more tossing and turning. For one thing she'd been married six years and with her husband beside her at night she was perfectly safe. Her childish fallacies had finally been laid to rest.

But waking up here and now had stirred some of those dormant memories.

Kelly's sofa was next to the window, so she only had to look over the top to see outside. Everything was in shadow. The other bungalows; the streets branching off from her close; the town in the distance. Total blackout. It was as though someone had covered the entire area with a blanket.

Or a shroud.

Trust Jeff to be away when she needed him most. He'd probably be enjoying himself in the hotel bar right about now – she knew what these so-called conferences were like. While she was here, on her own. In the dark. Kelly leaned in closer. No, not a light to be seen. Not—

There was something moving at the window.

Startled, Kelly pulled back. She could only see a vague outline, but that was enough. She inched forwards again. Was there someone outside? A face at the window?

It moved again. Sweet Jesus, it was behind her! Something with protruding eyes and a wide, gaping mouth. Kelly lost her balance and fell backwards. She landed awkwardly, the hardback novel jabbing into her spine.

Cursing, she flung it away into oblivion. *Get a grip on yourself. It was just your reflection, that's all.* But that doubting little voice was talking to her again, reminding her that reflections don't move of their own accord.

Saying that something was coming for her.

Kelly started to rise, slowly, carefully. Dammit, this was all her own fault. She should have taken up her sister's offer. Gone to stay with her for the weekend. But it would have been like admitting she couldn't cope. Fran would just love that. She'd been bad enough to live with when they were little. Kelly wasn't about to give her the satisfaction. Although by this stage even Fran's company was starting to look pretty appealing.

What to do now? A light! She should go and get a light.

As she staggered around the living room, trying to work out in which direction the door lay, an unwelcome thought crossed her mind. Why had no one else in her neighbourhood done the same? When Kelly had looked out of the window she'd seen none of the usual flickering of candles. No erratic torch beams flashing. What did this tell her? That the electricity had only just gone off. Or maybe, just maybe, something had happened to those people before they could—

She was doing it again. Scaring herself silly for no reason. It was all in her imagination. Now she'd get to the kitchen, find the torch, and shed some light on the situation.

Kelly followed the wall around, fingertips tentatively reaching out, half expecting to touch something nasty and slimy despite what she'd just told herself. Before she had too long to dwell on this, she came upon the open door and sighed with relief. She was no longer trapped in that room, in a confined space. Here was the hallway, and further up, the kitchen.

Still Kelly hesitated before stepping out into what felt like a dank, empty cavern, or some kind of disused railway tunnel with no beginning and no end. Perhaps *it* wanted her to come out. That might be part of *its* plan.

Stupid! Stupid!

Kelly dug her nails into the palms of her hands, the pain taking her mind off things for a blessed moment. She pressed on regardless, dragged into limbo. Kelly couldn't see the floor, so was it still there? For all she knew she could be falling into a pit and at the very bottom, waiting for her, would be—

Something brushed her arm as she moved through the hall. Kelly rounded on it and heard a crash as an assortment of objects fell to the floor. The plastic clatter of a telephone, coins jangling in a collection box, the tinkling as a photograph frame shattered. She'd bumped into the hall table.

Calm down. Have to calm down. Kelly's heart was fluttering and she felt sick. What the hell was wrong with her? She was falling apart, and all because of a tiny power cut. Kelly bent down and groped around for the phone. The line was dead. But whether it was due to the fall or not, she had no way of knowing.

Steeling herself, she carried on down the hallway. Her bedroom would be on the right coming up any second, with the spare room directly opposite. Ignoring these, Kelly made for the open space of the kitchen. She lost her grip on the wall for a second and found herself wading in a sea of nothingness.

She collided with the edge of a work-surface and stepped back, only to bang her head on the extractor fan. But this was a good thing. Now she could work out where the overhead cupboard was in relation to the oven. Inside there was the torch, a really powerful one Jeff had been given for joining that motor rescue service. In addition to an ordinary beam there was also a fluorescent strip down the side, which had the capacity to illuminate an entire room.

Smiling, Kelly opened the cupboard door. Everything would be all right once she had the torch in her hands. She could chase away her demons in no time. Standing on her toes, Kelly searched around inside. The torch wasn't where it was supposed to be. *No, this isn't happening, we always keep it in here!*

Wait. Now she remembered. Not two weeks ago Jeff had used it to poke about up in the loft, clearing some space for his old junk. But what had he done with it? Bloody hell, she was forever telling him to put things back when he'd finished with them.

Access to the loft was through the spare room, so she'd try in there first. Knowing Jeff he'd probably left it on the sideboard or something. *But not up* in *the loft, please not up there!* She heard laughing. *It* knew she would have to double back, and *it* was mocking her. Watching, safe in the knowledge that she could see nothing. *It* had come when she was at her most vulnerable, just like when she was a kid.

But she'd show *it!* Kelly could beat this thing yet. Wasn't far to the spare room, a few short metres. She could run if she had to.

Kelly turned and started to move forwards. Again it was hard to tell where she was going. She prayed that her internal radar would guide her, take her safely to her destination.

She had only managed a few steps when she heard the noise. A rough scratching – like that of sharpened claws – echoing all around. The laughing grew louder. Kelly made a dash for the spare room. This wasn't her imagination, this was real. There was something in here with her, fuelled by the energy of the night; the thing from her youth that would not leave her alone. Images returned to plague her. *It* had waited so long for the chance to savour her spirit. So long. Now that opportunity had arisen.

Kelly began to panic and took short, sharp breaths. Without realising, she plunged headlong into sorrow's arms. *It* grabbed her by the shoulders. She felt hands there, clutching. Strong hands. The blackness given form. Kelly twirled out of *its* grasp, swinging her fists round until they struck something. Tumbling, she caught a glimpse of *its* contours.

The monster groaned. Kelly heard the flapping of wings, could picture those appendages which grew out of the black.

You're dreaming. Can't you see that it's all a dream, you're still on the couch in the living room and none of this is happening? None of this is real, Kelly!

But dream or no dream, she couldn't just wait for this thing to attack again. On the floor she crawled backwards to avoid *its* talons.

'Kelly,' *it* whispered, coming closer, closer.

She put her hand out, feeling for something she could use as a weapon. Kelly's fingers came across a shard of glass from the ruined picture frame. Quickly, she grabbed the makeshift dagger and brought it up with all of her might. A warm wetness jetted across her face and she realised her aim had been true. The shape gurgled, then seemed to be absorbed by *its* dense surroundings.

She'd done it. The monstrosity was defeated. She felt stronger than she'd ever felt in her life.

That was when the lights came back on, and Kelly slipped even further into madness.

The scene was unreal, still part of her nightmare. On the floor was Jeff's prone body, his raincoat flowing behind, a bloody pool welling beneath his chin where the glass jutted out. Behind him was the open front door, his key still in the lock, scratch marks around the wood. She could imagine what he'd been trying to say: *'Kelly, guess what? The conference was rubbish so I thought I'd surprise you. I know how much you hate being on your own at night.'*

To her left was the discarded book she'd been flipping through when she dropped to sleep. One of those pulpy horror stories Jeff warned her about reading because they always made her so jumpy. Next to it was the broken picture frame. Her wedding photograph.

Kelly sat there on the floor, rocking back and forth. She wept, but they were more than just tears for Jeff. She cried for herself, because she knew that after all these years the darkness, the *shadows*, had finally won. She'd never sleep with her husband beside her again. Never be safe again.

As if to underline this fact Kelly heard the laughing again, inside her head.

And it wasn't long before she too began to black out.

The Cyclops

The Cyclops had been with him all of his life. As far back as he could remember.

When had it first latched onto him? In the womb? He used to imagine it somehow burrowing into his mother as she slept, gaining access to her maturing son inside. Or afterwards, lying in his cot, peacefully dreaming away the days – his only thoughts random nonsense and a desire to feed, to suckle? A parasite, draining his mother of milk. A parasite, just like the Cyclops.

No, not like that *thing*. His mother had loved him and cared for him willingly. The Cyclops commanded him, took him over. There was no interdependence. No symbiosis. The Cyclops was his master. It had been ever since it melded with him (*whenever* that occurred), nestling its way inside him, curled up next to his skin. A vile stinking abomination with no thought for anything but its own desires, its own pleasure.

So what was it, this Cyclops? He was damned if he knew. He only saw its head – if you could call it that – every now and again when he could bring himself to look at it. The main section was buried deep within him; it fluttered sometimes just to let him know it was there. But the bit you could see was slimy, revolting. Its one shiny black eye stared out malevolently, searching – hence the nickname he'd given it.

As far as he could tell, it was invisible to everyone else. Only he could see it, or feel it. Certainly his mother had never noticed it during his formative years, but then it *had* remained physically dormant for much of that time – a side-effect of the joining, he supposed. He kept it covered under his clothes mostly anyway. Up to the age of ten or so, it prepared itself: it was sustained by his bodily fluids, expelled its own waste, appropriated his nerve-endings and spent long hours working on his mind. At first only probing, then squeezing harder and harder. Establishing the link that would ensure its dominance. He'd tried to resist it, but the pain it inflicted taught him to comply. The Cyclops never spoke to him directly. It was too strange, too *different*. For all he knew it didn't even have a language of its own. But it was smart, and in time he began to understand it a little *too* well. Its thoughts, its edicts.

Its cravings.

It also grew stronger and began to move around, as it liked to do so frequently these days. Early adolescence was a bizarre time for him. He'd never fitted in at school because he was never allowed a free hand to interact with the other children. The Cyclops was always there, listening, telling him what to do. If he came across as an idiot, it was hardly his fault. He would've loved to have joined in with their games, been a member of their gangs. It just wasn't to be. He couldn't trust himself. He couldn't trust the Cyclops. Was there any wonder he bunked off so often? The Cyclops didn't care. It preferred to be alone with him anyway. To *work* on him further. His mother blamed herself, for isolating him from his father, for shunning the man – shunning all men come to that. She'd tried to do her best by the boy: to be both a mum and a dad. But it was clear he needed some kind of male role model. A patriarch if you like.

Enter Uncle Bob. A nice bloke, always smiling and joking, his mother had met him through a friend of a friend. Uncle Bob used to come round every weekend, with flowers for his mother and crisps and sweets for him. He liked Uncle Bob; Uncle Bob made them both laugh. But for some reason the Cyclops hated him. Loathed the very thought of him, let alone his presence. Perhaps it felt threatened, was afraid this man would somehow see it. *Somehow discover the Cyclops.* He attempted to reason with it, to settle it down. To mollify it. All to no avail. The Cyclops wanted Uncle Bob out, so out he had to go.

That was when he learnt just how powerful the wretch had become. How much control it could exert over him and his actions. It made him…do things, awful things to Uncle Bob. Spit at him, throw punches. Shout, scream and swear. It drove a deliberate wedge between his mother and her admirer. Astonishingly, Uncle Bob stuck it out for quite a while, possibly in the hope that it might be a phase: the infamous troubled teenager syndrome. But no relationship was worth this. He hadn't bargained on a problem child as part of the deal. A ready-made family, yes, he could cope with that; after all it wouldn't be more than a few years before the kid was grown up. But the spawn of Satan attacking him as soon as he set foot over the threshold? Forget it, he could live without them.

His mother cried the day she and Uncle Bob split up. He'd felt terrible, riddled with shame. He wanted to go to her and tell her that it wasn't him. *He'd* liked Uncle Bob. It was the Cyclops. Instead he simply listened to her through the bedroom door, sobbing her heart out. If he could have sworn revenge against the Cyclops without it knowing, he would have done so right that minute. But he said nothing, did nothing. And his mother died a broken and lonely woman some ten years later.

Everything changed after Uncle Bob departed. It knew it had total dominion over him now. Could get him to do whatever it wanted – and so it began to plan its first strike.

Nothing too daring to start with. A simple operation, just something to oil the wheels. To set them in motion. He journeyed out one night, alone, lying to his mother about where he was going. To placate the Cyclops. Stealthily he crept through the streets, shaking with fear, but driven on by his mandate. He had no choice but to obey. Further and further he went, away from the city, out into the suburbs. Into the quiet, secluded cul-de-sacs. Until he found what he was looking for at the back of a row of bungalows.

A rectangle of light floating over one of the gardens, virtually the only luminescence there. He came closer to the source, a bathroom window; the curtains wide. Why bother closing them, when the bungalow backed on to woodland and fields? From a discreet distance, he watched. And, through him, the Cyclops watched too, as the woman entered, mid-thirties with dark hair tied back. Slowly, she shed her clothes: jumper, jeans, shoes and socks. She stood there in her underwear, the whiteness stark against tan skin. Climbing out of these quickly, she hopped into the shower.

He crept closer still. He didn't want to see, but the Cyclops did – properly. So he released it. The shower spray bounced off the woman's body, some beads clinging to her, others dripping down to collect in the bath-tub below. He gaped at the way she massaged herself with shower gel. The way it made her glisten, slick and lustrous. She closed her eyes, lost in a world of her own, pulling the band out of her hair so that it fell in damp tangles over her shoulders.

It urged him even closer. It had to see. To see *more*. He tried to fight it, oh Lord how he tried. But the Cyclops, as always, was stronger. He knew what it wanted.

He pressed up to the glass. So close now he could reach out and touch her were it not for the transparent barrier between them. The Cyclops needed to—

She opened her eyes. Saw the figure at her window.

And screamed.

The Cyclops 'told' him to run. He could not be caught this soon. So he ran, faster than the wind, hopping over fences, tripping over flagstones. But he made it away from that estate safely, telling himself she'd only caught a glimpse...not enough to identify him even if he lived in the area. Just an indistinct outline, a reflection at her bathroom window. All his fear of the night was gone now, replaced by the dread of being seen. Of being apprehended doing what the Cyclops had ordained.

Never again, he told himself. *Never again!*

It was very late when he arrived home. His mother didn't hear him come in; the sleeping tablets her doctor had prescribed did their job most nights of the week. How he wished he could take some himself that evening; not enough to kill him (although the thought had crossed his mind), just enough to make him forget what he'd done. The dirtiness. The invasion of privacy.

All for the Cyclops.

But he was amazed at how fast he fell asleep, even without the aid of medication – a mixture of nervous exhaustion and bodily fatigue drawing him under. And as he slept he dreamt of the woman in the shower. The minutes spent recording her face, her body, had paid off. It was an exact reproduction of reality, except he was in there with her this time. It was pleasant. She lathered his chest, throwing her head back and laughing. They kissed, her soft lips squashed against his.

'Is this love?' he found the courage to ask, and she giggled again.

Then she saw the Cyclops. Even in his dreams he couldn't escape this parasite. Indeed, it almost seemed like the Cyclops was manipulating his psyche – which, to a large extent, it probably was. Gaining as much gratification from these images as him. More, if anything.

The woman screamed again, just as she'd done when she saw him at the window. A replay of that precise moment in fact, then a freeze-frame of her open mouth. The dream was over and the nightmare had begun.

When he awoke he discovered the Cyclops was already up. He stared into its dark, glassy eye and scowled. He felt like throwing up, but didn't. If the freaking bastard had been blessed with a mouth it might have smirked then.

The thought of what he'd done hounded him for weeks. He saw the phantom of that frightened woman's face wherever he went, but no one came looking for him. He was never arrested and placed in jail. Even if he had been he could have blamed the Cyclops; maybe sought help from the doctors. They might've been able to remove it.

He didn't know if that was at all possible without killing him too. The Cyclops never let him think about such things for any great length of time. So now he had to acknowledge that they were inextricably bound together.

As one.

The images of the woman didn't satiate the Cyclops for long. A month, six weeks at the most. Then it began to press him again. For more mental pictures, more stimuli. He held off as long as he could, battling the Cyclops for all he was worth, the oath he'd sworn to himself still ringing in his ears:

Never again! Never again!

But the agony it brought to bear was too much for him. Intense, but impossible to describe, it even caused him to pass out for a minute or two once. The Cyclops hadn't meant for that to happen, hadn't realised its own strength. He'd fallen over and nearly split his head open on the dresser – his mother rushing in to see what the thump was, only to find him prostrate on the floor.

That earned him a day in bed, a legitimate day off school. But no doctors. The Cyclops made his mother promise. No doctors.

As he lay there, looking up at the ceiling, he knew the Cyclops was regretting its actions. All those years, all that effort, would have been for naught if he'd died. It would hate to have to start from scratch with a new host, not when it was so close... He realised that the Cyclops needed him alive and well. Could that be used to his advantage?

It didn't cause the Cyclops to relent, though. How could it? No sooner was he back on his feet than it was niggling him again, but in more subtle ways. Wrecking his concentration, stabbing him with short, sharp bursts of discomfort; nothing that could damage him permanently. Every day became a guessing game as to what it would do next, and in the end it shoved him right up to the brink. After a further few weeks he stopped resisting and went along with the Cyclops once more.

Out on another midnight trawl.

He was the Cyclops' arms and legs, its transportation. He derived no enjoyment from the excursions. The creeping about, the spying. It forced him to become more and more adventurous. So he could 'record' the footage for ease of reference. He – it – built up quite a library. There was the blonde woman getting ready for bed, slipping into a baggy red T-shirt before climbing under the covers; the tall, sophisticated office lady just getting in from a late working dinner, stripping off her tweed suit and throwing it in the laundry basket; and the Cyclops' favourite, the curly-haired woman they caught on the living-room floor, already bare, rubbing oil all over her body, arching her back when she reached certain areas. It could access these memories whenever it liked, without his say-so. Waking or sleeping, it didn't worry the Cyclops. He could be eating his dinner, a microwave lasagna on the settee, and the Cyclops would activate them, feeding itself on the renderings. Compelling him to watch those oblivious women again and again. Their most intimate moments anything but.

For years this went on. He could not deny the Cyclops. But then, towards the zenith of his teens, it pushed him over the edge. And suddenly there was no turning back.

He could never forget the first, the same as he couldn't forget the woman in the shower, her screaming (her laughing) face.

Is this love?

The Cyclops had spotted her arriving home. Alone.

Instead of dragging him round the back to watch through a window, it took him over completely. Before he even knew what was happening, he'd pushed the woman through her front door and closed it behind them. His temples throbbed when he resisted the Cyclops, as he tried to get out of there. His intended writhed under him as he gripped one hand around her throat, cutting off her cries for help. The other hand pressing against the side of his own head, to quell the palpitations.

The Cyclops had its way that night. It made him... He couldn't stop it, couldn't do a blessed thing. He was just as much a victim as the girl beneath him, and he strove to make her understand that.

'It's not me. I'm not doing this!'

She became even more terrified, and he couldn't exactly blame her. How could he convince her that he was being directed by some kind of malicious, twisted fungus? At the end of the day it didn't make any difference. The Cyclops saw to that. It could leave no witnesses to this deed.

He was the one who sobbed in his room that night, as the Cyclops relaxed its hold on him – now it was over. The girl and the woman in the shower became interchangeable in his thoughts, both screaming now. Both—

Once the Cyclops had tasted, had touched, there was to be no dissuading it. Each progressive assault seemed to make it more energetic, as if it was somehow sucking the very fear out of its quarry and turning it into energy... *Or food?* Was that what the Cyclops did? Was that what it required to survive? He didn't have the answers and probably never would.

The Cyclops went on for as long as it dared in this neck of the woods. Always so careful, never as clumsy as the first time – and always making him wear gloves. The women who assembled on street corners were the easiest targets. They went willingly with him, but soon changed their minds once they discovered his – *its* – true intentions. The Cyclops, and what it must take from them.

Then came the time to move on, before he attracted too much attention. He travelled abroad, informing his mother it was a backpacking trip, and didn't come home for six years. There was so much scope for the Cyclops in foreign parts, the police that much slacker.

He used to think as he wandered down crowed streets, *if you had any idea what walks among you... What 'lives' inside of me. As part of me.* But how could they? He could hardly tell them and the Cyclops only revealed itself to the chosen few. They seemed to see it near the end, before they died. When it could camouflage itself no longer.

It was around this time that he began to drink. The Cyclops permitted it; hell, the Cyclops *encouraged* it – the alcohol making him even more compliant. But never too much. Never to the point of inebriation. The Cyclops did share his flesh and blood when all was said and done.

He returned home when he discovered his mother was terminally ill, but was too late to say goodbye. The Cyclops didn't care about his grief, it just wanted to take up where it had left off. Again it went on the rampage, always the same. The Cyclops was never satisfied. It made him regularly roam around the country, to throw off the scent in case anyone might be looking for them. But no one ever found them. The crimes went unpunished, which pleased the Cyclops, yet frustrated him.

Numbed to the slaughter and turpitude, his old self – *his real self* – rotted away. His only solace was the next beer. The Cyclops governed completely. It didn't mind – why should it, so long as it was getting its way?

Strangely enough, it was during one of these random forays that he came closer to the truth. He'd been acting on autopilot again (he didn't make the effort to explain his behaviour these days) when he caught sight of himself in a full-length mirror. The shock was like a punch in the guts. There was something about what he was doing that reminded him of...

Leaving the woman barely conscious, but still alive – red indentations marring her neck – he covered up the Cyclops, exited her house, and ran. It couldn't stop him, it was taken by surprise and more than a little drained by the night's exploits. He ran into the blackness, just as he'd done so many years ago when the lady in the shower screamed. And awkward remembrances came back to him from childhood, from so far back he couldn't ascertain his age. Two, three...surely no older than that. Hearing noises and doddering out to see what they were.

A man with his mother.

Not Uncle Bob, too early for that. And although she had never shown him pictures, he somehow knew that this was his father. The man his mother escaped from when he was but an infant. A man he had never seen, never been in contact with.

A man who also knew the ways of the Cyclops.

It had hidden these recollections from him, but now he drew them up from the deep well of his mind and drank in their sights. His father wore the parasite with pride, enraptured by its attachment to his body.

The noises he'd heard became perceptions now, his father and the Cyclops forcing themselves upon his mother – empty beer cans on the floor beside them. Her shrieks in agony at his violation, one hand reaching for her neck (small wonder she had fled soon after – in fear of her life!).

His ugly face turned towards the youngster, mouthing the question: 'Is this love?'

There could be no confusion, no doubt remaining. His father had passed on the legacy of this filthy organism. Indeed, *he* was more than likely a product of its lust, the result of a filthy Cyclops rape.

Half-crazed, he made it back to the flat he now rented and fell to the kitchen floor, banging the linoleum with his fists. If only he'd known...if only...

The Cyclops was snapping out of its daze, becoming aware of what was happening. Of the anger and hatred building. It wanted to quash this rebellion, to buck up and defend itself. But that was impossible.

Or was it?

His hand went to the counter and pulled down the bottle, part-filled with beer. That would calm him down, it thought. That would—

Before it could prevent him, he'd turned the bottle around, grasping it by the neck. He smashed it down on the side of the counter. There would be no more defilement, no more killing. He refused to carry on his father's legacy. To maintain the Cyclops and then, eventually, pass on its genes.

He freed it from the confines of his clothing. The parasite looked at him with its one black eye, pathetic and weakened. Like a shrivelled slug. All control lost, trying to evoke sympathy. For a moment it *almost* worked; he *almost* dropped the bottle.

But the detestation, the potent and vengeful loathing hit back. It was now or never. He had to rid himself – rid the world – of the contemptible, nauseating, thoroughly evil Cyclops, and hang the consequences to his own person.

Wearing a lopsided grin, he stabbed at it. Slashing with the bottle's ragged edges, ignoring the pain, the oozing blood and beer.

Plunging it deep, oh so deep between his legs.

Until he was sure the Cyclops was dead.

And he was at last free from its grip.

R.S.V.P.

23rd July

Mr A.J. Farnsworth (Managing Director)
Huntley Insurance Brokers
13 Umbridge Street
Chetterton
C23 3RA

Dear Mr Farnsworth,

Thank you for considering me for the position advertised in The Gazette last month, and for the interview you granted me two weeks ago. Your letter arrived promptly this morning, stating that you do not find me suitable for the job. Please, I urge you to continue reading. Do not simply cast this aside as you have done my services.

Firstly I feel I must respond to some of the issues you raised in your letter (thank you, by the way, for composing the letter yourself, even if your secretary did type it — so much more personal than the standard photocopied ones). I understand that I have not worked in some time, due mainly to circumstances beyond my control, as I stated at the interview and in my C.V. (which, you kindly pointed out, was disappointingly short and lacking in qualifications). But this in itself would not necessarily have prevented me from working for your firm. If anything, I would have given one hundred and ten percent to repay you for offering me a chance. For giving me a break. I'm positive, despite what you might say, that I could have handled the work quite easily if someone had been willing to show me the ropes. However this is sadly all academic now, isn't it?

I can't begin to tell you how much this post would have meant to me and my loved ones, my girlfriend and child. We were all looking forward to it, to being a normal, happy family again. You say you found my attitude off-putting, and it's funny you should mention that. Mary, my partner, is always telling me I lose my temper too quickly, but then I've had a lot to put up with over the years. Sorry, do bear with me, I'm getting to the point. You haven't stopped reading this, I hope?

199

It's very important that you carry on reading...

You see, I've taken out a little insurance policy of my own. Just in case. I've had a lot of time on my hands lately. Time to think, to watch. To watch your family wave you off in the mornings as you go to your cushy little job in your expensive car and...they remind me a great deal of my own family. We all have responsibilities, you know.

That's why, Mr Farnsworth, I visited your house again this morning, to explain it to them. To show them your letter. And guess what? They agree with me, your daughters and your wife. They say that your behaviour has been absolutely intolerable, so they decided to come along with me instead...after a little gentle persuasion. To replace my...my own family now that they've gone.

Ah, ah, ah. Before you reach for the phone to call the police, consider this. Do you ever want to see them again, Mr Farnsworth? If you bring in outsiders I doubt very much that it will happen. And don't bother trying to trace me, I no longer live at the number on my application form. Also the courier who delivered this has no idea of my true whereabouts (I gave him my old address, clever eh?). So that's that.

I know what you must be thinking, what have I done to them? (After all, they have been with me for a good few hours now.) Are they alive or are they dead? And this brings me to the purpose of my letter. To find out you're just going to have to meet with me, aren't you? Then we can discuss my future at your company. I think you'll agree now that you acted rather hastily in dismissing me, yes? I can use my initiative when I have to, Mr Farnsworth, and this goes to prove it. I have so much to offer, if only I could make you understand.

The alleyway behind McDonalds. Tonight. Come alone, I'll know if you don't.

Thank you for your precious time, Mr Farnsworth, and I look forward to seeing you again soon.

Yours truly,

S. Rawlings (aspiring insurance broker).

A Nightmare on 34th Street

Christmas Eve.

A time of loving, of giving. Peace on Earth and good will to all men (or should that be 'persons' in this politically correct day and age?). Yeah, right. Officer Mal Docherty hadn't seen much evidence of Peace on Earth recently, hadn't seen much evidence in all his years on the job, come to think of it. Yes, it was true that the crime rate had gone down in New York, so the figures said. But here on the streets, down here you saw plenty. Muggings, stabbings...and shootings – there were never any shortage of those. The last one he'd seen involved a drugs case back in August. Mal and his partner, Norman Young, had provided back-up for the cops in charge, and they'd witnessed the worst possible outcome of a deal gone sour. Mal could see the blood now, exploding out of the victim's chest as the bullet... He shook his head; he'd seen worse anyway. Much worse.

'Here y'go, Tee,' said Harry Grace, handing over two steaming cups of coffee to Mal. 'That'll keep you going for a while.'

'Thanks, Harry.' Mal had been coming to Harry's stall ever since it became part of his beat a few years ago. Harry made the best damned cup of java you'd ever tasted, and his hot dogs and doughnuts weren't so shabby either. The large man with salt and pepper hair and a glowing red nose that would give Rudolph a run for his money leant against his cart, grinning as Mal fished about in his pocket for change.

'No need for that, Tee. On the house tonight. It's Christmas!'

Mal looked up and down the street, surveying the scene. The swell of bodies filling up the space, bobbing in and out of stores – most notably *Crosby's*, the biggest store on 34th Street – all doing their last minute shopping. Not too far away a Salvation Army band was playing 'O Come All Ye Faithful'. Quite who the faithful were, Mal had no idea, but the bandleader was conducting the music for all he was worth in case they happened to show up. Lights glimmered in the darkness, the festive decorations illuminating the whole area. Above, giant screens advertised everything from aftershave or perfume at one end of the present scale, to outrageously expensive sports cars at the other: a stocking filler for the man or woman who has everything.

'So it is,' said Mal. 'God bless us every one.' He raised his coffee in salute, then took a sip, the liquid warming him up temporarily. It was freezing out here tonight, the weathermen – sorry, weather-*people* – promising snow again before the evening was out, to top up the layer that had already settled the day before last. Mal wasn't looking forward to working on Christmas Eve, of all nights. But he and Norm had drawn the shitty straw once again so he'd just have to accept the fact that he was on shift till well after midnight. It meant he'd miss all the preparations that were going on back at his home. His children, Lauren (seven) and Brad (five) getting all excited, ready to put out the mince pies and sherry for Santa, Wendy helping them make out their wish lists, a tradition from Mal's own childhood. Then they'd put them under the tree in the hopes they'd be replaced with brightly coloured packages tied up with bows the next morning. That's really what it was all about, the innocence of kids – their belief in the magic. Mal missed that now he was a grown-up.

'You been watchin' too many old movies, Tee,' said Harry.

'Yeah,' replied Mal. There were plenty on TV to choose from at the moment, the titles more of an irony nowadays: *It's a Wonderful Life...* Is that right? Still, better than living in the real world, he supposed. 'Well, cheers, Harry. You have a good one, won't you?'

'You too, Tee. Say hello to the missus and the little ones from me.'

Mal raised both coffee cups now, and turned his back on the vendor. He made his way past the crowds, back to the distinctive white and blue patrol car parked on the opposite side of the road. In shop windows he saw his reflection: the uniform of an NYPD cop, peak cap, padded jacket and belt, with baton and gun hanging from it. Mal sometimes wondered why he'd ever joined the ranks of the boys in blue. To make a difference? To make the city a safer place for your average citizen, if such a thing existed? To help create a decent world for his children, give them something concrete to believe in? At times it just felt like he was fighting a losing battle.

The lights changed as he got to them, the signal stating he was able to cross safely. Norm sat in the passenger side of the vehicle. He wound down the window as Mal approached, eager to take possession of his drink. The sounds of the radio wafted Mal's way: U2's 'Angel of Harlem' playing on a non-stop Christmas station Norm had found. Mal heard the lyrics talking about New York looking like a Christmas tree, how tonight it belonged to Bono, and thought how appropriate the first part was. New York *did* look like a Christmas tree that night, with all the decorations and lights, while the real thing – a giant tree not too far away – was attracting ever more visitors. But the city did not belong to that famous singer, didn't belong to anyone. It was an entity in its own right, one which shouldn't be judged by looks alone.

'About time,' Norm called out through the gap in the window, 'I was beginning to think you were grinding the beans yourself.' He took the cup from his partner and drank a mouthful, the coffee sticking to parts of his moustache. Norm looked at Mal. 'No doughnuts tonight?'

'Like I said before, Norm, you can do without them.' Mal pointed to the policeman's paunch, hanging over his belt. 'Save some room for that turkey tomorrow.' Mal knew that even though they were separated, Norm's wife, Cynthia, would be cooking a huge spread the next day for him – Mal always got a report back about it when the pair met up again. And she made enough to feed most of the division.

'I can always find room for one of Harry's doughnuts,' Norm assured him.

'I'm sure.' Mal drank more of his coffee and looked back over at the crowd again, seeing the faces this time. None of the people on the streets of New York tonight seemed particularly happy, or festive. They looked stressed, impatient, irritable. Christmas had become almost a mirror of modern day society in a way. Everything had to be done in a hurry and there was more pressure than ever to get things right: to keep up. Lose your footing on the treadmill and you were a goner. The ads showed a perfect world that couldn't possibly exist, and was all but impossible to live up to. Happy families, friends, lovers, all gathered around the fire playing games and having fun. The reality? Most family get-togethers ended in rows, most parties relied on booze to kick start them – and as for those on their own at this time of year, thinking they were missing out, well there was no wonder the suicide rate rocketed between December 24th and 26th...

'What're you thinking about?' asked Norm.

'Mmm? Oh, nothin' much. Nothin'…' Mal's sentence tailed off as he noticed a disturbance out on the street. There were a handful of folk piling out of *Crosby's*, a couple of maroon-suited staff following them. But these people didn't look stressed; at least, not in the same way the other New Yorkers did. They looked more panicked than anything, tumbling out of the entranceway, arms flailing as they did so.

'Norm?'

'Still here.'

'Norm, take a look across the road.' Mal pointed in the direction of *Crosby's* and what was rapidly becoming a small-scale riot of sorts.

Norm frowned. 'Somethin's up.'

Mal glanced back at him. 'No shit, Sherlock. Your finely honed police skills tell you that? Here,' he said, handing Norm the other coffee cup, 'hold this. I'm going to check it out.'

Mal made his way back across the street, not bothering to wait for the traffic signals to change this time. Instead he dodged in and out of the cars, earning a blast on the horn from one yellow taxi-cab. The police officer pushed past the gathering crowds to get to the people in the entranceway. Just what the hell was going on? A fire maybe? That would explain the pandemonium. Or, heaven forbid, something worse. Something manmade? Surely this city had seen enough of that kind of thing to last a million lifetimes?

'Okay, okay, what's the problem here?' Mal asked, his hand on one woman's shoulder.

She turned, a look of surprise and bewilderment on her face.

'Ma'am? Can you tell me what's going on?'

Still she stared at him, dumbstruck, so Mal looked around for someone else who could help. One of *Crosby's* staff came up, eager to oblige. 'Officer, oh thank the Lord!'

'What's happened, sir?'

'There's…' The man paused, not knowing quite how to explain the situation. 'There's been an incident, one of—'

Then Mal heard it: the distinctive blast of gunfire, coming from inside. Somebody in the crowd screamed and there was even more commotion.

Mal grabbed the member of staff before he could be swallowed up by the churning mass of bodies.

He looked the man in the eyes. 'How many?'

'Just one guy, he's gone nuts!'

More shots rang out.

'There are still people inside,' said the man from *Crosby's*. 'Children...'

'See that squad car over there, go tell the officer inside to radio for assistance.'

'I...yes, I think someone's called the authorities.'

'Go tell him anyway!'

The man nodded and began to push back through the crowd. It took a second or so for Mal to lose sight of him completely.

Alright, Malcolm Docherty, what should you do? Back-up's probably on the way right now. Wait for it to arrive? Might be too late by then – and that guy said there were people inside...children. I have no choice, have to do something!

Mal had to go inside.

Fighting against the tide of humans that were still pouring from the store, he headed for the doors, and headed inside *Crosby's* department store.

~

It had actually been less than a week since Mal had been in here, last Saturday to be precise; but it had been under such different circumstances. That day he'd been looking forward to visiting the store, bringing Lauren and Brad to town to see Santa in his den. In spite of the superficiality of it all, word had it that the fella they'd hired this year was good: extremely convincing and a wow with the kids. Mal had to admit that was right. They'd queued for hours on his day off just so his little boy and girl could sit on Father Christmas' lap. Had it been worth it? You bet. Just to see their cherubic faces light up as they entered the grotto – decorated with candy-coloured stripes, balloons, fairies, huge fluffy bears, and trees laden with baubles, stars and chocolate treats. There was even a toy train chuffing around tracks above the parents' and children's heads.

When Lauren and Brad were finally allowed up to the podium, where

Santa sat in all his glory, dressed in the obligatory red and white outfit, they'd both beamed so broadly all Mal could see were teeth.

'Ho, ho, ho,' Santa had said, also smiling – although you could only just see it behind his big white bushy beard. Brad and Lauren took their turn to whisper in St Nicholas' ear, while female helpers dressed as elves readied presents to give them when they were done. As Mal took their hands to lead them away, Santa pulled down his half-moon glasses and winked. Nice memories, and something to hang on to when everything else was gloomy.

All Mal could think was what a shame this had to happen here. A damn shame that whatever might unfold now would wipe out that memory and replace it with something completely different, something like—

Bang-bang-bang-bang-bang!

Mal heard the shots as he walked through the foyer, another handful of shoppers running past him. They were coming from the direction of the grotto he'd visited. Obviously someone else had been pondering the nature of this season a little too much, and had come up with their own way of coping with it. Mal broke into a run himself. But he ran in the opposite direction to the fleeing customers – drawing his own weapon as he went. There hadn't been too many occasions when he'd had call to discharge his pistol, and only one instance when he'd had no choice but to... Mal hoped with all his heart it wouldn't come to that again tonight.

Not tonight.

The first thing he saw as he entered the grotto was the train on the tracks above his head. It had been derailed and now hung down like a limp member, flaccid and useless. There was a break in the tracks, ragged pieces sticking out where the blast had hit it. Mal crept further inside, his forehead dripping with sweat – partly due to the change in temperature and partly to his anxiety at what he might find in here.

It was like a snapshot from some kind of nightmare, the grotto transformed into a hellish underworld. Bullets had riddled the brightly coloured walls, the fluffy bears and the mock presents on display. Parts of the scenery had been almost shredded in half by the gunfire, baubles on trees shattered. Mal saw an elf helper propped up against some steps, holding her arm. A stark redness was pouring through her fingers, dripping down her lime green costume. Their eyes met, and for a moment he saw a glimmer of hope in them.

Then a hail of gunfire splattered the wall behind him. Mal ducked, rolling over on his shoulder and spreading himself on the ground, flat. He tried to work out the position of the shooter based on where the bullets had come from. It was all but impossible; the whole thing had happened too quickly. From his place on the floor he could see more bodies, feet upon feet. He couldn't tell whether the people they belonged to were just injured, like the elf, or... Mal could hear children crying, adults half-screaming and half whimpering with fright. Jesus, who would do something like this?

Mal crawled along on his belly, wriggling like a snake. His hostage and siege training flashed through his mind. He should try to engage this person in conversation somehow, get them talking. At least then they wouldn't be shooting anyone. But who was to say this guy even *wanted* to talk? Only one way to find out.

'Hey,' shouted Mal. 'Hey you!'

Silence.

Mal tried again. 'Hey, I want to talk to you.'

Stupid! What a stupid fucking thing to—

'Don't want to talk,' came the answer in a voice that was deep, gruff, and on edge. It was capped off by another shot.

Mal flinched, but persevered. 'Then just listen, okay?'

Nothing.

'You can't be doing this. Look, put down your weapon and we'll sort all this out peaceably, okay?'

'You can't sort anything out. No one can!'

Good, thought Mal, *you've engaged him...keep going.* 'Why, what's the problem? There's nothing that can't be fixed.'

'That's what you say.'

'So, tell me about it. What is it, money, your job? Something more personal?'

'My job! Hah! That's a good one. '

Okay, so it's work. He's lost his job or something, maybe his family too? That's enough to set anyone off, at any time of year.

'Can't be as bad as all that, can it?'

'It's worse! They…they never stop coming.'

'Who, who don't stop coming?' Mal raised his head slightly, figuring he just about had an angle on the direction of the voice. Over on his far left. Then he saw the gunman, and it turned his blood colder than a winter's day in Lapland.

There, by the side of Santa's golden throne he stood; bottle of whiskey in one hand and a rifle in the other. By his feet was a sack of other weapons – Mal saw a machine gun poking out of the top – and tucked in his black belt were two automatic pistols. 'The letters,' said Father Christmas. 'The children, the presents…'

'Oh my God,' Mal whispered under his breath. It was the same man who'd been bouncing Lauren and Brad up and down on his knee, who'd winked at them as they left. Mal couldn't believe the turnaround though, from a happy, gentle fellow to raging lunatic; eyes wild, buttons undone halfway down his scarlet tunic.

'I just can't take it anymore,' shouted the man. 'It's the same every year! They never stop coming. *Never!*'

'Listen… What's your name?'

'You know my name. My *names*.'

He couldn't be serious, surely? 'No, your real name.'

'You know that as well, deep down.'

'Right, okay. Look, it's only once a year. It's just a job.'

The man laughed. 'Once a year, but for *sooo* many years, so many decades, so many centuries. On and on, never-ending. And it's not just a job; you can't quit, there's no way out. No way. It's too much for me, too much. I can't stand it anymore.'

'All right, I can help.' *Or at least get you some help*, thought Mal.

'No, no you can't. It's too late for that, much too late.'

Mal raised himself up a little, so he could see the Santa but duck down again quickly if need be.

'Ha! I know you,' said the man, waving his bottle in Mal's direction.

Mal was surprised he remembered, given the amount of people who must have passed through here. 'Er…yeah, I was in with my children.' Talking about Brad and Lauren made him look around for the other kids in the grotto. There were several hiding behind a mock-up of Father Christmas' sleigh, some more at the rear of a particularly large present. They looked terrified.

'No, I mean I *know* you, Malcolm.'

How did he know Mal's name? Must've mentioned it when he was here, that's the only thing he could think. 'I don't think so.'

'Oh yes, I know you. Remember that year you went on and on at your folks about that toy garage? Yes, the one with the little car wash and bell. They told you they couldn't afford it and you cried. Still arrived though, didn't it? You got your wish.'

'What the f... How did you know about that?' But then it wouldn't be that hard to guess, most guys his age would've wanted one of those as a boy. And his parents...well, they'd found the money from somewhere to get it for him.

'I know a lot of things, Malcolm. So many things. I know what a naughty boy you've been in your time as well. Haven't you?'

'Naughty...?'

'Does Wendy know about that female officer? No, I don't think she does, does she?'

Mal's mind was reeling. Now *that* was impossible, nobody knew about the fling he'd had with Barbara Kelly, not even Norm.

'And the druggie. Wasn't your fault, though. You did what you had to.'

'Shut up!'

'Just like we all do.'

'I said shut up!' Mal stood and raised his pistol, aiming straight for the man's head.

'Go on, do it then,' said the Santa. 'Wouldn't be the first time, would it?'

The crying got louder and now there was more screaming. 'I mean it,' shouted Mal. His hand was shaking, finger twitching on the trigger.

'Can't you see? All this,' Father Christmas nodded at the den, 'all this is bullshit. The world's changed, son. You know it, I know it. Everything's gone bad.'

'Including you.'

Santa didn't answer him, but Mal could see a tear trickling down his cheek, heading for the forest of white below.

'It really isn't too late, you know,' said Mal.

'Isn't it? You really believe that? You really believe in anything anymore?'

Mal fell silent.

'Thought so.' Santa raised his rifle, ready to shoot. Mal briefly saw a picture of the drug addict he'd killed all those months ago, and froze. He heard the crying of the children – of the adults – in that store. Did he really want to do this in front of them? Time was running out and he had to make up his mind.

There was a shot. Santa dropped his gun and his whiskey. Another blast echoed around the room, then the man was falling over, toppling against the golden throne. He raised a bloodied hand to clutch at the chair arm, but it slipped off, too wet to find purchase.

Mal looked down at his pistol, expecting to see the tell-tale smoke rising from the barrel. But then he realised he hadn't been the one who'd fired. He glanced over his shoulder and saw Norm there, along with a number of SWAT officers and, unless he was mistaken, a few Feds too.

They swarmed in, checking on casualties, ushering the children to safety, securing the area. Mal moved forwards with Norm and the SWAT team to find the man dressed as Santa keeled over on the floor. They snatched the handguns from his belt, kicked away his rifle, and trained their own weapons on him. Somebody called for a paramedic, and Mal noticed that a few had already entered the grotto to treat the wounded. He feared it would be too late for this particular casualty, however.

Father Christmas coughed, and smiled at Mal. 'Ho...ho...ho...' he wheezed. Then he winked from behind his pair of cracked half-moon glasses, before closing his eyes forever.

'You alright?' Norm asked his partner.

Mal nodded. Physically he was fine, if a little shaken up.

'Jeez Louise, look at the hardware in that sack,' said one of the SWAT guys. 'Guess not everyone wants video games for Christmas.'

Mal turned and started to walk away.

Norm jogged up alongside him. 'Hey, where are you going?'

'Home,' said Mal.

'What about the report? Hey...Mal, hey wait up!'

But Officer Malcolm Docherty was already on his way out of the store.

~

It began snowing while Mal walked the streets, but he barely even noticed. And it was close to twelve by the time he arrived back home. Mal let himself in, heading straight for Lauren and Brad's rooms first. They were fast asleep, their innocent faces as pale as angels on the pillows.

Mal left them in peace (heavenly peace...?) grabbed a Bud from the fridge, and walked into the lounge. The TV was on – the end of some stupid Christmas special featuring a variety of Z list celebs. Wendy was dosing on the couch; she only stirred slightly when Mal came in. He took a gulp from the bottle just as a newsflash came up on the television.

'*...in Crosby's tonight. The shootings left several people injured but only one person dead, the gunman – who has since been identified as a Mr Christopher Cringle. A spokesperson for Crosby's said, "He has only been in the employ of this store for the last month, and his credentials seemed very impressive..."*'

Mal switched off the set and took another swig of beer. The clock on the mantle chimed the hour. His eyes were drawn to the tree in the corner of the room, and the wish lists below it. He wondered whether those wishes would ever be granted, now that...

No, he didn't want to think about it. Didn't even want to consider the outrageous possibility that one of the last shining lights, one of the last symbols of hope, was no more. That *He'd* been tainted by this world, driven mad by the demands placed upon him.

Cringle had just been some nut in a Santa suit, the things he'd said lucky guesses. Just another person who'd lost it and gone ape with America's favourite adult toys.

'*I know you...You've been a bad boy...*'

Mal took out his notepad and pen, and scribbled something down. He walked over to the tree, bent over, left the note there. Then he joined his wife on the couch, slumping down beside her.

And waited till morning to see if his wish really would come true.

Sin

When the box arrived, it was treated as suspicious from the start.

For one thing, it was left on the steps of the police station, rather than being delivered with the rest of the post. Nothing was signed for, and it was delivered very early; it was still quite dark outside. The parcel was simply left, and reported by some of the early morning shift heading in to work. One young officer called Wells even made a joke about it, affecting Brad Pitt's gravely tones as he asked 'What's in the box? What's in the fucking box?'

Not particularly funny, given that the whole station was being evacuated at the time and the bomb squad was called in to make sure the package was safe. From a distance, they all watched as men dressed in heavily-padded clothing approached the oblong and went about their business, finally signalling that it wasn't an explosive device; not that anyone had ever targeted their small station, in their small town (which had only recently been granted city status – some argued prematurely). He'd never thought it was. Somehow he'd known this was connected with the case, his detective's intuition or 'Spider-sense' he'd always relied on – that and the size and shape of the box.

Because, when the people who had opened it reported back on the contents, they confirmed that not only wasn't it about to go off and take out half the street, that is wasn't in fact Gwyneth Paltrow's head either, they said that instead it was what looked like a foot. A human foot, severed at the ankle.

The killer had finally given one back...

As DI Patrick Hammond approached the – now unwrapped and open – box to peer inside, he felt his stomach rolling. Not because of the colour of the foot, grey almost white, nor the fact that from his angle he could see right down inside to the crimson meat packed around the bone, bits of ragged flesh skirting the edges where the foot had been sawn off. It was more because he knew whose foot this was, even before he spotted the star tattoo just below the ankle bone, standing out more than ever now against the starkness of the dead skin.

Knew it belonged to *her*, the woman he loved.

Wouldn't take the pathologist Dr Foxborough to verify that the foot belonged to one of the most recent...no, *the* most recent victim. Wouldn't take matching this against any of the corpses that had been stacking up these past few months in the morgue: all missing one foot; the left or the right, it didn't seem to matter which. This one particular foot they wouldn't be able to match against a corpse they had back there, because she was still missing – an abductee.

And now amputee, his mind provided; sometimes it just didn't know when to shut up. Hammond fought to hold back the tears at this, fought to control the memories that were coming back to him, of kissing that foot, of kissing the toes covered in ruby red nail polish – which were still that same colour, if more than a little faded and chipped now. It helped with his composure that his boss, DCI Eddie Balfour – a man who bore more than a passing resemblance to Homer Simpson, right down to the yellow tinge of his skin which was due to a liver complaint – was now standing beside him.

'Fuck,' the balding man simply whispered, which simultaneously said nothing and everything at once. It was a good job the press were being held back behind a cordon, otherwise they might have taken that as an official statement – and it was as good as any, Hammond supposed. Probably more than he could muster himself. Then Balfour asked his DI: 'What do you make of it?'

Hammond opened his mouth, and closed it again just as quickly. Shook his head. It was better not to speak at that moment, better to say nothing than let it all spill out.

'Looks like a job for Sherlock Holmes to me,' said a voice from behind them, that same wet behind the ears tosser Wells who'd been doing the Pitt impressions earlier on.

'Come again?' asked Balfour.

'Well, y'know, the game is a foot,' the officer clarified, then sniggered. Hammond looked at the ground, gritted his teeth, the clenching of his jaw causing a muscle in his cheek to twitch. He felt like lunging for the man, pounding his head into the pavement – but gallows humour was part and parcel (very poor choice of words) of their job. How many crime scenes had he visited and made jokes at, because he didn't know the vics, because if you didn't you'd go stark, staring mad. Poor unfortunates who'd had their hands bound behind their backs and hung, only to be met with gags like 'He'll be tied up for a while...'; people stabbed, only for some smart arse to state they 'Got the point..'; electrocutions that were 'Just shocking', and if it had been delivered by this pillock then no doubt the Connery accent would have been wheeled out. Different, though, when it was someone you knew, wasn't it? Someone you cared more about than anyone – anything – in this whole world. Loved so much, but couldn't show that you did. A secret love that—

'You get it?' prompted the young lad. 'That's what he used to say, Sherlock Hol—'

Release valve or no release valve, Hammond was seconds away from having this joker.

'Yes, yes,' said Balfour, waving the officer away like the nuisance he was; like a fly buzzing round that didn't know how close it had come to getting swatted. 'Very good. You'll be live at the Apollo doing stand-up in no time... If you're not careful.'

The officer got the hint about his job and sauntered off. 'Twat,' Hammond couldn't help muttering.

When he looked up again, he saw that Balfour was watching him, studying him. He had to be careful with that kind of shit – not because he was ashamed or anything, but because he would get taken off the case. He'd be no use to anyone then, especially *her*. 'This one's really getting to you, isn't it?'

Hammond gave a half shrug that was perhaps a little too exaggerated. 'Shouldn't have got this far. We should have had the bastard by now. Before...' He nodded at the box, but couldn't bring himself to look at it again.

Balfour placed a hand on his shoulder. 'Don't beat yourself up about it.' What he actually meant and what had been coming across since this investigation began, especially in certain narrow-minded quarters was: 'What's the big deal? They're only prostitutes.' Papers had said pretty much the same thing, after sensationalising those first few disappearances; letters columns especially, commenting that these women knew the risks, that they kept putting themselves out there amongst all these perverts – what did they expect to happen? Wasn't as simple as that, wasn't as clear cut. Yes, there might have been a time when Hammond would have agreed, but he knew so much about that world now – so much about the women who inhabited it. Knew one intimately. To him, it *was* a big deal – not least because these were people, living breathing people (or had been), some of them with families – hell, some only did this *because* they had families to support. But maybe he'd been underestimating Balfour, because when he continued the man said: 'We have a lead now, at any rate. Our biggest clue yet.'

Or maybe he was just keen to get this one sorted, get it off the books because it was making them all look bad. If the press got hold of this new turn of events, it would like as not send them into another feeding frenzy. Either way, it was time to take a step back now and let Foxborough and the SOCOs do their work.

Take a step back? If only he could.

She certainly wouldn't be able to now, would she? His mind said, at it again – reminding him of what she'd lost. Maybe even her life? It explained why he'd not been able to get hold of her in days, all that worry hadn't been wasted after all. Every morning Hammond would wake up expecting there to be another body; expecting it to be hers. Though not expecting this, never expecting this...

Hadn't he begged her not to keep going out there? In fact the last time they'd seen each other they'd argued about it, and he regretted that bitterly. She'd seen it as him telling her what to do when that was the last thing he wanted – nobody could ever tell her what to do, she was much too strong for that. No, he just wanted her to be safe and – be honest – he was getting to the point where the thought of all those hands on her, what those men she went with did to her, was driving him crazy.

Should have said something, should have told her how you really *feel.*

That he wanted to spend the rest of his life with her, take her away to the coast like she'd talked about that time, wash away all this dirt and grime and filth. Live the life he...they'd always wanted, that she'd been trying to save up for all these years and failing. That although he couldn't promise her the world, he could at least give her his heart, his devotion.

But he hadn't said any of those things, had he? Didn't seem the time or place when they were having a slanging match, and suddenly things were coming out of his mouth that he really didn't mean:

'If that's how you want it, then fuck off and get yourself killed.'

Be careful what you wish for… Hammond was wishing for something else entirely now, though, wasn't he? Something he'd asked Foxborough about when they visited him later.

'Is the vic…is she still alive, Doctor?'

Foxborough had looked up at him from his position over the metal table, those bulging eyes rotating in his direction like gun turrets ready to fire; mouth open and poised to shoot him with information that could wound or kill as effectively as any bullet. 'She was when the foot was severed anyway, that I *can* tell you.'

Hammond closed his own eyes, rubbed his face. Not quite the answer he was looking for, but it would do. It gave him hope. Wasn't a dead body, just a dead right foot: there on the table, staring up at him as accusingly as Foxborough.

'Of course, chances of re-attachment now are slim – it's way past the six to twelve hour window, and that's if it had been packed in ice.'

So, that perfect body was mutilated for life. She'd never be whole again, and it was all his fault. If only he'd got to the bottom of this earlier. If only—

'There were no clues as to the identity of the person who did this from the foot, the wrapping or box. No prints, DNA… Nothing,' Foxborough told them, as if he thought he was being helpful.

'But we do know who the victim is, thanks to Inspector Hammond,' Balfour had said from his position beside him again. Hammond had told them he'd spoken to a few of the contacts he'd cultivated on this case, asked who hadn't been seen in a while – it wasn't a lie, he had made sure she hadn't been around lately on her usual patch. Said it like he hadn't known immediately who the foot belonged to, said it as if he hadn't really known the vic at all and wasn't biting back the yelp that almost followed when he spoke her name.

'And we have a lead on who left the package,' Balfour added. 'CCTV outside the station picked up the license plate of the delivery van – driven by one Mr Harry Millard. We're confident he had nothing to do with it, seeing as he didn't make any attempt to disguise himself as he left it on the steps. He was just doing his job, basically.'

'He didn't think it strange that he had instructions to leave it on the steps?' asked Foxborough, poking at the foot again with one of his instruments.

Balfour shrugged. 'Christ knows. To be honest, after speaking with him I'm not sure the man's all there.' He tapped the side of his head. 'If you know what I mean?'

'Your average delivery man, then,' said Foxborough without any hint of humour this time; Foxborough didn't really do jokes, and if he did they were so deadpan they weren't really recognised as such.

'Anyway, he checks out – mainly because we have more CCTV from the depot where the delivery was arranged, of the actual person who paid for it.' A solidly built man, wearing a padded coat, jeans and hoodie, which was up; who kept his head turned or tilted away from the camera – had probably scoped the place out beforehand a few times – and paid in cash so there was no card to trace. The woman who'd served him couldn't remember much more than they'd seen themselves, because they dealt with so many people in a day. Nevertheless, the grainy picture was being circulated around the troops and through the media – the only time they actually were of use. Nothing as of yet.

Hammond had spent a long time staring at that image, staring at his enemy. The person who had done this to her…to so many others before her. He recalled the first of them now, left in a skip down an alleyway like so much trash; some would argue that she was, that it was where she belonged. But Maggie Graham hadn't deserved that end – *nobody* deserved that. Not even animals deserved to be treated so poorly; and some of those same people would put their pets above the human lives in question here.

Maggie, staring up, glassy-eyed, with her tongue lolling out black – a thin red line around her neck where she'd been garrotted. Staring up from her final resting place amongst the crisp packets, beer bottles and half-empty cartons of junk food – her frizzy hair actually containing bits of that food. They hadn't noticed the missing left foot until some of that rubbish had been cleared away, each bit taken to be painstakingly examined – the skip itself scrutinised for prints and anything else that might have given the killer away, though they'd yielded the same results as this most recent find. It had been removed quite clumsily really; torn away from the ankle when the saw had nearly finished its job, like a lumberjack hacking impatiently at branches. They had no idea why, until the next body had been found washed up out of the local canal.

Phoebe James was missing that same appendage, except it was the right not the left. While Maggie still had her clothes on, half of Phoebe's were torn or missing, though whether that was to do with being in the water for so long was debatable. She was a younger than Maggie's 38, but strangely looked older – and that definitely had nothing to do with the canal's attentions, because Hammond had seen photos of her when she was still alive. Drug and alcohol abuse was to blame, something he suspected she did to take her mind off her job and which had become a vicious circle; the only way she could now pay for her cravings. Phoebe had been garrotted as well, the same MO. That was when they knew they had a multiple murderer on their hands. When they found victims three and four – Willow Clark and Vera Humphreys (the oldest of the bunch at 45), one in a car park and the other in woods not that far away – they knew they were definitely dealing with a serial killer.

To begin with, certain resources had been at their disposal, in spite of the fact that recent budget cuts had meant even beat patrols had become a luxury of late. Stake-outs to watch these 'ladies of the night' – as someone poetically called them; it was the politest term Hammond had heard during all this time – even an undercover officer posted on a few street corners for a week or two. WPC Charlotte (Charlie) Grant, the subject of many a male fantasy at their station, even before they saw her done up in that plastered on make-up, wearing a leather mini-skirt and low-cut top. Hammond had winced at the dirty language she had to put up with as she walked through corridors on her way to do her duty – the wolf whistles and propositions, from single and married officers alike. To her credit, she'd given back as good as she got – she'd learned to do that very quickly when she joined the force, rather than running off to report it as so many of her colleagues had done and come up against brick walls. But that still didn't make it right.

Keeping an eye on her those evenings in his unmarked car, Hammond had been given a first-hand taster of the life of those women who risked everything out here. Seeing the trouble she'd gotten into a few times; though again Charlie had handled herself well, only having to pull her badge a couple of times. They'd been false alarms, of course; not the guy they were looking for. He never showed on those evenings, or at least he never had a crack at Charlie.

But Hammond couldn't help thinking, as he watched her putting her own life on the line for a different reason altogether, that as good looking as Charlie was, she still wasn't a patch on his girl. On *her*.

On his Ella.

Only that wasn't what she called herself, wasn't even what she wanted *him* to call her...not at first anyway. That name had slipped out when she hadn't been focussed one night, when she'd had a bit too much to drink; and he'd tried to find out more, but she'd clammed up on that occasion. If she'd been with anyone else but him, they might have forced her to tell – forced her to do a lot more besides. But he didn't; he respected her privacy. Respected *her*, actually.

A surprise really, given how they'd met. It had been a private bash thrown by a local 'businessman' a year or more ago, to get both members of the criminal underworld and a corrupt police force on side. Hammond couldn't say that he was entirely comfortable with both fraternities rubbing shoulders at the shin-dig, but was well aware of how it all worked in this town – corrupt politicians mediating between them half the time. Backs were scratched on a regular basis, the odd blind eye turned; checks and balances, was how it had been explained to him. The alcohol had flowed – and probably much harder stuff out of sight – and as part of the evening's entertainment, 'escorts' had been laid on (though it was clear to anyone with half a brain that these girls hadn't come from any kind of established escort company). A string of them had been paraded in front of Hammond, and he'd been asked to pick which one he wanted: black; oriental; Indian... 'Whatever floats your boat,' he'd been told, by the fellow who'd brought them in. A snivelling little man who seemed to live to please.

Back in the day, back before Ella, he probably wouldn't have hesitated

– just like the married Balfour, pointing out a thin, athletic girl, the exact opposite of himself. They'd then disappeared upstairs in the hotel where the party was being held. If he was being honest, Hammond was about to refuse the offer...when he saw *her*. She looked stunning, with that golden hair taken up and in that blue off-the-shoulder dress which clung to every curve of her; a choker at the neck completing the outfit (he really hoped now that hadn't been an omen of things to come...).

But he wasn't looking at her body – not really. It was those equally blue eyes he spotted first, being fanned by huge black eyelashes; that cute button nose and lips that looked naturally red, though he could have been wrong. Her expression, aided by the fair eyebrows that were slightly raised, was one of innocence – at odds with the profession he knew even then she was in. It didn't so much make him want to *have* her, as protect her – not that she needed it, as he later discovered. No, Ella was tough – and she'd been through so much.

While he was standing there, gaping, probably even had his mouth wide open, one of the other men in the room came over and approached her. Hammond recognised him as a lowlife called Nichols, involved in hardcore fetish webcam sites and not averse to knocking his performers about if the rumours were correct. 'Hi there, beautiful,' he said, practically drooling over Ella. He rubbed a finger down her cheek and across her chin, which made Hammond's stomach turn; particularly when he saw those blue eyes of hers brush the floor.

He couldn't help himself – before he knew it, he was cutting in, grabbing Nichols' arm and lowering it. 'I think you'll find she's spoken for,' Hammond had said, as if he was some half-arsed knight of old.

'That so?' replied the man, snatching his arm away.

Hammond didn't want any trouble, not here, so he looked over to the guy who'd told him he could pick whichever girl he wanted. A guy who also knew he was a copper. 'Gentlemen, gentlemen... I'm sure we can work something out,' he'd said in those same sycophantic tones.

'I'm sure we can,' said Hammond, eyes narrowing – a threat he couldn't really carry out implied; to look a bit more carefully into Nichols' affairs, perhaps?

'Look, look... Plenty more to choose from,' said the intermediary, his voice practically begging Nichols to let it go. There was a moment or so, when the criminal looked from Ella, to Hammond, to the toadying man – a moment when it could have gone either way – then thankfully he backed off, hands raised. No harm, no foul. The sycophant led him over to the other girls and he seemed happy enough to go with a brunette who had a chest that looked like it had been inflated with a bicycle pump. Leaving Hammond with Ella...except he hadn't known she was Ella back then. Back then, she'd introduced herself as:

'Sindy.'

'With a "C"?' he'd asked her, like *that* mattered.

She'd shaken her head.

Like the doll, then? he'd thought to himself, but didn't say it. *A plaything – from her childhood?*

'I'm Hammond. Patrick.'

Already, she was gesturing for them to leave, to head upstairs. Hammond went with her, more because he wanted to get away from everyone else than anything, but found himself tongue-tied as they headed for the lift. She pressed the button and stepped inside, so he followed – would have followed her anywhere, he realised at that moment. As they ascended, he caught her looking across at him, and she smiled, said: 'I'm glad.'

'Sorry?' Hammond replied, eventually finding his voice.

'Glad it was you,' she explained. 'And not him.'

'Oh,' he said.

When they got to the room, one of those allocated for use by 'guests' at the party, she'd entered first again and he'd trailed her inside. She'd told him to make himself comfortable while she poured a glass of champagne from a bottle provided. He took off his jacket, loosened his tie, and sat on the bed, accepting the glass gratefully from Sindy. But when she suddenly stepped back and reached around, pulling down the zipper on the back of her dress, he stood up again. 'No, no...wait...don't.'

She'd looked puzzled then, and he felt terrible – didn't want her to think he didn't find her attractive. It wasn't that; dear God, it *so* wasn't that. He just didn't want to spoil things – the sight of her in that dress, the illusion of her, the...perfectness of her. 'Oh, no. I don't mean... I just...'

Then a look of realisation washed over her face. 'You want me to keep my clothes on? I get it.'

He shook his head and the bewildered expression returned. 'Can we just... I mean, is it okay if we just spend some time together?'

The concept was clearly alien to her. She was probably used to men grabbing and tearing at her, not being able to wait to get her out of her clothes and into bed. 'Okay...' she said, unsure. Hammond wasn't quite sure what he was doing, either.

He nodded for Sindy to sit down on the bed with him and they sat in silence for a while, until one of them – he could never remember which – broke it with some nonsense. Chit-chat about nothing really, what they'd seen on the TV recently, at the cinema, what kind of food they liked...awkward at first, but then flowing more easily. The rest was just a blur, his mouth working, words coming out, but concentrating, fixated on her face – those eyes!

Right up until the moment she noticed the clock. 'Is that the time – listen, I've really got to go.'

'But it's only...' Hammond followed her gaze to the bedside clock and realised it was almost midnight; not late, but not really early either.

'They only paid us until twelve,' she explained.

'Then maybe we could...' he began, but she was already standing, already walking towards the door. 'No, wait!' he called after her. '*I'll* pay you.'

Sindy turned the handle, shaking her head. 'No. I really should be going. I enjoyed meeting you, though, Pat. I honestly did.'

And suddenly she was gone, as quickly as she'd appeared in the first place. Dipping in and out of his life. Hammond raced to the door, but the lift was already descending. He stabbed at the buttons, but it didn't stop. He raced to the stairs, raced down them, though by the time he reached the foyer, there was no sign of Sindy. Hardly anyone around at all from the party, in fact.

He'd spoken to the people who'd organised it, however, asked about her – and it was as he'd thought, Sindy hadn't been hired via any kind of agency, but through recommendations. 'I'm not surprised you want to see her again, the things she can do...' one guy he'd spoken to had said and Hammond's lip curled.

It took him a while to track her down, a week or so and on his own time, but it was what he did – as a detective (*can't track her down now, though, can you? as much as you'd like to*). She'd been in an area of town notorious for that kind of activity when he spotted her, leaning back against a wall and having a drag on a cigarette. Her hair was down over her shoulders this time, clothing much less classy than it had been the night of the party; in fact the coat with the fake fur collar looked positively shabby. Not that any of it mattered to Hammond, not even a little bit. To him, she looked Heaven-sent in the glow from the street-lamp.

He'd crawled up to the curb, risking all kinds of trouble – risking his career, but not caring. Then she'd kicked back off the wall, gone to engage her next client only to find Hammond leaning across as the passenger side window came down. 'Patrick?' she'd said, looking left and right – probably wondering if she was about to get arrested, knowing now as she did what line of work he was in. 'W-What are you doing here?'

He found that he couldn't really answer that, now he'd been asked. So he just said, 'I was wondering… if maybe you'd like a coffee or something?'

'A coffee?' She glanced about her again, nervous. 'I'm working. You… you really shouldn't be here.'

'Then tell me to go away.'

She opened her mouth to speak and he could've sworn his heart missed a few beats until the words came out, fearful that Sindy was just going to tell him to get lost. 'Please,' she said then. 'I can't…'

He was bringing out his wallet then, opening it up – really putting himself in the frame if he got caught. There was a time and a place, and out in public wasn't it. 'If it's money then…'

'Put that away, Patrick.' She climbed into the car with him and he drove off, taking her for that coffee. It had been the start of his seeing her on a semi-regular basis; whenever he could, and wherever. He'd taken her for coffees, drinks, meals, even out to see films a couple of times – but hadn't wanted to rush anything else. Sindy had always refused any offer of cash, which only fed into his delusions that he was…what, dating her? He'd often ask himself just what the hell he thought he was doing. If he got caught, a copper seeing a prossie – and not in the usual way – it would be the end of him, even in this town. But then he'd think of that face again and all would be right with his world.

He was keenly aware of the age difference as well, Hammond being a good few years older than Sindy, but she never made an issue of it – then again, why would she? Sindy was used to dealing with men of all ages and making them feel good about themselves. No, it wasn't just that – *couldn't* be that! There was something more between them, he could feel it; could sense it with that same detective's sense which told him when things weren't right, when people – even expert liars – were hiding the truth.

Expert liars like a woman who could be anyone for anybody? Could play any part, from a dominatrix to a school girl? Hammond always shook away the thoughts before they could take hold – it would only ruin how he thought of her, his Sindy...his Ella.

They'd slept together eventually, of course they had – at his flat, never hers – though the first couple of times they'd come close, he hadn't been able to bring himself to. 'It's okay,' she'd told him. 'It happens to everyone sometimes.' He'd nodded, not able to explain it was the sight of Sindy in all her glory that had done it, the reality even more breath-taking than he could have possibly imagined; the thought that all he could offer her was his lacking body, past its prime but every molecule of it hers if she wanted. Then it had happened, and it was like nothing he'd ever experienced before. All the others in the past, including Karen who he'd almost married, were like shadows – pale imitations of the real thing.

Real emotions, real feelings. Real...love.

The subject had come up more than a few times after that, about their respective occupations. He'd even felt brave enough, after talking about his own history – growing up in a family where you either landed on one side of the law or the other, and sometimes straddled both – to ask her how she'd gotten into this game, if you'd pardon the expression. He thought she wasn't going to answer him at first – it took so much for her to let her guard down, to properly trust. But then he found out why. She'd spoken in vagaries about a dead father, and about how things had changed after that; about a step-mother she hadn't seen eye-to-eye with and had her own kids anyway; about running away, living rough from the age of 16 – about a woman called Ruth who'd taken her under her wing for a little while and shown her the ropes of that particular world, before moving on to bigger and better things. Last she'd heard of the woman she'd married rich, taken on a daughter of her own.

It had been a start, though, and this job was a way for her to earn a bit of money and not be reliant on anyone. Be self-sufficient. But oh, those dreams of the coast...of being by the sea. She'd always loved the sea.

Not the time nor the place to talk about her jacking it all in, just being with him – even if it meant moving to somewhere else entirely. And the more Hammond left it, the harder it became; the more he felt it would look like trying to strong-arm her, that he was trying to take over her life, tell her what to do. That hadn't happened until the murders began...

Then he'd started, subtly at first with the warnings – that it wasn't safe out there. 'Patrick, it never *has* been,' she would tell him.

Finally, in the end, he'd argued with her about it; hadn't been able to get her to see reason. To see the danger. He'd even offered her the money if she'd stay off the streets, which she'd taken quite badly. That had led to the row, and those words he wanted to take back so badly. That he couldn't now she was gone; now that bits of her were being sent to them. The first time their killer had kept the body (no, they didn't *know* she was dead) and just dumped the foot. A reversal of all the other times – but why?

The cutting off of the feet had led them to conclude they might be dealing with a fetishist, which in turn had led to them trawling sites where they hung out; sites like the ones Nichols ran (he'd actually been a suspect for all of five minutes). Or more specifically a young DC called Crabtree, who was an IT specialist, had been trawling them. He'd come up with some interesting finds as well, but nothing that ever amounted to anything concrete. This one threw everything into confusion, though; why would their perp give the foot away instead of keeping it as a trophy, as he must have done with the others?

Why. Keep. Sindy (Ella)?

Hammond had spent a couple of very sleepless nights – on top of the ones where he'd been worrying about her – trying to figure it out, but drawing a blank. Of course, it's always when you're trying of think of an answer that something else hits you. Something which turned out this time to be just as important.

'It's been fucking staring us in the face, don't you see?' he'd said to Balfour. The man's expression told him that he clearly hadn't. 'The box. The box that the foot was delivered in.'

'What about it?' asked Balfour, still looking confused.

'It was a *shoe* box,' Hammond said.

'So what? Probably just because it was the right size and shape for a foot.'

Hammond shook his head. 'He could have used *any* kind of box... Didn't Crabtree say that a lot of the weirdos on those sites were into shoes as well?'

'And you're suggesting we arrest everyone who bought a pair of shoes in the last...what, ten years?' Balfour laughed.

'I'm saying what if our guy used that box because he had it to hand. What if he's around this kind of shit all the time? Works in a shoe shop, or a factory that—'

'Hammond, you're reaching. Whoever this is wouldn't be that stupid, not after covering themselves like they have.'

'Didn't one of those knobs from the local college who came in to talk to us about psychology say that deep down all these creeps *want* to get caught?'

Balfour sighed. 'We don't have the manpower to go talking to everyone in shoe factories all over the land, on the off chance your flights of fancy are right.'

'Just give me a few people. Look,' he said as she wandered past, causing the woman to pause, 'give me Charlie Grant – she's not assigned to anything at the moment. She knows the case.'

Reluctantly, Balfour agreed: Charlie, plus a couple of other PCs, until the weekend – that's all he could spare. So they headed off to talk to those who had any kind of connection to the trade. There was a mall not that far outside of town, so they started there – Hammond and Charlie. Two large stores, but staffed with tweenies who barely had a brain cell to share amongst them. Certainly nobody who could have engineered half the things they'd seen, or would have wanted to. He'd caught Charlie examining the items on offer more than once and just rolled his eyes at her. 'What?' she'd said in return. 'Women and shoes...'

But it was as they'd grabbed a quick lunch of Mega-Burgers and fries there in the 'Oasis' that she'd said to him: 'This is personal for you, isn't it?'

Wasn't just shoes women were known for, Hammond thought to himself, it was also their intuition; more powerful than anything he could muster. 'How do you mean?'

Charlie took a sip of her coke before answering. 'I've seen you with this, like a dog with a bone. You care about those girls, don't you?'

'Of course,' Hammond said, but didn't clarify that he cared about one more than any of the others.

'I like that,' said Charlie, smiling at him and taking a bite of her burger. 'You're a nice guy, Pat, you know that?'

He offered a smile back, but said nothing in return. A few years ago, before he'd met Ella, he would have been in there like a rat up a drainpipe. Wouldn't have worked out, obviously, but that wouldn't have stopped him with a woman like Charlie; shit, he'd have been getting down on his hands and knees and kissing the ground that she might be interested. But there was no-one else for him now, never would be. That's what made it personal, and that's why he could never tell anyone about it.

They checked out a couple more places that afternoon, but it wasn't until the following day that there was a development. Nothing was reported by the other officers, and it was the last store on their list – a mom and pop place as the Americans might have called it, name of Wilkinson's – that bore fruit. It was run by an elderly man who had owned the place since the 1960s and also offered shoe repairs, as well as selling new ones. They'd talked to him, looked around the place, chatted to the assistants, and come up empty; no odd feelings that anything was wrong, nothing. It was only as they were leaving and Hammond happened to look up – his 'Spider-sense' swiftly and forcefully kicking in – that he saw the curtains twitch in the flat above the shop. Could have been anything, just someone being nosy, but Hammond insisted on going back inside and asking about it. About who exactly lived *above* the store.

'Well... I do,' said Mr Wilkinson. 'Why?'

'Alone?' demanded Hammond.

The white-haired man had scratched his head. 'Since my wife passed away. There's my son, of course. But he's only been back a few...'

Hammond wasn't listening anymore, had already clocked someone through the open side door – heading down the stairs, sloping away towards the back of the building. He pushed Mr Wilkinson aside, probably a little too roughly but then he wasn't thinking clearly; he was thinking only of Ella. Then Hammond was out through the back door and in pursuit, the man ahead of him running down the rear alley – and though it was only from the back, Hammond could see that he might well be a match for the person on that CCTV footage. That he might well be their guy.

'Stop!' he shouted, even though in all his years on the force that tactic had never, ever worked. In spite of his size, the man was fast and it had been a while since Hammond had set foot inside a gym, let along used any of the equipment. He was lucky, though, in that there was a fence at the far end of the alley. The man leapt at it, scrambling to get over the top, but Hammond had his legs before he could reach that height. 'Oh no you don't,' he grunted, holding on to the writing figure. Wilkinson's son kicked back, catching Hammond in the cheek and pitching him backwards. Seconds later, he was up and over, leaving the Inspector behind.

It took Hammond a bit longer to clamber over the fence, but he made it – and still had the man in sight: just. He was running towards the road now, not stopping even for the traffic. Hammond ran as fast as he could after him, halting cars coming from the left and right, one clipping him as it braked. 'Bastard!' he growled, not even sure himself if he meant the driver or the man he was chasing.

There was a park ahead, and Hammond knew if the man reached that he'd be lost. The detective put on a spurt, but had no chance of catching his quarry before he reached the gates. Then, out of nowhere, Charlie entered stage left and flew at the guy – tackling him and bringing him to the ground. Hammond couldn't help grinning. She was already cuffing the man as Hammond joined them, winded and trying to catch his breath. 'Thought I'd skirt around,' she told him. 'You did a good job of distracting him, though.'

Hammond nodded his thanks to the woman and she nodded back – still having no idea what this actually meant to him.

~

The suspect had spoken not a word on the drive back in the car, and continued to remain silent in the interview room – even after a grilling from both Balfour and Hammond.

'You sure this is our guy?' his boss had asked when they'd taken a break.

'Why else would he have run?' argued Hammond.

'If I saw your ugly mug coming, I'd probably do a runner as well,' replied Balfour, but he conceded his inspector had a point. Why would the man have fled if he didn't have *something* to hide?

Turned out he did – not in the shop itself, which was scoured inch by inch, but in a shed on the allotment Toby Wilkinson's father owned but didn't really use any more. Toby had made use of it, though, as they'd discovered when they searched it and found all the missing – all the severed – feet inside, plus the handsaw that had been used to detach them; not to mention what else they'd seen when a black light had been flashed around the place.

'The sick fuck,' Balfour had whispered after he'd been told.

When Hammond confronted the man with photos from the scene, he'd looked up at the inspector and smirked; the grin threatening to split his fleshy face in two. Then that grin had turned into a giggle, before evolving into a full blown guffaw.

'You think this is *funny*?' Hammond had snarled, rising and banging his fist down on the photos.

'Easy,' Balfour cautioned, placing a hand on Hammond's arm – nodding over at the camera to remind him that the interview was being recorded for posterity.

Hammond nodded and took his seat again. The last thing they wanted was for Toby to get off because of a cry of police brutality – although right at that moment all Hammond wanted to do was ram his fist into that face; ram it so hard it exploded out the back of the man's skull. But there was something he needed to know first.

'So you kept the feet, dumped the rest of their bodies...'

'Only bit I needed,' said Wilkinson, who'd become a bit more talkative once he knew they had their evidence; even confessed to using thick bootlaces he'd then disposed of as his murder weapon of choice. He'd grown up around shoes, around feet – helped out in the shop sometimes, though he'd had to stop because the temptation was too much he'd admitted. The temptation to kiss the feet of female customers, to lick them (and Hammond again had to switch off the memories of doing the same with Ella). Inside that shed he'd been able to do whatever he liked with them, though, whenever he liked. It didn't bear thinking about.

'But why change it up? Why send us the foot this time?' Balfour enquired.

'And,' Hammond asked yet again, 'where is the rest of her? Is she even still alive?'

Toby Wilkinson simply shook his head, the remains of that smirk lingering. Hammond grimaced, his hand still balled into a fist.

'Answer me, *damn you!*'

'Patrick,' Balfour warned again.

'Tell me!' Hammond said, getting up once more and rounding the table. Grabbing Wilkinson and screaming into his face, removing all traces of that smile. 'Tell me you little shit, or so help me I'll—'

Balfour was there in a flash, pulling Hammond away. '*Inspector!*' But it took a couple more PCs to actually wrestle him out of the room. 'What the hell has gotten into you?' asked the DCI when they were outside.

'What's the matter, did he put his foot in it?' said the smart-arse Wells; just passing by, wrong time, wrong place.

Definitely the wrong thing to say.

Hammond lashed out before anyone could stop him, striking the man with a fist that was still looking for a target. He backed off, backed away – looking around at startled faces, then down at the ground, at the copper rubbing his jaw. Then his eyes found Charlie in the corridor; she'd seen what had happened and they exchanged a look. Her lip was trembling and Hammond thought he saw her eyes watering – because she knew for sure now. Knew what she'd only suspected before.

He got out of there before anyone had a chance to say anything, left the station and got into his old Nissan, driving away at speed. Hammond got about a mile from there before he had to pull over; before he started slamming the steering wheel.

Before he started crying himself. Crying, and thinking that he might never, ever stop.

~

In light of what had happened, both inside the interview room and just outside it, Hammond was taken off the case and suspended.

The comedian Wells decided not to press charges, especially after Balfour explained that it was in his best career interests not to. It was all put down to the stress of such a high-profile investigation, although Charlie had called, left messages to say that if he needed to talk she was a good listener. Hammond didn't need to talk, he needed to know what had happened to Ella.

Had Wilkinson garrotted her, like the rest? Would she be found in some skip or washed up on the banks of the canal? It seemed less likely, the more time that passed, they'd ever get the answer – and especially when Hammond wasn't allowed access to the prisoner. And seemingly all but impossible once Wilkinson took his own life whilst in custody. He'd bitten into his wrists to open up his veins after being visited by a distraught father who'd essentially disowned him. Those family ties having more impact than any screaming policemen. You could take away belts and laces, but if someone was determined they could still find a way to end it and take their mysteries with them.

Mysteries like Ella.

Hammond would dream about her, when he could get to sleep that was – often with the aid of large amounts of vodka. In those dreams she would be running towards him on a beach, like in all those god-awful romance movies. It was usually the thing that tipped him off he was dreaming in the first place, the running; but he would try to push that to the back of his mind and enjoy the fact he was with her again, even if he knew it wasn't real. He could look into those blue eyes, stroke that golden hair and kiss those lips. Then he'd wake abruptly, be wrenched away from her all over again and end up reaching for the vodka.

At some point he decided that he should visit her home. Not the one she had in town, that dingy bed-sit she'd tried to keep hidden, but he'd followed her to one night anyway just to be able to picture where she was when she wasn't with him (and not have to think about her with all those other guys). That had also given Hammond her second name, Tyrell, which was on the lease.

No, the place she'd come from. The place she'd told him about… if nothing else, her mother – her step-mother – had a right to know exactly what had happened to her daughter, face-to-face rather than just being told about it impersonally on the phone. If he couldn't have any part in Ella's future, then perhaps he could connect with her past. Sure, they hadn't got on (which family ever really did?), but they *were* still family – and family was all important. Family ties…

So, he'd got the address and set off – locating the property in a nice little corner of the suburbs. Looking at all those houses, it was hard to imagine why Ella had left in the first place; he certainly wouldn't have done. Cushy, very cushy. Her mother was one Hester Tyrell, who was at Number 24, Langley Avenue: a white, two storey property with a 4x4 outside on the driveway that made the Nissan he was parking up look like a horse and cart by comparison. This family had money then, maybe not fortunes but they were doing all right. Again, he wondered what kind of argument could have led to Ella storming off and never coming back…

'If that's how you want it, then fuck off and get yourself killed.'

He closed his eyes, breathing slowly in and out. Had to keep it together, at least long enough to get through this. Hammond climbed out and walked up the driveway, admiring the pretty arrangements of flowers in the front garden, the tiny tree in the middle of the lawn. When he reached the front door – ringing the bell as he did so – Hammond was surprised to see it open almost immediately. Standing there was a woman with dark grey hair, streaked through with lighter shades of the same colour. She was wearing a maroon dress that covered every inch of her, right up to the neck, and over the top of that a shawl – the effect of which was to make her look much older than she probably was. 'Yes?' she asked eventually, her voice tinged with more than a hint of suspicion.

'Er... hell-hello. My name's Patrick Hammond, I hope you don't mind me dropping by but—'

'If you're selling something, then...'

He held up a hand. 'No, no. Nothing like that. I know...well, I knew your daughter.'

She looked at him sideways then, her suspicion deepening. 'Which one?'

It was his turn to pause, then he remembered this woman had kids of her own. 'Your step-daughter, Ella.'

Hester Tyrell's face soured at the name.

'I was part of the investigation leading up to what happened,' Hammond clarified.

'A policeman?' Hammond nodded. 'Then I suppose you'd better come inside.'

He was shown into and through a hallway with a set of stairs ahead, then ushered right into a living room. The décor did little to dispel the old-fashioned air, tasteful but stuck somewhere in the mid-1930s. Hester Tyrell bid him to take a seat on the sofa, which had elaborately-carved wooden arms and was just as hard as it looked. 'I...I expect you were told what happened,' Hammond began. 'About Ella's...disappearance.'

The woman took a seat opposite him, but didn't lean back – instead keeping her posture very straight. Hammond had to wonder whether she'd ever really relaxed in her life. The fact she answered the door so quickly meant that she must have seen him pull up outside through those net curtains, the bay window affording her a view of the entire street from this angle. 'I was informed, yes. Terrible business...but then, that was the kind of world she lived in, wasn't it.'

A statement of fact, not a question; Hammond ignored it. 'I was wondering if you might be able to shed some light on her background at all? About her time living with you?'

Hester Tyrell let out a long breath. 'She was a wilful child, right from the start. I should probably have thought twice about taking her on, but then I did so love her father.'

'Mr Tyrell?'

She nodded. 'He sadly passed away when she...when Ella was still only a little girl, really. Ten, eleven. She was the apple of that man's eye – and, between us, he was much too lenient with her. I did my best, but...well, it explains a lot about where she ended up. A streetwalker! I ask you, how in God's name...' The woman shook her head in despair. 'The shame of it. I'm glad we never had anything to do with each other after she left.'

It was Hammond's turn to sigh. This wasn't exactly how he pictured the conversation going. 'And you never re-married? No boyfriends or anything? No man of the house?'

'Mr Hammond,' she said seriously, inching forwards but still keeping her back rigid, 'I have loved only two men in my entire life, and I married them both. There have certainly never been any... "boyfriends", as you call them. Only suitors. Two of them, who courted me. The first, my sweet Kenneth, blessed me with my girls...but only after we were wed.'

Suitors? Fucking hell, thought Hammond. The décor wasn't the only thing stuck in the past.

'Anything else would have been a sin, as you can probably appreciate.'

'Oh, definitely,' he replied, then straight away regretted the sarcasm in his voice. He needn't have worried, it wasn't even noticed as the woman continued her sermon:

'It's values such as these I have tried to instil in my daughters now that they're older,' she stated, matter-of-factly. 'I keep telling them, when it's the right one, you just know – don't you think?'

Now *that* Hammond did agree with. It was how he had felt the first time he clapped eyes on Ella.

As if reading his mind, she now asked: 'So how did *you* know my step-daughter, exactly, Mr Hammond? Just through the case?'

'We were... I'm...I was her friend,' he thought would be the safest answer.

She stared at him. 'I see. And the man who did all this, he came to a bad end I understand.'

'He did.'

'His guilt finally catching up with him. Agent of the Devil,' Mrs Tyrell told Hammond. 'Oh, would you look at me,' she suddenly said after a pause, 'where are my manners? I haven't even offered you a drink. Tea, coffee?'

'Coffee, please,' he said, 'if you have it.'

'Of course, just bear with me...' He rose when she did, out of politeness. But when she disappeared into the kitchen – through an open doorway inside the living room – he couldn't help wandering around and looking at some of the pictures on the wall, hanging over the fireplace: photos of Hester's daughters when they were small, wearing knitted cardigans and with their hair cut short. There were no photos of Ella on display, however. Various religious mantras covered another wall, including one that caught his eye, footprints on a beach: *During your times of trial and suffering, when you see only one set of footprints*, the text said, *it was when I carried you.*

'Do you take milk, sugar?' a voice wafted in from the other room.

'Oh...er, black please,' Hammond answered. It was then that he heard the creaking from upstairs, floorboards above him. Could have been the house settling, but it sounded a lot like a person. 'Mrs Tyrell, are we alone in the house?' he called.

'Oh yes, quite alone,' came the reply. 'Apart from the cat, of course – he's probably hiding, doesn't like strangers, you see.'

Could be a cat, he supposed, but Hammond's Spider-sense was tingling like mad. He made his way across the room to the door Hester Tyrell had disappeared through. 'So there's just you and...' He stopped, the kitchen was empty – no sign of Hester Tyrell. What he did see, when he looked across the way, was a coat hanging from the back door, which was swinging open. A coat he recognised: the padded jacket from that CCTV footage he'd studied so long and so hard.

No man of the house, my foo... Hammond thought, then was suddenly aware of someone behind him, someone swinging something which connected with his left arm as he turned and sent it numb. He was shoved backwards into a small kitchen table by the large figure that had struck him; the large figure who must have been upstairs all this time. Hammond just about had time to move sideways before what he could now see was a cricket bat came crashing down onto the table beside him.

As he rolled off and onto the floor he took in the sight of the sturdy guy in front, a hoodie pulled up over his head. The bat was drawn back again, ready to take another swipe at Hammond, but he was ready this time.

Barrelling into his attacker, he shoved him against the wall, causing all the air to explode out of the man's body. Hammond brought up the back of his head, catching the guy under the chin and whipping his head back. Hammond retreated a step or two, tried moving his left arm, but found he couldn't; it was definitely broken. He didn't have much time to think about this, though, because the man was coming at him again, swiping the bat from side to side. He lunged and Hammond ducked, the bat striking one of the cupboards and smashing the wood to pieces, smashing some of the crockery inside as well.

Hammond punched the man in the face with his good hand, felt the satisfying splinter of bone as the nose exploded with redness. The man dropped the bat, hands going to his face, before Hammond followed this up with a knee to the stomach. The big man doubled over, as Hammond scooped up the bat and brought that down on the back of his head. His attacker fell forward and sideways, unconscious or dead – it didn't matter to Hammond.

'Thanks for this,' he growled as he carried the bat out through the back door and into the garden. Hammond quickly spotted where Mrs Tyrell must have gone, one door still open on what looked like a coal bunker. He should be calling for back-up, waiting until it arrived before going after the woman, but he had only one thing on his mind: Ella. This woman, her stepmother, was – as insane as it sounded – somehow responsible for what had happened to her, and he was going to get to the bottom of it no matter what.

Hammond reached the bunker, looked down at the steps which descended into the darkness. That wasn't completely true, there was a flickering light down there – breaking up the black. 'Mrs Tyrell... I'm coming down there now, and just to warn you, I'm armed.' It wasn't a lie, and though he would have preferred to have an armed response unit with him, or even a pistol himself, the weight of the bat was quite comforting as he made his way down those steps.

There were several of them, taking him what must have been deep under the garden – perhaps the property had come with this place originally? In any event, Hammond found the bottom step at last, looking around for the source of the light, which appeared to be some kind of lamp fitted to the wall. There was indeed coal still down here, for the fire inside the house he assumed, but there was also something else. And, as his eyes adjusted to the dimness, he finally saw what it was.

Chained to the back of the bunker, slumped forward with matted hair over its face, was a body. Naked and filthy, Hammond could see this was a woman, a naked woman, and it was a testament to the state of her that he didn't recognise Ella until his eyes dropped to take in the stump at the end of her right leg; the wound cauterised but still angry-looking.

'My...My God...' he finally breathed out, taking a step towards her. Ella wasn't moving; and like the person who'd attacked him in the kitchen, it was unclear whether she was alive or dead.

'Your *God?*' came a voice off to the side of him, unmistakably Mrs Tyrell's. 'Do you even have a God, Mr Hammond, liar and fornicator that you are?'

He was having trouble processing any of this, didn't know how to answer. Hammond just wanted to go to Ella, to get her down from there. Mrs Tyrell stepped between them, casting a look backwards at her step-daughter. 'She's where she belongs, your whore, in the filth and the dirt. Always wild, she was. Always unruly... I tried my best, tried to get her to follow the right path – but nothing ever worked, not even when I was forced to...correct her. Forced to punish her by locking her down here. Imagine how horrified I was when I finally discovered where she'd gone when she ran away, what she'd been up to. And there was only one way I could see to help her, to *stop* her.'

A streetwalker! Not any more...

'The others,' Hammond managed. 'You used what was happening to do this?'

Hester Tyrell let out a shrill laugh. 'Of course not. Of course I didn't use it. I *initiated* it!'

Hammond's face screwed up. 'You did what?'

'That agent of the Devil... He wasn't hard to find, on one of those perverted sites you must have looked into yourself. Wasn't hard to manipulate – he was halfway there already. An agent of the Devil to destroy the Devil's work. So much sin... so much...'

'Sin? Jesus! What do you call murder?'

'Do not blaspheme!' Mrs Tyrell shrieked. 'And I did not kill *anyone*.'

'No, not you personally. But you sent the box, didn't you? You led us to him,' spat Hammond.

'I knew someone would put everything together, you're *detectives* after all. Doing good deeds...well, some of the time. And it was an offering. An atonement of sorts, her road back to a righteous path.'

'What was to stop him from turning you in? Wilkinson?'

'Oh, Heavens,' she touched her chest, 'I never even met the maggot.'

'No, you had help. Your friend back there in the kitchen.'

'My...my friend?'

'Or whatever you want to call him, your fucking suitor – whatever. Look, just get out of the way.'

'My...? I don't understand.'

'It doesn't matter, don't you get it? He's in a pool of blood back there. Now get the fuck out of the—'

The scream that followed didn't come from Mrs Tyrell; it came from behind him. Hammond wasn't expecting it, wasn't prepared for it – for the notion that Mrs Tyrell might have had more than one helper; yet another guy, and for someone who thought all that was a sin she sure put it about. He whirled and began bringing the bat up, but it was knocked out of his hand by something else: a coal shovel, wielded by this newcomer. A shovel they then swung, missing Hammond only by inches – their intention to open him up.

'Shit!' he said, stumbling backwards and losing his footing because of a rogue piece of coal on the ground. Hammond landed awkwardly, banging his injured arm – the pain was incredible.

The scream turned into a voice: 'What did you do to her?'

In spite of the agony he was in, Hammond couldn't help thinking: *who?*

'Anna... Mum, what did he do to Anna?' The man looked over towards Mrs Tyrell, before stepping forward so Hammond could see his...*her* face, framed by that same haircut he'd seen in those photos.

'I don't know, Diana,' answered Mrs Tyrell.

Fuck! thought Hammond – it hadn't been a man at all, not in the CCTV footage at the post depot, not in the kitchen with the bat; probably not even in the contact with Wilkinson on those sites! These were Tyrell's children, hers and Kenneth's girls – though easily mistaken for men at first glance, built as they were. Ella's damned step-sisters! Diana moved forwards, holding the shovel high like the Sword of Damocles over Hammond. 'He can't be allowed to live,' she stated.

'An eye for an eye?' said Hester Tyrell, like it was the most reasonable thing in the world.

'How about,' said Hammond, getting his breath back, 'turning the other fucking cheek!' He threw the piece of coal he'd tripped on, striking Diana in the face – hard – causing her to drop the shovel and giving Hammond time enough to get to his feet, to kick out at the woman. She went backwards, striking the bunker wall, which shook and rained coal dust on her. Biting down the pain, Hammond snatched up the shovel and ran into her with it, this time like a jousting knight. The blade rammed into her stomach, and she hawked up blood.

Now it was her mother's turn to scream, running at Hammond and drawing a kitchen knife she'd had behind her back. He turned to face her and was slashed across the chest for his trouble. 'You crazy bitch!' he shouted, head-butting the woman.

Hester Tyrell staggered backwards, a cut opening on her brow. She snarled, then came at him again with the knife, holding it out in front of her. Hammond sidestepped her, then stuck his leg out, which sent her flying. He looked around for the only weapon left, snatching up the bat and hitting Mrs Tyrell as she was starting to pick herself up off the floor. Hammond's breath was coming in short bursts, slowing up finally. He looked up and over at the other body, slumped and held by chains.

Family ties...

'Ella,' he said, dropping the bat and shambling across to her. Even after all this, she wasn't moving; not even a twitch.

'*I did not kill* anyone!'

Hammond hoped against hope Tyrell had been telling the truth. Of course, one of those equally deranged daughters might have done the honours. He reached out, fingers trembling, and repeated her name. 'Ella... Ella, it's Patrick.'

Her skin was cold as he lifted her head up, but then she'd been in this place probably for weeks. 'Ella...*please!*'

He couldn't see her eyes, because the hair was still hanging over them – couldn't see whether they were open or closed. But then there was a breath, a whisper, and he could see her smile beneath the dirt. 'I...I knew you'd come,' she managed. 'I...I made a wish...'

Hammond moved forward, letting her head rest on his shoulder, and now he cried simple tears of joy.

~

It was warm in the sun.

Warm on the beach as they walked along it. Ella wouldn't be running anytime soon, but the prosthetic he'd helped her with that morning, as she sat on the bed and he'd attached it to her stump, enabled to her make her way along the sand – arm in arm with Hammond. She got him to stop for a minute, and he thought it might be because she was sore, but it was only so she could look out over the sea. He'd found out why she loved it so much, the coast – it was where she'd lived growing up with her parents, her real parents. And then her and her dad – before he met Hester, before he'd died.

The things that woman, that *family* had put Ella through afterwards... Hammond didn't wonder any more about why she'd left, about what had put her on the road to where she'd ended up. She'd finally let him in – trusted him with everything.

'You okay?' he asked her, brushing a strand of that golden hair out of her face now he was able to; using the hand that was only recently free of a cast that reached up to his elbow.

'Yeah,' she answered, and smiled. She knew how much he loved her – should do, because he told her a million times a day. In fact, they told each other. Knew that the foot thing didn't bother him in the slightest, that she was still perfect in his eyes. He'd even drawn that star on it in marker pen, to replace the tattoo, to make her feel better.

'It was never a star,' she said as he did it, taking the pen from him and adding a stick underneath. 'A wand. A magic wand, like the kind your fairy godmother uses.'

'My fairy what?' he'd asked.

'Never mind,' Ella had replied with a laugh.

As she watched the ocean, he watched her. He'd never let anything happen to her again, and she never wanted him to. They'd agreed to both leave their former lives behind and start afresh, out here. It had been the best thing either of them had ever done. Of course, the past has a way of coming back to haunt you – and news had reached them that week about the trial coming up.

'You sure you're okay?' he asked her again.

'Oh, yeah...' She looked at him with those blue eyes. 'I am. Just thinking about, well, y'know.'

'I do,' he told her.

'What do you think will happen to them?'

'If there's any justice, the judge will lock 'em up and throw away the key,' Hammond answered. Incredibly, all three of the Tyrells had survived what happened, though with extensive injuries. Diana would never walk again, he'd been told, and there was a certain kind of justice in that alone. He just wished it was all three of them. Hammond put his arm around her shoulder. 'I'll make sure of it,' he promised her, knowing that with both their testimonies it should be enough to see the trio put away for life.

Then they could get on with their own lives. Maybe marry, have kids someday? They were subjects he hadn't dared broach, but he would, when the time was right; he wouldn't put things off again. Ella had enough on her mind for the time being, though; enough on her plate. She'd get through it, of course, she was strong, tough. Actually, they'd both get through it as a couple.

'Come on,' she said, starting to walk again and he fell in step at the side of her. 'You can buy me an ice cream.'

He chuckled. 'With pleasure.' And as they walked, he took one last look over his shoulder. Two sets of footprints, side-by-side. But if Ella happened to get tired, or her leg was aching, Hammond would pick her up and carry her in his arms. Then there would be only one pair.

Because then, as always from this point on, after the trials and suffering were behind them, they would still be together.

They would be one.

Suit of Lies

It has been said that they form a web, a tissue...but they do nothing of the kind.

He knows what they really make – their texture, cut, their unmistakable uniqueness. For much of his life he has woven the thread. Actually that's not strictly true. The thread has woven *itself* – he has merely provided the raw material. From an early age he has done this, since Benjamin learned to think, walk and talk he spouted his untruths.

Not that it was entirely his fault. His parents set him upon that track. To begin with, whenever he did something wrong and they asked him about it, he would always admit his blame. Take the time he inadvertently kicked over the dog's water and food...

'Oh, just look at the mess. Benjamin! Did you do that?'

'Y-Yes.' His reward for honesty was a smacked pair of legs. 'That's very naughty. Let this be a lesson to you.'

It was a lesson all right. Next time the dog would get the blame.

And so it began. Slowly but surely he learnt as he grew, that if you were ever to get on in this world, if you were ever to get what you wanted, you had to lie. They were small at first, so small you hardly noticed them. White lies. So white they were almost invisible, translucent fibs.

'Have you washed your hands before eating?'

'Yes.'

'Did you play nice with Rosy from next door?'

'Yes.' *The fact that she wet the bed that night was nothing to do with him...*

'Was that a bad word I just heard you say?'

'No.'

So on and so forth. Sometimes he got away with it, sometimes he didn't. But, as the saying goes, practice makes perfect. And the more he told, the better he became at it. The more he told, the more convincing he became as well. Straight, poker-faced. Totally unreadable.

Only then was he able to move up a level.

The lies, especially after he started school, came thick and fast. They took on a life of their own occasionally, developed into elaborate pantomimes that required skill and perfect timing to pull off – not to mention a surplus of slower kids to take the rap. For example, how on Earth he'd got away with the felt-pen graffiti scandal in the toilets he still didn't know to this day. A combination of quick-talking and Robbie Kemp being in the cubicle next door might've had something to do with it.

'It was Robbie, Miss Chambers. I swear. Robbie!'

He could still see Robbie being hauled out of the boys' lavs by his ear...could almost feel the lobe straining fit to tear, in an era when such actions didn't result in the school being sued and the teacher facing child abuse charges.

Strangely enough that was the first time he noticed the effect of his lies, too. Not the effect on poor old Robbie – for that was self-evident – but rather the immediate after-effect of telling the lie.

It was as Benjamin walked past the mirrors in the toilets that he saw the words still hanging in the air around him. Small, black words and letters, buzzing around his head like flies. He stopped and stared, blinking at the peculiar phenomenon. But then at his age weren't all phenomena peculiar, and even the strangest things accepted without question?

The lies finally settled on him, at his shoulder. He tried to brush them off but found that they'd stuck fast to him. And now they were knitting themselves together, intertwining, forming a tiny little square.

'Benjamin!' Miss Chambers had shouted. 'Come along at once.' The headmaster's office awaited.

So he'd gone and repeated his story, hands in pockets to hide the felt marks on his fingers. He made such a case that he even had Robbie believing it himself. But he never once forgot the threads, nor the square – which, by the end of the day, was somehow even larger.

Benjamin was eager to see if it would happen again, and maybe this had something to do with fixing him in his ways. It certainly didn't help. More lies, more words, more material. It seemed to be a part of him, whether he had his ordinary clothes on or not. Even when he took a bath, or got undressed ready for bed, the growing patchwork of lie-fibres would be there at his shoulder.

Benjamin would pretend to be sick to get days off school – easy to feign a stomach ache or a flu – just so he could study the upshot of those lies. Those...*fabrications*. Only later would he grasp the true significance of that word, for the untruths *were* manipulating themselves into a sort of 'material', covering his shoulder and upper arm now. He'd asked his mum once about it, but she didn't seem to see the thing at all. Or maybe she didn't want to see.

'What're you talking about, Benjamin?' Never Benny or Ben; always Benjamin. 'Have you been watching those silly cartoons again?'

'No.' Benjamin looked up and to his astonishment saw a small black *No* float out of his mouth, because *of course* he'd been watching cartoons, couldn't get enough of the things if the truth be known (ha!). His eyes followed the word as it joined its brethren, and they welcomed this small but powerful addition to their ranks with open arms. The more the merrier. The more the thicker, and velvetier...

The worse the lie, the more letters he would add to the cloth, and the more substantial those letters would be. Just like at that birthday party when he was ten, and he deliberately pushed his cousin Faith down the stairs, breaking her arm. It was her own fault, she'd been badgering him the whole time about borrowing his Etch-a-Sketch – his fucking new Etch-a-Sketch, mind! – so he'd seized the opportunity during a dizzying game of tag.

Cue ambulance, and more fast-talking. 'I didn't mean to, it was an accident. You know how clumsy she is anyway.' Words, blacker than black. Words to cover up hate and hurt. To cover up the top of his arm as well, spreading down across his chest. Benjamin, though, had grown used to the substance by now. Had lived with it just as someone might live with a mole or a birthmark, although *they* don't usually get bigger or seep through your proper clothing when you aren't looking.

A good job he had adjusted, because in the years to come, through adolescence and into young adulthood, the material would spread even more. Yet, having said that, he did find he could control it more now, could choose whether to display it or conceal it. But every time he bullied some innocent boy and denied responsibility...every time he and his gang (a gang he formed quite early on in secondary school) vandalised or generally terrorised...every time he'd sweet talk some girl into putting out, and later claim that he'd done nothing of the sort, particularly if complications arose...every time he stole or stopped out late or did errands for the local faces...the suit of lies would gain a little bit more in essence and durability.

By the age of seventeen, it was already down to his waist, having encased his arms and settled completely across his broad shoulders. Just as the 'jacket' had grown, so too had he, into a handsome youth with twinkling eyes and a charming grin. A wide boy, but dangerous with it. So dangerous that the joy riding he encouraged his friends to participate in finally resulted in a crash that left one member of his gang paralysed, and another with a punctured lung. Benjamin, who'd been in the passenger seat, had belted up before the journey began and so escaped any serious injury. He also escaped any serious blame or repercussions. It wasn't his idea, you see. He hadn't egged the others on or talked them into doing it.

More lies; but they got him out of a tight spot once again.

Unfortunately the families of his cohorts didn't see it that way. Nor did the local villains who used him occasionally for services rendered; his brush with the law made them nervous. So it was time for him to leave the area, make his way down south to seek out his true destiny. He told his mum and dad he was going to town one day, then never came back. A small falsehood really, but with tremendous repercussions.

It wouldn't be the last.

Benjamin worked in a succession of jobs on his travels, paying for his journey to a better mode of life. Selling used cars offered him a decent living for a while ('One previous owner, very careful driver, hardly ever used it...' Cut-'n'-shuts? he didn't know the meaning of the word), as did telesales after that ('Can you afford to take out life insurance, sir? Can you afford *not* to, that's the question?'). But they never really satisfied him. Nor did the succession of faceless women he bedded in his early twenties, telling them yes of course he loved them, of course he'd stay with them – that no way was he like all the other bastards out there. Nevertheless, he'd always move on in the end.

No, it was the big cities that offered him the most opportunity. He somehow found himself involved in investments, in stocks and shares.

This was how he came to make his fortune. This was where his talents truly came into their own: juggling figures, buttering up clients, conning...no, *persuading* people to part with their hard-earned just to furnish him with a big house – a des-res complete with swimming pool – and a sports car (personalised number plate, 160 mph on a good day, 200 on a bad one). And the clothes, don't forget the clothes...silk shirts, handmade ties, designer suits – not that any of these could match the suit that had shaped itself around him during this time. Benjamin liked that one the best of all. He'd become very comfortable with it in fact, so comfortable he took pride in adding more blackened phrases to it, would stop and admire it in shop windows, the jacket done and the trousers coming along nicely. It was almost his mission to complete it, to try and finish the suit.

Benjamin was becoming a man of many words. All of them false.

He also settled for just the one woman; well, he married her at any rate. Penelope was the daughter of one of his work associates and he really thought he'd loved her there for a while. She was so...so...Penelope. Unlike all the others, he didn't lie to her. Not at first. He meant what he said, even if that didn't do anything to enhance the suit. It was getting its fill from other sources anyway.

'...and forsaking all others, as long as you both shall live?'

'I do.'

Except he didn't, did he? Benjamin could only curb his appetite for so long. The women were there, and the affairs were a buzz. He'd been stupid to think he could spend the rest of his life with that single, solitary woman. God, she was just so...sooooo Penelope. The only thing now was that she'd take him for all he'd got if he tried to wriggle out of it. Besides, he secretly enjoyed all the planning, the subterfuge, the 'I was just having drinks with the boys at the club,'s, and the 'I completely lost track of time,'s. Plus, of course, it all added to the suit's finery.

Consequently, for a long time things were fantastic. They were the best few years of his life, bar none. He even branched out into other areas of business, making even more money out of back-handers and decidedly dodgy deals. It was an easy racket, and he covered his tracks at every turn.

Then, one day, everything just started to go wrong. A friend...(more of an acquaintance really, for Benjamin never really had any *true* friends; he was constantly using them, betraying them and letting them down)...anyway, this person once told him something that had stuck with him, albeit at the back of his mind. A sage piece of advice if he had but known it, except Benjamin dismissed it with all the casualness of a fortune cookie prediction.

They had said to him:

'You know, whatever you do in this life, good or bad, always comes back to you threefold. Karma I think they call it. Oh, you can get away with anything for a while – and though it may seem like the bad people get all the luck in this world, it'll catch up with them sometime. I firmly believe that. You get your "reward" eventually.'

Benjamin's own eventually came when the stock market took its first sucker-punch.

Like so many other brokers, he danced around the inevitability of it all, made promises down phone-lines that he could never, ever keep; made assurances that were worth nothing on paper or in the ether.

'Don't worry, it's just a temporary thing. What's a few points here or there? The market's well on its way to recovery. Just give it a bit more time.' He said this while he withdrew large amounts of cash from the system, covering his own back, in more ways than one, and making sure that when the other boot fell he'd still be sitting oh-so pretty. It didn't matter about the suicides that would pave his escape.

At the same time, however, several of the apartment blocks built by a construction firm he'd invested in had been found to be hazardous in the extreme. Benjamin denied ordering all the cost cutting, palmed it off again on the little man. But he couldn't do that when the reporter from the *Daily Archer* came a-calling, claiming he'd done some investigating of his own. Not only could he tie Benjamin in to several illegal porn and drugs operations in the East End – blame his teenage roots – but he also had proof that the high-flyer had been diddling his taxes for years.

A meeting to pay the man off had led to another push down another flight of stairs: concrete ones. This time the victim hadn't survived. Another kind of investigation was bound to ensue...

Not only that, but Benjamin's string of other women were becoming more and more demanding. It was growing harder to keep track of them all, and Penelope was becoming very suspicious indeed.

So the lies flowed like booze at a bachelor party. More elaborate pantomimes than even he could've contemplated at school. Still the suit was always hungry for more. Craving them, feasting off his paranoia and insecurities. It became fat on the profits of his wrongdoings. When he looked in the mirror or a shop window now, he hardly recognised the thing, and there was no chance of concealing it. No longer smart and elegant, it weighed him down, added pounds to him, and seemed to be growing out of all proportion. Just growing and growing and—

Everything spun out of control. There were too many balls in the air for Benjamin to handle. His lies were no longer convincing, his memory jumbled and confused. His reward? He lost everything. The money, the prestige, the power, his marriage.

Then eventually he lost his very freedom, thanks to an eyewitness testimony to the reporter's death.

'I sentence you to life imprisonment!'

But it didn't matter anyway. The suit, and in particular the jacket, now trailing down over each arm, was binding him, contorting him and pinning him back. Trapping him inside it until he couldn't possibly hope to break free. Making a mockery of him and the man he'd once been.

So yes, as he sat alone in his cell, Benjamin did contemplate what the nature of his condition actually was. What the lies made up. Why the suit had come to him – unless all the liars and cheaters of this world had their own suits, of course.

As he did so, his arms snapped back around him, cocooning him, Benjamin still told his lies. He simply couldn't help it. He lied over and over again, to his fellow inmates – when he was allowed to see any – and to his keepers. But most significantly to himself, pretended that everything was going to be all right. Pretended that this hadn't really happened to him, that the suit wouldn't squeeze the life out of him one day, or cover his face and choke him in the night. Pretended that the suit of lies didn't *really* exist in fact, which was, perhaps, the biggest lie anyone had *ever* told.

And maybe, just maybe…

The most dangerous lie of them all.

A Suspicious Mind

I'm caught in a trap,
I can't look back.
Because you've taken out my
Eyeballs baby.

Oh why can't you see...
What this is doing to me,
All your hooks,
And spikes, now baby?

We can't go on together,
With your suspicious mind,
And we can't live our dreams,
With your suspicious mind.

When that old friend I know,
Dropped in to say hello.
Nothing happened,
I swear now baby.

There's no need for that.
For the power saw.
Can't we just talk about this,
Now baby?

We can't go on together,
With your suspicious mind,
And I can't live it seems,
With—

About the Author

Paul B. Kane is an award-winning writer and editor based in Derbyshire, UK. His short story collections – as Paul Kane – include *Alone (In the Dark)*, *Touching the Flame*, *FunnyBones*, *Peripheral Visions*, *Shadow Writer*, *The Adventures of Dalton Quayle*, *The Butterfly Man and Other Stories*, *The Spaces Between*, *Ghosts* and *Monsters*. His novellas include *Signs of Life*, *The Lazarus Condition*, *RED* and *Pain Cages*. He is the author of such novels as *Of Darkness and Light*, *The Gemini Factor* and the bestselling *Arrowhead* trilogy (*Arrowhead*, *Broken Arrow* and *Arrowland*, gathered together in the sell-out omnibus edition *Hooded Man*), a post-apocalyptic reworking of the Robin Hood mythology. His latest novels are *Lunar* (which is set to be turned into a feature film), *Sleeper(s)* (a modern, horror version of *Sleeping Beauty*), the short YA novel *The Rainbow Man* (as P.B. Kane), the sequel to *RED* – *Blood RED* – and the bestselling award-winning *Sherlock Holmes and the Servants of Hell* from Solaris.

He has also written for comics, most notably for the *Dead Roots* zombie anthology alongside writers such as James Moran (*Torchwood*, *Cockneys vs. Zombies*) and Jason Arnopp (*Dr Who*, *Friday The 13th*, *The Last Days of Jack Sparks*) and as part of the team turning *Clive Barker's Books of Blood* into motion comics for Seraphim/MadeFire. Paul is co-editor of the anthologies: *Hellbound Hearts* (Simon & Schuster), stories based around the mythology that spawned *Hellraiser*; *The Mammoth Book of Body Horror* (Constable & Robinson/Running Press), featuring the likes of Stephen King and James Herbert; *A Carnivàle of Horror* (PS Publishing) featuring Ray Bradbury and Joe Hill; and *Beyond Rue Morgue* (Titan), stories based around Poe's detective, Dupin.

His non-fiction books are: *The Hellraiser Films and Their Legacy*; *Voices in the Dark*; and *Shadow Writer – The Non-Fiction. Vol. 1: Reviews* and *Vol. 2: Articles and Essays*. His genre journalism has appeared in the likes of *SFX*, *Fangoria*, *Dreamwatch*, *Gorezone*, *Rue Morgue* and *DeathRay*. He has been a guest at many conventions, including: Alt. Fiction five times; the first SFX Weekender; Thought Bubble in 2011; Derbyshire Literary Festival and Off the Shelf in 2012; Monster Mash and Event Horizon in 2013; Edge-

Lit in 2014; HorrorCon, Liverpool Horror Festival and Grimm up North in 2015; plus The Dublin Ghost Story Festival and Sledge-Lit in 2016. In addition he has been a panellist at FantasyCon and the World Fantasy Convention, was a fiction judge for Sci-Fi London 2016 and is currently serving as co-chair of the UK arm of the Horror Writers Association.

His work has been optioned for film and television, and his zombie story 'Dead Time' was turned into an episode of the Lionsgate/NBC TV series *Fear Itself*, adapted by Steve Niles (*30 Days of Night*) and directed by Darren Lynn Bousman (*SAW II-IV*). He also scripted *The Opportunity*, which premiered at the Cannes Film Festival, *Wind Chimes* (directed by Brad Watson [*7th Dimension*] which sold to TV), *The Weeping Woman* – filmed by award-winning director Mark Steensland and starring Tony-nominated actor Stephen Geoffreys (*Fright Night*) – and *Confidence*, starring *Hellraiser* and *Nightbreed*'s Simon Bamford. You can find out more at his website **www.shadow-writer.co.uk**, which has featured such guest writers as Dean Koontz, Robert Kirkman, Charlaine Harris and Guillermo del Toro.

Also by Paul B. Kane
(as Paul Kane unless stated):

Novels

Arrowhead

Broken Arrow

Arrowland

Hooded Man (Omnibus)

The Gemini Factor

Of Darkness and Light

Lunar

Sleeper(s)

The Rainbow Man (as P.B. Kane)

Blood RED

Sherlock Holmes and the Servants of Hell

Forthcoming: Before & Deep RED

Novellas & Novelettes

Signs of Life

The Lazarus Condition

Dalton Quayle Rides Out

RED

Pain Cages

Creakers (chapbook)

The Curse of the Wolf

Flaming Arrow

The Bric-a-Brac Man

The P.I.'s Tale

Snow

The PI's Tale

The Crimson Mystery

The Rot

Collections

Alone (In the Dark)
Touching the Flame
FunnyBones
Peripheral Visions
The Adventures of Dalton Quayle
Shadow Writer
The Butterfly Man and Other Stories
The Spaces Between
Ghosts
Monsters
The Dead Trilogy
Forthcoming: Disexistence & Shadow Casting

Editor & Co-Editor

Shadow Writers Vol. 1 & 2
Terror Tales #1-4
Top International Horror
Albions Alptraume: Zombies
The British Fantasy Society: A Celebration
Hellbound Hearts
The Mammoth Book of Body Horror
A Carnivàle of Horror: Dark Tales from the Fairground
Beyond Rue Morgue
Forthcoming: Dark Mirages

Non-Fiction

Contemporary North American Film Directors: A Wallflower Critical
Guide (Major Contributor)
Cinema Macabre (Contributor)
The Hellraiser Films and Their Legacy
Voices in the Dark
Shadow Writer – The Non-Fiction. Vol. 1: Reviews
Shadow Writer – The Non-Fiction. Vol. 2: Articles & Essays